"Are you claimed for this dance?"

Isabella hesitated. "No," she said. "I am not."

The major's face hardened. He'd seen the hesitation.

Shame made her flush. "It would be my pleasure to dance with you, Major."

Major Reynolds offered her his arm. "Then let us join a set." Politely spoken, but she heard an edge of irony in his voice.

Isabella fanned herself, hoping to take the heat from her cheeks, and laid her hand lightly on the major's sleeve. The hard angles of his face, the severe cut of his coat, the darkness of the cloth, matched one another.

They walked onto the dance floor amid the murmur of conversation and rustle of fabric. Isabella heard the word *ogre* whispered to her right.

The major had heard the whisper. Anger glinted in his eyes. He halted. "Perhaps you would prefer not to dance, Lady Isabella? You can hardly wish to be seen with an ogre." The major's voice was light, his expression sardonic.

"You are mistaken," Isabella said, taking her place opposite him. She met his eyes—cold and hard and so clear they seemed to look right through her—and curtsied as the musicians played the opening chords. She understood why society was afraid of him. *Not the scar, but his eyes.*

* * *

Beauty and the Scarred Hero
Harlequin® Historical #277—February 2010

EMILY MAY

grew up in a house full of books—her mother worked as a proofreader and librarian, and her father is a well-known New Zealand novelist. Emily has studied a wide number of subjects, including geology and geophysics, canine behavior and ancient Greek. Her varied career includes stints as a field assistant in Antarctica and a waitress on the Isle of Skye. Most recently she has worked in the wine industry in Marlborough, New Zealand.

Emily loves to travel and has lived in Sweden, backpacked in Europe and traveled overland in the Middle East, China and North Africa. She enjoys climbing hills, yoga workouts, watching reruns of *Buffy the Vampire Slayer* and reading. She is especially fond of Georgette Heyer's Regency and Georgian novels.

Emily writes Regency romances as Emily May and dark, romantic fantasy novels as Emily Gee (www.emilygee.com).

Beauty and the Scarred Hero

EMILY MAY

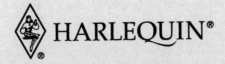

HARLEQUIN®

TORONTO • NEW YORK • LONDON
AMSTERDAM • PARIS • SYDNEY • HAMBURG
STOCKHOLM • ATHENS • TOKYO • MILAN • MADRID
PRAGUE • WARSAW • BUDAPEST • AUCKLAND

Recycling programs
for this product may
not exist in your area.

ISBN-13: 978-0-373-30586-5

BEAUTY AND THE SCARRED HERO

Beauty and the Scarred Hero was written during a year spent traveling in North America. I would like to dedicate this book to Brooke (Sonoma) and Sandii (Redondo Beach) in whose homes I wrote many words.

I would also like to acknowledge the following libraries, where I spent many hours, days and weeks working on this book:

In Canada, the public library in Sault Ste. Marie (Ontario) and the Morrin Centre (English Library) and Bibliothèque Gabrielle-Roy, both in Quebec City (Quebec).

In the U.S., the public libraries in Burlington (Vermont); Moab and Kanab (Utah); Flagstaff and Willcox (Arizona); Santa Fe, Deming and Silver City (New Mexico); Sonoma, Sacramento and Salinas (California); the Seattle central library and the branch libraries in Fremont and Ballard, as well as the Bainbridge Island and Port Angeles public libraries (Washington). And lastly, my favorite library: Lake Oswego in Oregon—I wish I could work there every day!

Chapter One

'This is a respectable establishment. It's not for the likes of you.'

Lady Isabella Knox, sister of the Duke of Middlebury, paused in the act of removing her gloves. She looked down at her dog. Rufus cocked his head and gazed back up at her with mismatched eyes. His tail wagged, brushing the muddy hem of her walking habit.

'I beg of you, don't turn me away.' The speaker was tearful, young and well bred.

'The Hogshead will take you.' The landlady's voice came clearly from the taproom, cold and dismissive.

'Oh, but please—' The girl's entreaty ended on a sob.

Isabella pulled one kidskin glove off, finger by finger. She glanced at the half-open door to the taproom and then at the staircase, at the top of which a comfortable and very private parlour awaited her. *Curiosity is a sin*, she told herself.

She heard brisk footsteps behind her: her maid Partridge.

'Fresh air,' Partridge muttered, shutting the parasol with a snap. 'Dirt and puddles and yokels gaping—'

Isabella raised a finger. 'Hush a moment, Partridge.'

'I beg you, please…' The girl sounded so like her niece Felicity that Isabella made up her mind. She stepped towards the taproom door. Rufus followed, his claws clicking briskly on the flagstones.

'A fine thing it would be if I let you put up here, with her ladyship in the house—'

Isabella laid her hand on the door. It swung open at her touch. She took in the taproom with a glance: the low, beamed ceiling, the wide fireplace, the landlady in her white apron and widow's cap, and the girl, pretty and tearstained, with a portmanteau at her feet.

The landlady drew herself up, stout and starched, and then sank into an obsequious curtsy. 'Your ladyship.'

'Mrs Botham.' Isabella looked at the girl. Yes, very like Felicity. Dark-haired and slender and scarcely out of the schoolroom. 'I couldn't help but overhear. Pray, don't turn this child out into the street on my account.'

The landlady straightened. Her face was round-cheeked, her complexion florid, her expression righteous. 'The Hogshead will do very well for her.'

Isabella looked at the girl's clothing. The green sarcenet pelisse, the straw bonnet trimmed with ribbon, the jaconet muslin gown, were neat and plain and well made. 'Do you think so?'

She spoke gently, but the colour in Mrs Botham's cheeks heightened.

The girl curtsied. 'Ma'am, if you please, I don't wish to put up at the Hogshead.'

'I should think not.' There was nothing common about the girl's vowels, or her curtsy. 'Where is your maid?'

The girl flushed. 'I don't have one, ma'am.'

'I run a respectable establishment—' Mrs Botham began.

'Precisely.' Isabella pulled off her other glove. 'Which is why this child must stay here.'

The girl cast her a grateful glance.

'Unfortunately I do not have suitable accommodation, your ladyship.' The landlady's smile was polite and insincere.

'I find that hard to believe,' Isabella said, beginning to lose her temper.

'Nothing suiting the young person's requirements.'

The girl flushed again. 'I can't afford a room,' she whispered. 'I thought…I thought I could sleep in the servants' quarters, but—'

'No money and no maid?' Isabella looked at her. 'You are in a predicament, aren't you, my dear?'

Tears welled in the girl's eyes.

'You may share my maid's bedchamber,' Isabella said. She heard Partridge sniff behind her and ignored it.

The landlady inhaled, swelling in her starched apron. 'I won't have a Fallen Woman in this house!'

'I'm not, ma'am! Indeed, I'm not!'

Do I care whether she is or not? Not when the girl was so young and so clearly in need of aid. 'A truckle bed in my maid's room,' Isabella said briskly. 'And refreshments in my parlour.' She folded her gloves and waited for the landlady to protest.

Mrs Botham inhaled again, her apron swelling, but uttered no sound.

'Come along, my dear.' Isabella smiled and held out her hand to the girl.

'My portmanteau?'

'One of the servants will bring it up, won't they, Mrs Botham?'

The landlady smiled tightly and nodded.

The girl clutched her hand. 'Come upstairs and have a cup of tea,' Isabella said as they exited the taproom, Rufus following closely at their heels. She ignored Partridge's silent disapproval. 'And do tell me your name, my dear.'

The girl's hand was small and damp and warm. 'My name is Harriet,' she confided as they climbed the staircase. Her gaze was worshipful. 'Harriet Durham.'

* * *

'Tell me, my dear…how is it you're in such a fix?'

Harriet's cheeks coloured. She looked down at her cup. 'I'm running away.'

'Running away?' Isabella sipped her tea and surveyed the girl's face. She could discern no boldness. Harriet had soft brown hair and soft brown eyes and an air of timidity. Her expression when she glanced at Rufus was wary. *Surely not the type of girl to run away?* 'From your parents?'

'My parents are dead.' Harriet looked up from her study of the teacup. 'I live with my grandfather.'

'You're running away from him?'

'Yes.' Harriet shivered. 'And from Major Reynolds.'

'Major Reynolds?' Isabella lowered her cup. 'Who is he?'

Tears filled Harriet's eyes. 'I'm to marry him.'

'And you do not wish to?'

Harriet shivered again. She shook her head. 'No.'

Isabella placed her teacup on the little cherrywood table beside her. The tabletop gleamed and the parlour had a pleasing smell of beeswax polish. Mrs Botham kept a very clean—and extremely respectable—establishment.

'Did you tell your grandfather that you do not wish to marry Major Reynolds?'

Harriet nodded. 'He said I was being foolish. And he shouted at me, and—' She groped for her handkerchief. The tiny lace-trimmed square of fabric was sodden.

Isabella picked up her teacup and sipped, while Harriet wiped her eyes. 'How old are you, my dear?' she asked once the girl had composed herself.

'Seventeen.'

Felicity's age. Too young to be in the world alone. 'Where are you going?'

'My Aunt Lavinia.' Harriet's smile was tremulous. 'Only I hadn't realised that the stage would be so slow, or that it would cost so much to take a room in an inn...' Tears suspended her voice.

Isabella placed her teacup on its saucer. She reached down to pat Rufus. His eyes opened, one blue, one brown, and his tail gave a thump on the floor. 'Where does your aunt live?'

'Penrith. In the Lake District.'

Isabella frowned. 'My dear child, do you realise how far that is?'

'Is it very distant from here?' Harriet twisted the handkerchief.

Isabella looked at the tears shining in the girl's eyes and decided not to answer that question. Instead she asked, 'Is your aunt expecting you?'

Harriet shook her head.

'But you're certain she'll give you refuge?'

'Oh, yes.' Harriet nodded. 'She said that I was always welcome to stay with her, only...only my grandfather wouldn't let me speak her name, or write to her, or...or—'

'How Gothic!' Isabella said lightly, to forestall more tears. 'What did she do to incur such wrath?'

'She married Mr Mortlock. Grandfather said he wasn't good enough—and Aunt Lavinia told him he was a tyrant and married Mr Mortlock anyway!' Admiration was patent in Harriet's voice. 'Only Mr Mortlock died, which Grandfather said served her right, and so now she lives alone.'

'How long ago was this?' Isabella asked.

'When I was a child.'

The girl was still a child. Too young to be forced into marriage—and too young to travel halfway across England on her own. Isabella glanced out the window at the roofs of Stony Stratford and the deepening dusk and made up her mind. *It's not really meddling. I'm merely helping her on a path she has already chosen.* 'I shall take you home with me,' she said. 'To London. And then—'

'London? Oh, no!' Harriet dropped the handkerchief in her agitation.

Rufus opened his eyes again. His ears pricked. He lifted his head and looked at Harriet.

'Why ever not, child?' Isabella said, resting her hand on Rufus's head, feeling the warmth and smoothness of his coat beneath her palm.

'Because he's there!'

'He? Your grandfather?'

'Major Reynolds!' Harriet's face twisted. 'If he should find me—'

'Major Reynolds will not find you,' Isabella said firmly, 'because you shall be at my house, quite snug and safe. And once we have received an assurance from your aunt that she's expecting you—for she may be away, you know!—then you shall travel to stay with her.'

'But Major Reynolds—'

Isabella looked at her with some amusement. 'Is he such an ogre, child?'

'An ogre?' Harriet shuddered. 'Oh, yes. Yes, he is!'

'Then I promise to keep you safe from him.'

'He will be very angry.' Harriet blinked back tears. 'My grandfather has already announced our engagement.'

Isabella experienced a moment's misgiving. If the engagement had been announced in the newspapers, then the scandal…

I should restore her to her grandfather.

The girl was as young as Felicity, with no parents to dote on her. *Even so, I should—*

She looked down at Rufus. He glanced up at her with his odd eyes and thumped his tail on the rug again, content, trusting.

'Tell me about Major Reynolds,' Isabella said, giving her own handkerchief to Harriet.

'He's a soldier.'

Isabella suppressed a smile. 'Yes, my dear, I had gathered that. Is he old, and what is his disposition?'

'Old? Oh, yes, ma'am. He's quite as old as you.' Harriet's cheeks coloured. 'I mean, he's *much* older than you. He's as old as my father…that is to say, as old as my father would be if he were—' She bit her lip.

That settled it, Isabella decided. She wasn't about to allow this child to be married to a man old enough to be her father.

'And as to his disposition, he looks so…so *stern*, and…and—'

'I collect he is quite an ogre,' Isabella said lightly, to avert more tears. 'Is he ugly too? I'm persuaded he must be!'

Harriet shivered. 'His face is quite scarred, ma'am. And he shouts and—'

Isabella's eyebrows rose. 'Major Reynolds has shouted at you?'

'No, ma'am,' the girl said, earnest and wide-eyed. 'But he's a military man, so I know that he will.'

Isabella suppressed another smile. 'You have experience of military men?'

Harriet nodded. 'They stomp, and they have loud voices, and they…they shout, and—'

Isabella had a moment of enlightenment. 'Your grandfather is a military man?'

'A colonel, ma'am.'

A maid tapped on the door and entered, bobbing a curtsy. Rufus sat up, alert. 'Just seeing to the shutters, your ladyship.'

They sat in silence while the maid placed more wood on the fire and lit the wax candles with a taper and then busied herself closing the shutters against the dusk.

'Then it's settled,' Isabella said briskly, once the woman was gone. 'You shall travel with me to London tomorrow and stay until we know that your aunt is ready to receive you.'

Harriet gripped the handkerchief tightly. 'And your husband, ma'am? Are you certain he will allow it?'

'I have no husband. A widowed cousin keeps house with me in London. She does not often venture out, and will be pleased to have your company.'

The girl's eyes widened. 'No husband?'

'Yes,' Isabella said, smiling. 'I know it's odd, but I find it very comfortable to live without one!'

'How is the child?' Isabella asked, as she sat in front of the mirror brushing her hair. The bedchamber was more shadows than candlelight.

'Asleep.'

Isabella laughed. 'Partridge, such disapprobation in one word!'

Partridge sniffed, and said nothing.

Isabella laid down the hairbrush. The tooled silver back glinted in the candlelight. 'You may tell me that I'm meddling, Partridge, and you are quite right!'

Partridge silently folded the day's clothes.

She *was* meddling, quite dreadfully, but Mrs Botham had annoyed her, with her bristling, pious indignation. 'She reminds me of Felicity.' Isabella ran a fingertip over the silver crest on the hairbrush. *I will stand in her mother's stead for a while.* 'We shall keep her reputation intact, until her aunt can claim her.'

Partridge sniffed again.

Isabella turned to look at her. 'You think I should return her to her grandfather? You are perfectly correct, my dear Partridge. Only I fear he has already disowned her!'

Partridge said nothing.

Isabella turned back to the mirror. She picked up the hairbrush again. A strand of hair was caught in the soft bristles. She pulled it out and wound it meditatively around her fingertip, where it gleamed like gold thread in the candlelight. Yes, she would take the place of Harriet's mother for a few days, although no one would think the girl her daughter; they were too dissimilar in appearance. Harriet was dark and dainty, whereas she was tall and fair. The goddess of the harvest, an admirer had once likened her to. He'd even penned a poem. *To the harvest goddess with her corn-ripe hair...*

Isabella snorted beneath her breath. She leaned closer to the mirror, but the light was too dim to discern the faint lines she knew were at her eyes. *And I am merely nine-and-twenty.* Too young to be Harriet's mother.

'She won't be with us long,' she said aloud to Partridge. 'She shall write to her aunt tomorrow—and to her grandfather, to inform him that she is safe in a respectable household.'

And Harriet must write to Major Reynolds too, to beg his pardon for jilting him. One must be polite, even to an ogre.

Partridge finally broke her silence: 'She's not one of your strays, Miss Isabella. I hope you don't live to regret this.'

Isabella met her own eyes in the mirror. *So do I.* 'Nonsense,' she said, with a light laugh. 'What can possibly go wrong? No one will ever know!'

Chapter Two

Major Nicholas Reynolds, late of the 95th Rifles, looked across the expanse of his desk, with its tidy piles of parchment and the sturdy inkpot and sharp-nibbed quills and the letter knife he'd picked up in Spain, and said, 'No.'

'But, sir—'

Nicholas sighed. He laid down his quill and pushed aside the letter he'd been writing. 'What did I say last time?'

'That you wouldn't pay off any more of my debts,' his nephew said sulkily, not meeting his eyes.

'Precisely. And I always keep my word, Charlie.'

He spoke quietly, but his nephew flushed, his cheeks reddening above the high points of his collar.

Nicholas sighed again. He rubbed his forehead. 'Did your father refuse to advance your allowance?'

'I haven't asked him,' Charlie said gruffly. 'You know how he is, sir. He'll scold me like a fishwife, and go on and on and and…'

Nicholas did know. He looked across the desk at his nephew. Charlie's hair was styled in the latest cut, his blue coat had padded shoulders, a nipped-in waist and extremely large gold buttons, and the intricacies of his neckcloth must have taken a good hour to achieve.

A bandbox creature. And Nicholas had no time for band-box creatures. There were more important things in life than one's clothing.

But beneath the extravagant attire was a young man who was in trouble.

Nicholas ran his fingertips lightly over the scar that ridged his cheek. *What to do?* He came to a decision. 'I'll buy that black horse of yours. How much do you want for him?'

'What?' Startled, Charlie looked up and met his eyes for the first time during the interview.

'How much for your black horse?'

'But…but I like that horse!'

'Then learn not to outrun the carpenter,' Nicholas said mildly.

Charlie flushed. His eyes lowered. 'Very well,' he said, sulky again.

He found his manners when Nicholas handed him a roll of guineas, stammering his thanks and bowing. Nicholas watched as he walked towards the door. Somewhere beneath the expensive, frivolous exterior was the rough-and-tumble boy who'd cared more for his horses than for his clothes. 'Charlie. Would you like a commission in the army?'

His nephew paused with his hand on the door knob. 'Sir?'

'A commission, Charlie. Would you like one?'

Charlie blinked. He looked slightly appalled. 'Thank you, sir, but…that is to say, I prefer…'

You prefer to be a man-milliner instead of a man.

'Let me know if you should ever change your mind.' Nicholas picked up his quill again, dismissing his nephew. He didn't look up as the door closed.

An hour later he finished his business correspondence and sealed the letters. At home he'd go for a ride, but in London there was little pleasure to be had in riding, with its busy streets and crowded parks and the *properness* of everything. There was no place for a man to gallop.

Unless he rode out to Richmond.

Nicholas glanced at the window. Fresh air. That's what he needed. Away from the fug of London. He pushed back his chair.

A footman knocked and opened the door. 'Your post, sir.'

Nicholas looked at the pile of invitations on the silver tray. This was another thing he disliked about town—all the balls and assemblies where the object wasn't to dance but to determine the eligibility of possible spouses. Looks, breeding, fortune—all were assessed in meticulous detail. *As if we were cattle at an auction.* 'Throw them in the fire.' He'd chosen a bride. The Marriage Mart—and all those appraising sideways glances—was behind him.

The footman halted. 'Sir?'

'Give them here,' Nicholas said impatiently, holding out his hand. 'And send round to the stables. I'd like Douro ready in twenty minutes.'

He went through the pile of letters swiftly, rejecting the invitations without reading them. A letter from Colonel Durham he put to one side. And there was another, written in a feminine hand that he didn't recognise. He reached for the letter knife, slit it open, and unfolded it, pausing as the butler knocked and opened the door.

'Sir? Lord Reynolds desires a word with you.'

Nicholas closed his eyes for a moment. He toyed—briefly—with the thought of not being home to his brother, then he opened his eyes and put down the letter. 'Send him in, Frye.'

He pushed out of the chair and walked across to the decanters. He needed brandy, if he was to talk with Gerald this early in the day.

'Nicholas! I must speak to you.'

'Brandy?' Nicholas asked, pouring himself a glass. He turned to face his brother.

It was like seeing himself in a mirror—only paler and soft with fat. No one would ever mistake him for Gerald, though, and not merely because of the scar. Gerald's clothes were as elaborate as his own were plain—the neckcloth extravagantly high, the waistcoat exotically embroidered. Fobs and seals and diamond pins adorned his person and tassels dangled from his boots. His hair was pomaded and he brought the scent of Steek's lavender water with him into the room. *Decked out like a prize pig at a fair*, Nicholas thought, barely managing to prevent his lip from curling.

Gerald shook his head. His eyebrows drew together. 'You gave my son money!'

Nicholas swallowed a mouthful of brandy. It was smoky on his tongue and warm in his throat. 'I bought that black horse of his.'

'To pay off his debts!'

Nicholas shrugged. 'I bought his horse. What he does with the money is up to him.'

His brother swung away. 'I give him a generous allowance,' he said, a bitter note in his voice. 'And yet he can never—' He swung back to face Nicholas. 'And you! Why does he come to you and not me!'

Because you scold like a fishwife. Nicholas shrugged again. 'He runs with a fast set,' he said. 'He would do better to find new friends.'

'And you encourage him by paying his debts!'

Nicholas sighed. 'Gerald—'

'I must request that you not give my son money,' Gerald said, with stiff pomposity.

'I didn't *give* him money,' Nicholas said, nettled. 'I bought his damned horse!'

'And I must ask that you don't put ideas into his head!'

'What ideas?'

'The army.'

'I don't think he's interested,' Nicholas said drily. Although it would do the boy good to learn there was more to life than clothes and gambling.

'I should forbid it!

'He's of age,' Nicholas pointed out. 'If he wishes to join the army, he may.'

'Not if I have any say in the matter!'

Nicholas discovered that his fingers were clenched around the glass. He relaxed them and drained the last of the brandy. 'Very well,' he said. 'I shan't mention it to him again.'

'Make certain you don't,' Gerald snapped. 'He pays far too much attention to what you say.'

'Does he?' Nicholas shrugged. 'I hadn't noticed.'

'He looks up to you as a hero.' The bitter note was back in Gerald's voice.

Nicholas was suddenly uncomfortable. He turned away and placed his empty glass on the sideboard. 'You have my word that I won't speak of it to him again,' he said, not looking at his brother.

But Gerald, with the tenacity that had earned him the nickname Terrier at Eton, persisted. 'I can think of nothing worse than for him to enter the army!'

'Really?' Nicholas turned back to face him. 'I can think of many worse things.'

Gerald flushed, hearing the sarcasm in his voice. 'The army—'

'A little discipline would do him good.'

Gerald stiffened. 'Are you implying that my son lacks—?'

'I'm not implying anything,' Nicholas said, impatient with the conversation. 'I'm merely saying that I think the army would do him good. And—' he held up his hand to forestall Gerald's interruption '—that you have my word I shan't mention the matter to him again.'

'Good!' Gerald snapped. 'Heaven forbid that my son should become like you!'

'Or you!' Nicholas retorted, stung into losing his temper.

Gerald drew himself up. 'What do you mean?'

Soft and useless is what I mean. 'Nothing,' he said. 'Forget it.'

'Damn it, Nicholas—'

Nicholas sighed and closed his eyes. Why did he always end up arguing with Gerald? 'Is that all?' he asked, opening his eyes. 'Because I have other business to attend to.' He walked back to his desk and sat down, reaching for the opened letter.

Gerald hesitated, and then turned on his heel and stalked across the study. 'I shall see you at Augusta's tonight,' he said, and shut the door with a snap.

Nicholas put down the letter. Damn it. Gussie's ball was this evening. He'd have to go.

He rubbed his face, feeling the scar beneath his fingers, the smoothness and roughness of his ruined cheek. *Why must we always argue?*

He knew the answer. Even when they were children it had been like this—no matter that Gerald was the eldest, the viscount; it was Nicholas people turned to for help. That Gerald's own son did it merely made it worse.

Nicholas sighed and opened his eyes. He looked down at the letter lying open on his desk. It was very short.

> Dear Sir,
> I regret that I find myself unable to marry you.
> Please accept my apologies.
> Harriet Durham

Nicholas pinched the bridge of his nose. He swore under his breath, quietly, and stood and walked to the sideboard and poured another brandy. He drank it slowly and deliberately. Then he went back to the desk and reached for Colonel Durham's letter. He slit it open with a swift, sharp movement.

The butler knocked on the door.

'What?' Nicholas said, frowning at him.

'Colonel Durham to see you, sir.'

Nicholas clenched his jaw. He exhaled sharply through his nose. 'Send him in.'

'Your horse, sir?'

Nicholas closed his eyes briefly. An ache was building in his temples. 'Another twenty minutes, Frye.'

'The weather, sir—'

He turned to look out of the window. A light, grey drizzle was falling. *Damn.* 'Twenty minutes,' he repeated. Because if he didn't gallop he was going to smash something.

He inhaled a deep breath, kept the thought of Richmond and Douro and a thundering gallop firmly in his mind, and turned to face Colonel Durham as Frye ushered him into the study.

The Colonel was a heavy man. He had the bearing of a soldier, despite his greying hair, and wore his clothes as if they were a uniform. Age hadn't been kind to him; his face had lost its flesh, falling into deep, ill-humoured wrinkles. Uncompromising furrows bracketed his mouth and pinched between his eyebrows.

Nicholas bowed. 'I was just about to read your letter, sir.'

'Don't bother,' the Colonel said brusquely. 'I had hoped to avert—' His mouth tightened. 'But it's too late.'

'Brandy, sir? Or shall I have Frye bring up a bottle of claret?'

'Brandy,' the colonel said, glaring at him.

He's embarrassed, Nicholas realised. *Embarrassed—and angry.*

Frye withdrew, closing the door. Nicholas walked across to the sideboard. He poured the Colonel a large glass of brandy and himself a small one. 'Please be seated, sir.'

Colonel Durham sat.

'I have received a letter from your granddaughter,' Nicholas said, handing him the brandy. 'I understand she wishes to terminate our engagement.'

Rage flushed the Colonel's face. He swallowed his

brandy, grimacing. 'I must apologise for my granddaughter's behaviour.'

Nicholas sat behind his desk. 'May I speak to her, sir?'

'Speak to her?' Colonel Durham uttered a harsh laugh. 'By all means. If you can find her!'

Nicholas frowned. 'I beg your pardon?'

'The stupid chit has run away!'

Nicholas placed his brandy glass carefully on the desk. 'Run away? Why?'

'Because she doesn't wish to marry you.'

Nicholas looked down at his brandy. There was a bitter taste in his mouth. 'If she had told me,' he said quietly, 'I would have withdrawn my suit—'

'Ridiculous nonsense!' Colonel Durham said. 'And so I told her.'

Nicholas raised his head. 'She spoke to you about it, sir?'

The Colonel nodded.

'And you said…?'

'That it was her duty to marry you.'

Nicholas positioned his glass precisely in the middle of his blotter. He could feel anger rising in him. 'And then she ran away?'

Colonel Durham's face reddened. 'She makes a fool out of me!'

No, Nicholas thought sourly. *She makes a fool out of me.* He drank a mouthful of brandy, not tasting it. 'Where is she?'

'I don't know, and I don't care! I've wiped my hands of her.'

Nicholas put down his glass. Colonel Durham was a rigid, narrow-minded bully—he'd known that before he'd offered for Harriet's hand—but to disown the girl, when she was so young, was… *Criminal, that's what it was.* 'She's only seventeen years old. You can hardly—'

'What business is it of yours?' the Colonel snapped.

Nicholas looked at him coldly. 'It is entirely my business.

If you recall, sir, it is *me* she is betrothed to.' *And me she ran away from.*

The Colonel's mouth twisted. 'Some interfering busybody has her.' He dug inside his coat and tossed a wad of paper on Nicholas's desk. 'Here.'

Nicholas separated the sheets of paper and smoothed them. Two letters. He recognised the writing.

> Dear Grandfather,
> I have gone to live with my aunt. I know it is my duty to marry Major Reynolds, but I find myself unable to.
> Your granddaughter, Harriet

He glanced at the Colonel. 'This is dated four days ago.'

Colonel Durham shifted in his chair, as if he heard the unspoken accusation. 'I thought it would be an easy matter to find her and bring her back.'

And then what? Nicholas didn't ask the question. The answer was obvious: the Colonel had intended to browbeat Harriet into marriage.

And I was never to know.

Anger surged inside him. He gritted his teeth together and read the second letter. It was dated yesterday.

> Dear Grandfather,
> Please do not be concerned for my safety. A kind benefactress has given me shelter until I can be united with my aunt.
> Your granddaughter, Harriet.

Nicholas put down the letter. 'Who is the benefactress?'

'I don't know. And I don't care!'

'You should.' His voice held a note of reprimand. 'Your granddaughter's safety is entirely in her hands.'

Colonel Durham's face grew redder. 'Without her interference, I would have had Harriet back by now. The matter could have been kept quiet! Now—'

'It can still be kept quiet,' Nicholas said calmly. His hands wanted to clench. He spread his fingers on the desk. 'No one need know why the engagement has been terminated.'

The Colonel's eyes slid away from him. 'I stopped at my club on the way here—' He cleared his throat. 'I may have uttered a few imprudent words.'

Nicholas exhaled through his teeth, silently. He didn't need to be told what Colonel Durham meant—the Colonel was a man of loud rages. By tonight half of London would know of Harriet's flight. *And because you couldn't control your temper, we will both feature in society's latest scandal.*

'Stupid girl!' Colonel Durham said savagely. 'If I could lay my hands on her, I'd horsewhip her!'

Nicholas looked at him with dislike. *It is you I'd like to horsewhip.* Anger was pushing upwards in his throat. 'I'll send a notice to the newspapers,' he said, speaking with careful politeness. 'Stating that my engagement to your granddaughter is terminated.' He stood and bowed. 'Good day, sir.'

The furrows in the Colonel's face deepened, showing his displeasure. For a moment it looked as if he would say more, then he pushed to his feet and nodded curtly. 'Good day.'

Nicholas watched him depart. Anger thumped inside his skull. He picked up the letters again. *I know it is my duty to marry Major Reynolds,* Harriet had written, *but I find myself unable to.*

He clenched his hands, crumpling the paper. Now he'd have to start again—attending balls and assemblies, dancing, making polite conversation, selecting a girl who was quiet and biddable and easily moulded into the wife he wanted—while the ton watched with sideways glances and amused whispers.

He threw the letters aside and went in search of his riding gloves.

Chapter Three

Isabella looked around the ballroom. She gave a sigh of pleasure. London. The gaiety, the busyness. 'I do love the Season.'

'Yes.' But her companion was frowning.

'Have you the headache, Gussie?'

'Headache?' Augusta Washburne's brow cleared. 'No, I'm cross.'

'Cross?' Isabella glanced around the ballroom again, her gaze catching on the shimmer of expensive fabric and the glitter of jewels, the bright flare of the candles in the chandeliers. The room was crowded to its furthest extent; beneath the music the babble of voices was loud. She could perceive no reason for Gussie to be cross. The ball was undeniably a success.

'It's this business with Nicholas!' Gussie said. 'Everyone's talking about it.'

'Nicholas?'

'What a dreadful squeeze, darling!' Lady Faraday swooped on Gussie. 'One can scarcely move!' She turned to Isabella, the three tall feathers in her turban swaying and nodding. Her gown was pink and trimmed with an astonishing number of flounces. 'Isabella, darling! You're finally back in town!'

'Sarah, how do you do?' Isabella said politely, but Lady Faraday had already turned back to Gussie, her eyes bright and expectant.

'What's this I hear about your cousin? Is it true? His bride ran away?'

Gussie's face tightened. She glanced at Isabella. 'Yes.'

Isabella's pleasure in the ball became tinged with unease. 'Your cousin?'

'Major Nicholas Reynolds.'

Isabella stared at Gussie. 'The ogre? He's your cousin?'

'Ogre?' Lady Faraday uttered a tittering laugh.

'Ogre?' said Gussie, in quite a different tone of voice. Her eyebrows pinched together again. 'Who called him that?'

Isabella bit the tip of her tongue. *Fool.* 'Major Reynolds is your cousin?'

Gussie nodded.

'And his bride has run away!' Lady Faraday exclaimed. 'Now tell me, Augusta—'

Her gleeful curiosity was too much for Isabella. 'Sarah, I do believe Mrs Drummond-Burrell is trying to catch your attention.'

'She is? Oh, pray excuse me—'

Isabella watched her go—feathers bobbing above the pink ball gown—and frowned. How had Lady Faraday known about Harriet? The child had written her letters barely a day ago, and yet already a gossip like Sarah Faraday—

'An ogre!' Gussie said. 'Where did you hear that?'

'Oh…I've received a number of callers,' Isabella said, skirting around the truth. 'You know how it is when one first arrives in town.'

Gussie's frown was fierce. 'But who *said* it?'

The temptation to lie was strong. Isabella moistened her lips. She looked down at her fan and spread the pierced ivory sticks. 'I heard…I believe it may have been the person who is sheltering Miss Durham.' *Not a lie. Not quite.*

Breath hissed between Gussie's teeth. 'She had no right!'
I know.

'Who is she?' Gussie demanded.

Isabella closed her fan. 'No one I have spoken to knows,'
she said, truthfully. She smoothed the long gloves up her
arms, deeply uncomfortable. 'I didn't realise Major Reynolds
was your cousin.'

'Second cousin. He's Lord Reynolds's brother.'

Isabella experienced a sinking sensation in her stomach.
The major was a nobleman? 'I don't believe I've met him.'

'He'll be here tonight,' Gussie said, turning to scan the
ballroom. 'I'll introduce you.'

'Oh.' Isabella followed her glance, suddenly nervous. 'But
perhaps he won't come if everyone is talking—'

'Nicholas is not a coward,' Gussie said staunchly.

'Oh,' Isabella said again. She swallowed. 'I look forward
to meeting him.'

Nicholas halted. He looked across the street. Flambeaux
burned and a red carpet had been laid up the steps. He braced
himself for what was to come: stares, whispers.

I don't have to attend. I can just turn and walk away.

On the heels of that thought came anger. He was used to
stares—his face made certain of that—and he was damned
if he was going to hide from tattlemongers!

Nicholas strode across the street and up the steps. He
handed his hat and gloves to a footman and walked up the
curving staircase towards the sound of music and the rise and
fall of voices, punctuated by laughter.

He was late. The ball was well underway. The large room
was stuffy, the air warm and over-scented, and the flowers in
the vases were wilting.

A *contredanse* was playing. Nicholas stood inside the
doorway, watching as the dancers went through their sets. His
gaze slid over débutantes in pale gowns, officers in uniform,

matrons with curling feathers in their headdresses. The officers and the matrons were of no interest; the débutantes were.

The dark-haired, laughing girl was pretty, but—*too bold*, he decided. He didn't want a *coquette* for a wife. Beside her in the set was a redhead who looked possible. Shy, not flirting—

'Nicholas! I had quite given up on you!'

Nicholas turned. 'Gussie.' He bowed. 'You must forgive me.'

'You are forgiven,' his cousin said with a laugh, and stood on tiptoe to kiss him.

'You look well,' Nicholas said, smiling. With her shining brown hair and shining brown eyes and the scattering of freckles on her nose, Gussie looked more like a schoolgirl than the mother of three children.

His cousin ignored the compliment. She clasped his hand tightly. 'Now, Nicholas, you must not run away!'

Nicholas lost his smile. 'As bad as that, is it?'

'You know how London gossips.' She pulled a face. 'But you must dance before you hide in the card room!'

'An order, Gussie?' He raised his eyebrows.

'Yes,' she said frankly, 'because you know what people will say if you don't!'

He did. It was another reason to dislike London: everyone watching and passing judgement.

'I have saved the next dance for you,' Gussie said. 'It's to be a waltz!'

'My timing is most fortunate, then,' he said lightly, smiling.

Gussie showed him a dimple. She placed her hand on his sleeve as the sets broke up and the dancers left the floor. There was barely room for anyone to move.

'Congratulations,' Nicholas said. 'A squeeze.'

'Yes,' Gussie said, with no attempt at modesty. 'It's most gratifying!'

Nicholas laughed at her candour. It took his attention from
the glances that were directed his way. No one was ill bred
enough to point, but he was aware of heads turning, a stir of
conversation. *Ignore them*, he told himself.

He had learned to hold his head up, to not hide his ruined
cheek; he would learn to ignore this. It couldn't last for ever;
the London gossips would be talking of someone else soon
enough.

He scanned the ballroom. Gerald stood in the far corner,
his fleshy, jowled face flushed with heat and alcohol. And
there was Gussie's husband, Lucas, in the company of a
striking blonde in a blue gown. Nicholas kept his gaze on the
blonde in a long moment of appreciation, liking her height,
her generous figure, her full mouth.

Gussie maintained a stream of light chatter as they took
their places on the dance floor, but once the music started, her
tone changed. 'I am very sorry, Nicholas, about what has
happened.'

Nicholas looked past her. *So am I*. He caught someone's
eye—a matron with three feathers in her hair and a pink
gown with an overabundance of flounces, who coloured at
being caught staring and hastily averted her gaze.

Nicholas's jaw tightened. He returned his attention to
Gussie.

'I should warn you…' She grimaced, a brief screwing up
of her face.

'Warn me?' He tried to laugh. 'Why?'

'Nicholas…you are being called an ogre.'

'What?' Nicholas almost halted in the middle of the
ballroom.

Habit—and the tug of Gussie's hand—kept him dancing.
'It's merely someone's foolishness!' she said. 'You must not
pay any attention to it!'

They danced in silence. Beneath the music was the murmur

of voices. He saw quick glances directed his way, lips shaping words. He didn't need to hear them to know what was being said.

If the name didn't suit him so well, he would laugh it off, but it fitted perfectly—the scarred face, the runaway bride. *An ogre.*

Anger built inside him, growing with each step that he took. He tasted it on his tongue, bitter—

'You must not think about it!' Gussie said, as the music came to an end.

Nicholas forced a smile. 'I assure you, I shall not.'

Gussie chose to believe him. 'Good,' she said, with a quick smile that showed her dimples. 'And now, Nicholas, I must introduce you to a particular friend of mine.'

He wanted to balk. His mood was too unpleasant—

'Her name is Isabella,' Gussie said, tucking her hand into his arm. 'Lady Isabella Knox. She was dancing with Lucas.' She stood slightly on tiptoe and glanced around the ballroom. 'Do you see them?'

The blonde? He saw her. She stood out among the débutantes and the matrons, tall and elegant and deliciously curved. Her hair was an extraordinary colour, like ripe wheat in sunlight.

Nicholas's mood improved slightly. *One more dance*, he decided. And then he would take his rage to the card room.

Chapter Four

There was no mistaking Major Reynolds. The scar was broad and livid on the left side of his face, stretching from temple to cheekbone to jaw. He was a soldier; that was clear as he escorted Gussie across the dance floor. It wasn't just the military cut of his clothes, it was the way he held himself, the unconscious air of authority, the alertness with which he scanned the room, the hardness of his mouth and eyes. *A dangerous man.*

Isabella looked away. She tried to concentrate on Lucas Washburne's conversation.

'The ogre comes,' a lady murmured behind her, and smothered a laugh.

Irritation surged in Isabella's chest. That wretched Sarah Faraday! How dare she spread—!

'Isabella, I'd like you to meet my cousin, Major Nicholas Reynolds.'

Isabella swallowed her irritation. She fixed a smile on her lips and turned her head.

Major Reynolds stood before her, tall, with cold eyes and a scarred face, precisely as Harriet had described.

No, not precisely. Major Reynolds wasn't old. Mid-thirties, at a guess.

'…ogre,' she heard whispered behind her.

The nervousness returned, tightening beneath her breast-bone. *If he discovers that I am the source of that appellation—*

'How do you do, Major Reynolds?' she said hastily, giving him her hand, hoping that guilt wasn't stamped across her face.

The Major made no sign that he had heard the whisper. 'It is a pleasure to meet you, Lady Isabella.' He bowed over her gloved fingers.

'Be warned, Nicholas!' Gussie said with a light, bubbling laugh. 'She will try to thrust a stray animal upon you.'

The Major released her hand. 'No lapdogs, I beg of you, ma'am.' His smile didn't reach his eyes.

Unease prickled over Isabella's skin. *He's angry.*

'It will more likely be a kitten with half a tail,' Gussie said. 'Or a flea-ridden puppy—'

'Both of which we have,' her husband said drily.

For a fleeting second the Major looked amused. He smiled faintly. The corner of his right eye creased slightly. The left side of his face, scarred, showed no sign of amusement.

The musicians began to tune their instruments again. 'The quadrille,' Lucas Washburne said, holding out his hand to his wife. 'This is our dance. If you will excuse us?'

Isabella watched them go. She transferred her gaze to Major Reynolds and smiled at him politely. 'How long have you been in town, Major?' She knew the answer. Harriet had told her in the carriage; Major Reynolds had come to town three weeks ago, in search of a bride.

A man who acts swiftly.

'Three weeks.' The Major's eyes were on her face. Their colour was disconcerting, a clear, chilly green. 'Are you claimed for this dance?'

Isabella hesitated. *I wish I was.* 'No,' she said. 'I am not.'

The Major's face hardened. He'd seen the hesitation.

Shame made her flush. 'It would be my pleasure to dance with you, Major,' she said, opening her fan.

Major Reynolds offered her his arm. 'Then let us join a set.' The words were politely spoken, but she heard an edge of irony in his voice.

Isabella bit her lip. She fanned herself, hoping to take the heat from her cheeks, and laid her hand lightly on the Major's sleeve. The cut of his coat was plain, almost austere, and the fabric was a green so dark it was nearly black. The hard angles of his face, the severe cut of his coat, the darkness of the cloth matched one another.

They walked on to the dance floor amid the murmur of conversation and rustle of fabric.

'How long have you been in town?' Major Reynolds asked.

Isabella heard the word *ogre* whispered to her right. 'I arrived two days ago,' she said hastily, loudly. 'On Saturday. I've been in Derbyshire, visiting my brother and making the acquaintance of my newest nephew.'

The Major had heard the whisper. Anger glinted in his eyes. He halted. 'Perhaps you would prefer not to dance, Lady Isabella?'

I would. But guilt made it impossible to take the proffered escape. 'Nonsense!' Isabella said, shutting the fan.

'You can hardly wish to dance with an ogre, ma'am.' The Major's voice was light, his expression sardonic, his eyes hard.

'You are mistaken,' Isabella said, lifting her chin and silently condemning Sarah Faraday to perdition.

Major Reynolds made no answer. He led her to a position in a set that was forming. His manner was quite composed. He paid no attention to the sideways glances, the whispers.

Isabella took her place opposite him. She met his eyes—cold and hard and so clear they seemed to look right through her—and curtsied as the musicians played the opening chords. She understood why Harriet was afraid of him. *Not the scar, but his eyes.*

She observed Major Reynolds obliquely as they danced. His resemblance to his brother was strong. The bones of his face were well shaped, his features regular. Without the scar he would have been an attractive man. With it…

An ogre.

Isabella bit her lip. She opened her fan again.

The Major had a soldier's physique; in that respect he didn't resemble Lord Reynolds. His body was lean, not fleshy, hard-muscled, not soft. Like his brother, his hair was the colour of honey—a shade between brown and gold—but his skin was bronzed from the sun. The scar covered the left side of his face, a thickly ridged burn, purplish-pink, barbaric, making him look half-savage.

Was it a legacy of Waterloo, the battle that had claimed so many of England's finest last year? Or did it date back to the conflict in Spain?

They weren't questions she could ask.

Major Reynolds moved through the quadrille with calm confidence, seemingly oblivious to the sideways glances, the muffled giggles, the whispers, that his progress afforded. Only his eyes, glittering with anger, showed that he was aware of the stir he was creating.

With each step that he took, Isabella's guilt grew. It had been unforgivable, uttering the word *ogre* in front of Sarah Faraday. The Major was no husband for Harriet, but he didn't deserve this. And however much she might blame Lady Faraday, she knew who was truly at fault: *Me. My wretched tongue did this.*

And with the guilt was a reluctant admiration. The Major had courage to hold his head up, the scar so bold across his cheek, in the face of so much attention.

There was no pleasure in the quadrille, in the steps of *l'été* and *la pastourelle*. Each half-heard whisper, each muffled giggle, served to enhance her guilt. *Shut up!* she wanted to hiss to the dark-haired débutante in the neighbouring set. Her hand itched to box the girl's ears.

The word she had uttered only a few hours ago was on everyone's lips. *I've turned him into an object of ridicule.* The worst of it was, she couldn't undo it.

The quadrille had never been so interminably long before, so filled with discomfort. Her relief, when the musicians played the last chord, was intense.

Major Reynolds escorted her from the dance floor, calm and smiling, with anger in his eyes. 'Thank you,' he said politely, bowing.

'It was a pleasure, Major.'

He acknowledged her words with a slight lifting of his eyebrows, a tiny, wry movement.

The wryness gave her courage. Isabella took a deep breath and laid her hand on his arm. 'Major Reynolds, you must dance every dance tonight.'

The wryness vanished. He seemed to stiffen. 'Must I?'

'Yes.' The bright, cold anger in his eyes was daunting, but she held tightly to her courage. 'Major, you must pay no attention to what is being said—and you must not leave early!'

His jaw seemed to harden. *He thinks me impertinent.*

Isabella took another deep breath. Guilt was lodged in her chest, a hard lump. 'Come,' she said, smiling, coaxing, aware of nervous perspiration prickling across her skin. *I owe him this.* 'I will dance the next waltz with you!'

'Charity, ma'am?' His eyes were bright and hard.

No, guilt. 'Not at all,' Isabella said, lifting her chin. 'I save my charity for animals!'

The Major smiled abruptly, a genuine smile that took the anger from his eyes. 'Lapdogs.'

He looked quite different, smiling. Isabella relaxed fractionally. 'They are usually much larger,' she said. 'And often quite ugly. It can be difficult to find them homes!'

Major Reynolds laughed. For a brief instant he looked almost boyish, not a battle-hardened soldier. 'Very well. The waltz.' He bowed. 'It has been a pleasure to meet you, Lady Isabella.'

Isabella watched as he walked around the perimeter of the ballroom. Heads turned as he passed. Someone laughed, and turned it hastily into a cough. *I did that.*

She couldn't take the word back, but she could try to undo the harm of it.

Her conscience demanded it.

Nicholas endured a cotillion, two country dances, and a *boulanger*—the latter with a partner who met his eyes once, blushed vividly, and stared steadfastly at the floor for the rest of the dance—before the second waltz was played. He didn't need to search for Lady Isabella Knox; he knew precisely where she was.

He returned his partner to her mother and walked around the ballroom.

'There he is. The ogre.'

It was a whisper, but loud enough to reach his ears. Nicholas gritted his teeth. He kept a determined smile on his face as he took the final steps that brought him to Lady Isabella's side. His mood lifted as he led her on to the dance floor. It lifted still further when the musicians began to play. They made their bows to each other. Lady Isabella gave him her hand. Nicholas drew her close. For the next few minutes he'd forget about runaway brides and—

'How has your evening been, Major Reynolds?'

He met Lady Isabella's eyes. They were a shade between grey and blue, and quite serious.

'I have had more comfortable evenings,' he admitted.

'Yes,' she said. 'So have I.' A small frown marred her brow. 'In fact, Major, I have given the matter some thought, and I think I know how to come about.'

He experienced a twinge of misgiving. 'You do?'

'Yes,' Lady Isabella said. 'You must become my beau!'

Surprise made him laugh. Heads turned as people looked at them. Nicholas ignored the stares. 'Your beau?' He shook his head and almost laughed again. 'I think your husband would have something to say about that!'

'I have no husband.'

No husband? He was suddenly aware of the curve of her waist beneath his palm in a way he hadn't been before, of her gloved hand clasping his, of the soft fullness of her lips—

'Knox was my father's name, Major Reynolds, not my husband's.'

Nicholas cleared his throat. 'Oh,' he said, inadequately.

'I am the eldest daughter of a duke. London does not laugh at me.' There was no arrogance in Lady Isabella's tone, merely a plain matter-of-factness. 'And if you are my beau—'

'London will not laugh at me.' He was abruptly angry. 'Thank you for the offer, Lady Isabella, but I do not need your—'

'It's not charity,' she said calmly, meeting his eyes.

His mouth tightened. 'No?'

'No. I don't like what has happened, Major Reynolds. It makes me quite cross!'

It seemed she told the truth: her lips pressed together and her eyebrows pinched into a frown. The frown faded as he watched. 'I do not like being cross,' she said, with that same matter-of-factness. 'So I should like to stop this gossip.' Her lips turned up in a smile. 'What do you say?'

His own anger wasn't so easy to relinquish. He frowned at her. 'Are you in the habit of taking beaux?'

'No,' she said, apparently unruffled by his disapproval. 'But given the circumstances, I am prepared to make an exception. It will only be for a week, two at the most.'

'No one would believe it,' Nicholas said flatly.

Her eyebrows rose. 'Why not?'

'In case you hadn't noticed, madam, I am somewhat disfigured.' There was a bitter edge to his words he hadn't intended.

Her gaze shifted to his cheek. Her brow furrowed again, faintly.

Nicholas gritted his teeth. He knew what she saw; he'd seen it often enough in the mirror: the thick ridges of scar tissue, the melted skin, the—

Lady Isabella met his eyes. She shrugged. 'It's not important.'

She meant it. He heard the truth in her voice.

Nicholas almost missed a step. He cleared his throat again. 'Madam—'

'I am an eccentric,' Lady Isabella said, with another light shrug of her shoulders. 'If I choose you as my beau, London will believe it.' She smiled at him, golden and beautiful. 'Now, how shall we go about it? Two dances tonight, and then…tomorrow I shall meet you in Hyde Park and take you up in my phaeton. Are you free in the afternoon, Major?'

He eyed her circumspectly.

'Well, Major Reynolds?'

He turned her offer over in his mind. As a charade it had its appeals. Playing beau to a woman as lovely as Lady Isabella, driving in Hyde Park with her, dancing… 'Very well,' he said, feeling almost cheerful. 'Yes.'

'Five o'clock in the park,' Lady Isabella said as the waltz ended. 'By the Stanhope Gate.'

Nicholas's ill humour returned as he escorted her from the dance floor. His ears heard the word *ogre*, half-whispered, to his right.

Lady Isabella heard it too. He saw her bite her lower lip. She glanced at him.

Nicholas smiled tightly. *If I knew to whom I owe that name, I'd—*

The candles in the chandeliers seemed to burn brighter for

a moment. The crystal drops glittered, as sharp-edged as shards of glass.

I can find out.

Nicholas inhaled, smelling the mingled scents of perfume and perspiration, and beneath them something darker: his own anger. Determination solidified inside him. He'd find out. It couldn't be impossible. Someone must know. Ladies always talked among themselves. Perhaps Gussie knew, or even Lady Isabella…

Nicholas looked at his companion with renewed interest. 'Lady Isabella?'

'Yes?'

'Do you know to whom I owe my sobriquet?' He tried to speak as lightly as he could, to hide the anger in his voice, but she must have heard it. Her cheeks flushed delicately. She opened her fan.

'Why do you wish to know, Major Reynolds?'

He shrugged. 'It's useful to know one's enemies.'

'Enemies?' She glanced at him quickly. 'I'm certain there was no malice intended, Major. Indeed, you must not think it!'

Nicholas's interest sharpened. 'You know who it was?'

Lady Isabella fingered the thin ivory sticks of her fan. They were painted with tiny roses, red and yellow and pink, with dark green leaves. She didn't meet his eyes. 'I believe it came from the lady who is sheltering Miss Durham.'

Harriet's kind benefactress. Anger flared in his belly.

Lady Isabella glanced up at him. 'But no one knows who she is.'

Someone must.

'I'm certain it wasn't ill meant, Major Reynolds! It was foolishness, nothing more. Pray, do not think about it!'

He smiled, tightly. 'I assure you, madam, I shall not.' He wouldn't think; he'd *do*. He'd find Harriet's benefactress, and when he did—

An eye for an eye. Her humiliation, in return for his own.

Chapter Five

Isabella took a deep breath as the phaeton entered Hyde Park by Stanhope Gate. *Be calm. Be confident.* But it was hard to be either calm or confident when she was this nervous.

She glanced down at Rufus. He, at least, was enjoying himself. He sat up, alert, his tongue hanging out and his ears pricked. His tail wagged, stirring the vandyked flounce that ornamented the hem of her carriage dress.

Isabella took another deep breath. She squared her shoulders and began to scan the thoroughfare. Curricles and a barouche, gentlemen on horseback, ladies walking—fashionable London had turned out to see and be seen. *Where are you, Major Reynolds?*

Despite the nerves, her conscience was easier. This was something she had to do. Her penance, if it could be called that. Not for sheltering Harriet—she had no qualms about her role as protector—but for her disastrous slip of the tongue last night.

Her fingers tightened on the reins. *There he is.*

The Major stood to one side of the drive, looking towards the Serpentine and the trees of Kensington Gardens. Isabella observed him as she slowed the horses to a walk. He wore a gentleman's clothes—dark brown coat and buckskin breeches and top hat—but even so he looked like a soldier. His attitude was alert as he waited, watchful and unsmiling.

Her opinion was the same as it had been last night: *a dangerous man*. He stood quietly and yet there was something hard-edged about his figure, his face. She had no difficulty believing that he had killed.

In profile the scar wasn't visible. The lines of his face— brow and cheekbone, nose and jaw—were strong. He was attractive—and then he turned his head, showing her his left cheek. The scar was vivid on his face, almost shocking. Something tightened inside her, a tiny recoil, at the pain it represented.

Isabella lifted her chin and fixed a smile on her face. 'Major Reynolds.' She brought the horses to a halt. 'Fancy meeting you here.'

His lips twitched. 'Yes,' he said. 'Fancy that.'

Some of Isabella's tension eased. Her smile felt more natural. 'Shall we take a turn around the park together?'

The Major bowed, with none of a dandy's flourishes. *Very much a soldier*, she thought, watching. 'I should be delighted,' he said.

Her groom jumped down and Major Reynolds climbed into the phaeton. Rufus, true to his mongrel origins, was not fastidious when it came to new acquaintances. He welcomed the Major eagerly and tried to lick his face.

'Not quite a lapdog,' the Major said.

Isabella looked at Rufus's long legs and unruly tail. 'Not quite.' She brought the horses to a walk again. 'Tell me, Major, did you receive an invitation to the Harringtons' ball tonight?'

'Yes,' he said, rubbing one of Rufus's ears. 'But I hadn't thought to go.' He glanced at her. His expression became wry. 'I take it I'm attending?'

'Yes,' said Isabella. 'We shall dance the first waltz and the closing dance.'

The Major stopped rubbing Rufus's ear. He sat back and observed her. 'The closing dance?'

'Yes.' Isabella said. *So that you shall not leave early.*

His eyes narrowed slightly.

Isabella smiled. 'And you may take me to supper, Major.'

Major Reynolds observed her a few seconds longer, and then said with the utmost politeness, 'It will be my pleasure, Lady Isabella.'

That cold, green gaze was oddly intimidating. Isabella cleared her throat. 'And tomorrow is Wednesday, which means Almack's.'

An expression of dismay briefly crossed the Major's face. 'Must I—?'

'Yes.'

Major Reynolds observed her for a moment. The set of his jaw was almost grim. 'Very well, madam.'

Isabella transferred her attention to the horses. 'Which dances would you like? A waltz and—'

'Two waltzes,' the Major said firmly.

She glanced at him, startled. 'Two?'

'If I am to endure Almack's, then it must be two waltzes.'

'Oh.' She was suddenly, disconcertingly, aware of him as a man. The broad, strong hands, the muscled length of his thigh, the sheer size of him as he sat alongside her. She swallowed and looked away. 'Now, we must meet as many people as possible,' she said briskly. 'Do you see anyone—? Oh, Lady Cowper! Are you ready, Major?'

An hour later, her jaw ached from smiling. Rufus lay across the Major's boots, asleep. 'I think that's enough for one day,' Isabella said.

'More than enough,' the Major said drily.

It was draining to be the object of so much attention. But the first step was now behind them, and in a few hours they'd

take the second. By midnight London would be talking about
Major Reynolds, and not merely to call him an ogre.

'We shall do this again tomorrow,' Isabella said, trying to
sound cheerful. *My penance.*

'If you think it necessary, Lady Isabella.' There was no inflection in the Major's voice.

She glanced at him. He had to have enjoyed the polite and
meaningless conversations, the bright-eyed curiosity, the
unspoken interest, even less than she had.

'Yes,' she said firmly. It was necessary. *I won't have you
laughed at because of me.* She bit her lip, wishing she could
apologise, but his face made it impossible—the hardness at
his mouth, the hardness in his eyes. 'I wish to be of assis-
tance, Major.' It was the closest she could come to an apology.
'If there is any way that I can help you in this matter, please
inform me.'

Major Reynolds looked at her for a few seconds in silence,
and then seemed to come to an abrupt decision. 'There is one
thing, madam.'

'Oh?'

'If you should discover the whereabouts of Miss Durham's
benefactress, I would be pleased to know it.' His voice was
light, but his eyes—

Cold. Angry.

Isabella swallowed.

'You may put me down here,' the Major said.

Isabella obeyed automatically, reining in the horses. Her
mouth was dry. *Don't panic.* She moistened her lips. 'Why
do you wish to know?'

His smile was hard-edged. 'I should like to make her acquaintance.'

'Why, Major?'

Major Reynolds touched the scar on his cheek. 'She
coined my new name, did she not?'

Isabella bit her lip. She nodded.

'Then I should like to make her acquaintance.' He lowered his hand. Anger glittered in his eyes. 'Have you heard anyone speak of the woman's identity? Or her whereabouts?'

Isabella shook her head. 'No one knows who she is,' she said hurriedly. *A lie.* She knew, and so did her cousin, Mrs Westin. And her maid, Partridge, and the other servants.

Too many people.

Major Reynolds accepted her words with a nod. He wore the clothes of a gentleman, but in every other way he was a soldier, his expression grim, his eyes cold. Ruthless. Dangerous.

She shivered.

'I intend to discover her location.'

Isabella didn't need to ask why: revenge.

Major Reynolds leapt lightly down from the phaeton. He looked up at her, his eyes narrowed against the sun. 'Thank you for your company, Lady Isabella.'

She attempted a smile. 'It has been a pleasure, Major.'

The Major bowed. 'Good day, madam.'

Isabella watched him go. *I lied to him.* But the shame she felt was eclipsed by another emotion: panic.

She had the sensation that she couldn't breathe. Fear prickled over her skin. Major Reynolds was hunting her.

The first thing Isabella did when she set foot in her house on Clarges Street was to send for her man of business; the second was to speak to her cousin.

Mrs Westin was in her sitting room, a comfortable chamber with walls of pale green and a white marble fireplace. Sèvres china adorned the mantelpiece: bowls and cache-pots and a particularly fine vase of deep blue, gilded with chinoiserie decoration. Figurines perched on side tables and peered from the glass-fronted mahogany cabinet, looking at her with tiny, painted eyes.

Mrs Westin was engaged in her favourite occupation:

knitting for the poor. Harriet sat on a chair alongside her, reading aloud from what Isabella recognised as An Improving Work. Mrs Westin, while never deprecating Isabella's preference for novels, refused to read such books herself.

Harriet looked up. 'Lady Isabella!' She put the book aside, rose and curtsied. Her expression was shyly adoring.

Isabella forced a smile. 'Hello, my dear. Would you be so kind as to give me a moment alone with my cousin?'

She waited until the door had shut behind Harriet before turning to her cousin. 'Elinor…'

Mrs Westin had laid down her knitting. She sat with her hands folded in her lap and an expression of mild enquiry in her faded blue eyes. 'Yes, my dear?'

'Elinor, I have come to ask you…' Isabella felt heat rise in her cheeks. She turned away and walked to stand at the window.

'Is everything quite all right, my dear?'

'Oh, yes! That is to say…' She turned resolutely back to face her cousin. 'Major Reynolds has it in his head to find me.'

Mrs Westin's brow creased. 'Find you? But I thought you were meeting him in Hyde Park today? Although I cannot see why it is *your* responsibility to stop London laughing at him. It has nothing to do with you!'

Isabella found herself unable to meet her cousin's eyes— or make a full confession. 'No, Elinor,' she said, looking down at her clasped hands, shame burning in her cheeks. 'You misunderstand. Major Reynolds means to discover where Harriet is staying. And…and he is very angry!'

'Oh,' said Mrs Westin. 'Oh, dear.'

'He shall be much in my company the next week or so, and…and it is likely that you shall meet him, and…' She glanced up, twisting her hands together. 'I have come to beg you to…to not tell him that Harriet is here, even if he should ask you.'

Mrs Westin's expression became one of gentle reproach. 'Thou shalt not lie, my dear Isabella,' she said in her soft voice. 'The good Lord commands it of us.'

Isabella's cheeks grew hotter. 'I know,' she said. 'But…but could you please not tell him that it is I who—'

'If Major Reynolds should ask me,' Mrs Westin said, picking up her knitting again, 'I shall tell him that I pay no attention to gossip. *That* is the truth.'

Isabella released the breath she'd been holding. 'Thank you, dearest Elinor.'

'You did quite right to rescue that poor child,' her cousin said, setting neat stitches of grey wool. 'But I should have thought you would have returned her to her grandfather. Surely he would not have been so hard-hearted as to turn her away. However, I'm sure you did what you thought was right!'

Isabella bit her lip.

'I own, I cannot like the subterfuge. There is something distasteful about it.'

Isabella agreed. *Extremely distasteful.* She'd not thought it would be, when she had so blithely offered Harriet sanctuary. But the lies she had uttered, the skirting around the truth, the begging of her cousin's complicity—

Abhorrent, that's what it was.

'And it must be said that Harriet should not have run away!' Mrs Westin glanced up from her knitting. 'One must always do one's duty to one's family, however unpleasant it may be.'

Isabella opened her mouth to disagree—*surely not an unhappy marriage!*—and then prudently closed it. Duty was the tenet Mrs Westin lived by; she continued to wear black for a husband she had neither loved nor liked.

'However, what's done is done, and we must make the best of it.'

'Yes.' Isabella managed a smile. 'Indeed we must.'

The interview with her cousin over, she hurried downstairs, but her man of business had not yet arrived. After a moment's indecision Isabella climbed the stairs again and sat purposefully down at the pianoforte. She turned the sheets of music, looking for the latest piece she'd purchased. Sonata No. 14, by Beethoven. She blew out a breath and sat still for a moment, her hands poised above the keys. *Calm.* Then she began to play.

The first movement was soft, almost a lamentation, but the music came jerkily from her fingertips, a choppy, disjointed sound. After a few minutes her ears could bear it no longer. Isabella pushed back the thimble-footed piano stool and went downstairs again, where she refrained from opening the front door and peering out into the street. Instead, she paced in the library while Rufus watched from the rug before the fireplace. The sturdy walnut mantel clock ticked the minutes away on its gilded face. Half an hour passed before the butler announced Mr Tremaine's arrival.

He bowed and advanced across the floor towards her. 'Good evening, Lady Isabella. How nice to see you back in London.'

Mr Tremaine was a stocky man with a square, blunt face and an air of solidity. The sight of him should have calmed her. It didn't. Mr Tremaine was no match for Major Reynolds.

'I understand you have urgent business for me, madam?'

'Yes.' She tried to smile. 'I need you to go to Stony Stratford, to an inn called the Rose and Crown.'

'Tonight?'

'Yes,' she said. 'As soon as possible.'

'And my task, madam?'

'You must speak to the landlady. A Mrs Botham.' She turned and walked to the fireplace. The clock kept time on the mantelpiece, *tick tick tick*. 'I stayed there three nights ago on my way back from Derbyshire. While I was there I made the acquaintance of a young lady. A Miss Harriet Durham.'

She glanced at Mr Tremaine. 'I need you to ensure that my name cannot be connected with hers. Either she was not there, or I was not there. I do not care which.'

'You wish me to, er...pay Mrs Botham?'

'Yes,' Isabella said, aware that she was flushing. 'You may draw upon my funds. I shall leave the sum up to you.'

Mr Tremaine bowed. 'Very well, madam. I will depart immediately.'

Isabella bit her lip as she watched the door close behind him. *First I lie, and now I bribe.* She looked down at her hands. They were clenched tightly together.

She released them and blew out a breath. A glance at the clock showed that it was time to prepare for the Harringtons' ball. Two dances with Major Reynolds, and supper.

Isabella squared her shoulders. 'I am not afraid of him,' she told Rufus, but deep inside herself she knew it was another lie. Major Reynolds would be a formidable enemy. If he ever found out—

Fear shivered over her skin.

'He won't find out!' she said to Rufus.

Rufus wagged his tail.

Chapter Six

Nicholas looked at himself dourly in the tall mahogany-framed mirror. He was dressed in the long-tailed coat, knee breeches and silk stockings that were requisite attire in the ballroom. Another evening of being stared at, he thought sourly. Of being laughed at.

His gaze rose to the scar on his cheek. *Lucky*, he told himself, lifting his hand to touch light fingertips to the ridges of melted skin. *I am lucky.* But he didn't feel lucky at this moment.

A footman entered, bearing a note. 'Sir?'

His mood lifted as he turned to take the note. It must be from Lady Isabella, crying off—

No, his name was inscribed in his brother's hand.

His mood became sourer. He broke the seal and unfolded the parchment, skimming the few lines of writing quickly. *Unfortunate circumstance…distressing for the family…* The final sentence arrested his gaze: *Therefore I judge it best for you to leave town.*

Nicholas felt a quick flare of anger. 'You judge, do you?' he said beneath his breath.

'Sir?' the footman asked.

Nicholas glanced at him.

'The servant who brought the note wishes to know if there will be a reply.'

'Indeed!' He strode down the stairs, his shoes making sharp slapping sounds, and into his study. At his desk he penned a curt note to his brother. The quill rasped across the paper: *I have no intention of leaving town like a dog with its tail between its legs.* He sealed the note briskly and handed it to the footman.

Nicholas turned to the long mirror that hung over the mantelpiece, adjusting the crisp muslin folds of his neckcloth. His mood was no longer unenthusiastic. Indeed, he felt almost martial, as if the Harringtons' ball was a battle to be fought.

A battle that included a waltz with Lady Isabella.

He turned away from the mirror. For all her golden-haired beauty, Lady Isabella was a better judge of how to handle this mess than his brother was. *Meet them head on.*

At the Harringtons' ball Nicholas had been aware of sniggers and amused sideways glances. He had also been aware of his brother's angry glare and early departure. At Almack's, the following night, there were fewer sniggers, and the glances were more speculative than amused. Neither Gerald nor his wife was present.

'It's working,' Lady Isabella said, as they danced their second waltz together. Gossip and music swirled around them, and beneath those sounds was the rustle of silk ball gowns and the soft scuff of dancing slippers on the polished floor.

'Yes.' But he had come no closer to finding Harriet's secret benefactress—nor to finding a bride of his own. Mothers who had previously regarded him with interest now viewed him with disfavour. *As if they truly believe I am an ogre.*

Although a few were still throwing their daughters at him, most notably Mrs Pennington.

'Tomorrow there's a balloon ascension at Turnham

Green,' Lady Isabella said, her gloved hand warm in his. 'I'm going with Lucas and Gussie and the two older children. Would you care to accompany us?'

It was phrased as a question; he knew what answer she expected. *Another opportunity to show ourselves together.*

'It would be my pleasure,' he said politely.

The true question was: how was he to find Harriet's bene-factress if he spent all his time in Lady Isabella's pocket? And, equally as important, how was he to find himself a bride?

'How are you at matchmaking?' he asked abruptly.

Lady Isabella's eyebrows went up. She studied him for a moment, with some curiosity. She wore a gown of Turkish red tonight, a warm, vivid colour. Above the crossed bodice her skin glowed, milk-white. Rubies and diamonds nestled in her golden hair. 'If you will forgive my impertinence, Major Reynolds…what is it you're looking for in a bride?'

Not a Pennington. A quiet, soft-voiced girl.

'I want peace and quiet,' Nicholas said. 'I want a marriage with no arguments.'

'Quiet,' Lady Isabella said. She glanced around the ball-room, a thoughtful crease on her brow. 'Have you considered Miss Thornton? She's—'

'Too old.'

'Too old?' Her eyes flew to his, startled. 'But she's barely two and twenty!'

'I want a young bride.' Too late, Nicholas realised that Lady Isabella was well past the age of two and twenty.

But Lady Isabella appeared not to have noticed the unin-tended insult. 'Why?' she asked, frankly.

Nicholas concentrated on his steps for a moment. He chose his words judiciously, careful not to give offence. 'While I was in the army, I observed that the more youthful a recruit is, the more easily he can be moulded into a soldier one wants to serve with.'

Lady Isabella surveyed him, the thoughtful crease still on her brow. 'You wish to mould your bride into a wife who suits you.'

Stated so baldly, it sounded…arrogant. 'Yes,' Nicholas said firmly. *I have nothing to be ashamed of*, he told himself, and yet his cheeks felt faintly hot, as if he flushed.

'And would you expect your wife to mould you into the husband she would like to have?'

'Mould me?' he said, affronted. 'Of course not!'

Lady Isabella's lips tucked in at the corners, as if she suppressed a smile.

'My wife would have no need to mould me,' Nicholas said stiffly.

Her lips tucked more deeply at the corners. 'You have no flaws, Major?'

Nicholas eyed her with suspicion. Was she laughing at him? 'None that a wife should care about,' he said, even more stiffly. *I sound like Gerald. Pompous.* 'Apart from the scar.'

Lady Isabella's mouth lost its tucked-in look. Her gaze touched his left cheek. 'The scar is unimportant,' she said. 'A woman who did not see that would be a poor wife.'

Nicholas cleared his throat. He found himself without any words to utter.

'Quiet and malleable,' she said, glancing around the ballroom again. 'And young. Are those your only criteria?'

He nodded.

Her eyes lighted on someone to his left. 'How about Miss Hyde? Have you considered her?'

He didn't turn his head to follow her gaze. He knew precisely what Miss Hyde looked like: hazel eyes, light brown hair, shy smile. She had been on his list of suitable brides. 'Unfortunately Miss Hyde's mother seems to believe I *am* an ogre.'

Lady Isabella's gaze jerked back to his face.

'No smoke without a fire, as they say.' His tone was light and wry, but it didn't elicit a smile.

Instead, Lady Isabella frowned and said tartly, 'Mrs Hyde is a very foolish woman!'

'She merely conforms to public opinion. And she is not the only mother in this room to do so.'

Lady Isabella's frown deepened. 'But surely—'

'Would you wish your daughter to marry a man rumoured to be an ogre?'

Lady Isabella bit her lip.

'No,' Nicholas agreed. 'Neither would I.' He smiled, but beneath the smile was anger. When he found Harriet's secret benefactress—

He almost misstepped. With effort he brought his attention back to Almack's, the waltz, his dance partner. She stood out from the débutantes in their pale silks and satins. It wasn't merely the richly coloured gown or her beauty; it was her manner, her easy confidence. In contrast to the young ladies who crowded the dance floor, Lady Isabella seemed entirely without vanity. She didn't preen or pose, she did nothing to draw attention to herself—and yet no man could be unaware of her presence in the ballroom.

She didn't fit the current fashion for slenderness. Her figure was ripe and womanly and—

Nicholas cleared his throat. *She is not the woman for me.* He knew what he wanted in a wife, and it was not Lady Isabella.

He glanced around the ballroom, noting the flicker of gazes hastily averted. Ladies watched from behind the cover of painted fans. He saw curiosity, amusement, incredulity. *London watches and wonders.*

The dance came to a close. His partner curtsied; he bowed.

'Now you may escort me to supper,' Lady Isabella said cheerfully.

Dry cake and tepid lemonade? Nicholas repressed a shudder of revulsion and extended his arm to her. 'It would be my pleasure.'

Nicholas drove to Turnham Green in his curricle, with Lady Isabella seated beside him and the groom perched behind. The day was perfect for a balloon ascension; the sky was the colour of duck eggs and the only clouds were high and to the east, a faint white swathe rippled like sand on a beach. The warm breeze was fragrant with the scents of summer, of grass and sunshine and wildflowers.

Nicholas found himself enjoying the excursion more than he had anticipated. It was amusing to watch Viscount Washburne play the father, lifting his son up on to his shoulders for a better view of the balloon as the envelope filled with gas, swinging his four-year-old daughter in the air until she shrieked with laughter. Except, he realised, Lucas wasn't playing at being a father, he was *being* a father, his attention wholly on his children, on his wife. *That is what I want. Life instead of death, laughter instead of the sounds of war.*

Envy came, sudden and unexpected—and so strong that he had to turn away. Behind him were the sounds of the ascension: excited voices, the creak of rope, a loud shout—*Stand back, ladies and gentlemen! Stand back!*—while inside him was a dark, bitter knot of emotion: jealousy.

For an instant he didn't recognise himself, didn't like himself—and then the familiar sense of who he was returned: a man in control of his thoughts and his emotions. The sound of the crowd swelled behind him—indrawn breaths, cries rising to shouts, *look, look!*

Nicholas turned around. The envy was gone. In its place was calmness, determination. He rested his gaze on Lucas Washburne and his family. *I will have that.* It was a promise to himself, a vow.

Lady Isabella turned to him. Wheat-gold ringlets framed her face beneath a straw bonnet lined with blue silk. 'How thrilling it must be to rise up into the air like that!'

'Very,' he said.

She looked absurdly youthful—her eyes as bright as a child's, her lips parted in delight—and quite extraordinarily beautiful. His attention was caught by the curve of her cheek and the perfect line of her throat, the rosy lips, the smooth skin.

Desire clenched in his belly, where only moments before had been jealousy. Nicholas pushed it hastily aside. 'Would you ride in a balloon if the opportunity arose, Lady Isabella?'

Her eyes brightened still further, as if he'd issued a challenge. 'Yes!'

But the question he wanted to ask, the question that burned on his tongue, the question he didn't dare ask, was, *Why are you not married?*

He asked Gussie later, while Lucas was swinging Grace in the air again and Lady Isabella was listening to young Timothy explain the intricacies of aerodynamics.

'Her fiancé died,' Gussie said quietly.

'Oh.' He glanced at Lady Isabella. 'Was it recent?'

'Ten years ago, I think. Or maybe eleven. Long before I met her.'

'Ten years!' His attention jerked back to Gussie. 'She must have loved him very much.'

Gussie lifted one shoulder in a shrug. 'I suppose she did.'

'But…' He glanced back at Lady Isabella. She was listening quite solemnly to Timothy's tangled explanation, her expression serious, a hint of laughter in her eyes. 'But does she not want children?'

'She has many nephews and nieces.' Gussie followed the direction of his gaze. 'Isabella is everyone's favourite aunt.'

But does she not want to be someone's mother?

'She should marry,' Nicholas said.

'Perhaps she doesn't want to.'

'But…' *But it's such a waste.*

He dared not say the words aloud, either to Gussie, or to Isabella as she sat beside him in the curricle on the way back to London. The barouche, with children, parents and nurse inside, was some distance behind them. Rufus, confined to the curricle while the ascension had taken place, was happily reposed across his mistress's feet.

'Were you terribly bored?' Lady Isabella asked.

'No,' Nicholas said, truthfully. 'Although I was less entranced than young Timothy.'

Her face lit with amusement. 'Was he not adorable? Such enthusiasm!'

Do you not want children of your own? He bit back the words and concentrated instead on his driving, trimming the reins slightly as the curricle passed over a narrow stone bridge.

Lady Isabella clutched his sleeve. 'Oh, stop! Stop!'

He reined in the horses, alarmed. 'What?'

But Lady Isabella was already scrambling from the curricle and didn't answer him.

'Get down,' Nicholas said to his groom. 'Hold them!' And he jumped down on to the road.

Isabella was hurrying back towards the bridge, but she didn't cross it; instead she cut across the grass towards the stream. Rufus loped alongside her, his ears up and his tail wagging, as if it were a game.

Nicholas followed at a run. The grass was shaded by trees and still wet with dew, despite the sun being high in the sky. 'What's wrong?'

Lady Isabella crouched on the edge of the bank and reached for something in the stream. 'A sack,' she said. 'It's moving. There's an animal in it.'

Nicholas halted alongside her. His boots were sodden. Lady Isabella's shoes, the hem of her gown, were saturated. She seemed oblivious to it.

'Are you certain?' He saw, now, what she was reaching for: a coarse brown sack, its neck bound with string, lying partly in the water. The fabric moved slightly, stirring with weak movement.

Lady Isabella didn't answer. She reached for the sack again. It was just beyond the reach of her fingers.

She stood and lifted her skirts and prepared to step into the water.

Nicholas uttered a silent sigh. 'Allow me,' he said.

Lady Isabella turned to him. 'Oh, would you? Quickly! Whatever's in there must be drowning!'

Nicholas stepped down into the stream. He bent and grabbed the sack. Water streamed from the coarse fabric.

He turned towards the bank, aware of tiny, high-pitched sounds of distress coming from the sack. Lady Isabella stood there, still holding her skirts up and allowing him a fine view of shapely, silk-clad ankles. Rufus stood alongside her, his head cocked and his ears pricked, as if he too had heard the tiny sounds.

Lady Isabella dropped her skirts and reached out her hands for the sack.

'It's wet,' he said. 'Your gown—'

'As if I care!'

Nicholas handed her the sack and climbed out. His boots were filled ankle-deep with water.

Lady Isabella crouched on the wet grass and undid the string with hasty fingers. She opened the sack carefully. The cries of distress became louder: squeaking, peeping noises.

'Kittens,' Lady Isabella said.

Nicholas stepped closer and peered inside. Kittens, wet and squirming. Rufus peered inside too, pushing his nose into the sack. His tail was wagging.

'I hope they're old enough…' Lady Isabella said, her tone worried. She lifted a tiny creature from the sack and examined it. The kitten shivered in the palm of her hand. It was grey, striped with black.

The Washburnes' barouche clattered over the bridge and halted alongside his curricle. 'Is everything all right?' Viscount Washburne called.

'Yes,' Nicholas said, taking a step towards the road. 'Just a sack of kittens.'

He realised his mistake as soon as he heard young Timothy's upraised voice. 'Kittens!'

Nicholas turned quickly back to Lady Isabella. 'I hope they're all alive,' he said in a low voice, 'because the children are coming.'

Lady Isabella glanced up. She looked past him and nodded.

'Kittens, Mama! Kittens!'

Lady Isabella pulled the shawl from her shoulders—a shawl that even he could see was of very expensive Norwich silk—and began to briskly dry the kitten she held. 'Here.' She handed it to him and reached into the sack for another.

Nicholas held the kitten, damp and shivering, and watched as Lucas and Gussie shepherded their children across the wet grass. Gussie's expression was concerned, Lucas's was merely resigned.

Six-year-old Timothy crouched to look in the sack. 'Where's the mother?'

'Not there, darling,' Isabella said as she dried another kitten, this one ginger with stripes.

'I want that one,' Grace said, holding on to her mother's skirt. 'It's pretty.'

Isabella smiled at her. 'But you already have a kitten, sweetheart.'

'But I want *that* one.' Grace reached out a cautious fingertip towards the shivering, mewing creature.

Nicholas watched as Gussie and Lucas exchanged a glance above their daughter's head. He saw resignation and amusement and acceptance, and swallowed a laugh.

'You already have a kitten, sweetheart. Don't you think she might be jealous if you brought another one home?'

Isabella said. 'But here, you may hold her for me while I dry her brothers and sisters.'

'I think they would be friends,' Grace announced, clasping the ginger kitten close to her chest.

The sack held five kittens. 'But what about the mother?' Timothy said worriedly.

'I shall be their mother,' Lady Isabella said, smiling at him. 'Until they are old enough to have homes of their own.'

'They're very small,' Timothy said dubiously, looking down at the kitten he held cupped in his hands.

Nicholas was privately dubious too, but he didn't express it aloud. Instead he fetched a blanket from the curricle. His boots squelched with every step he took.

'Thank you,' Lady Isabella said, when they were in the curricle again, the kittens bundled in the blanket on her lap and the barouche once more behind them. 'I'm sorry. Your boots…' She bit her lip. 'You must be quite uncomfortable.'

'I was a soldier, ma'am. Wet boots are nothing.'

Her gaze flicked to his cheek, and then down to the bundle on her lap. 'Well…thank you. I am very grateful.'

He took in her appearance—the muddied, grass-stained gown, the wet hem and wetter shoes, the ruined shawl lying on the floor of the curricle. 'Your maid will not be pleased with you.'

She met his eyes again. To his surprise, she grinned. Her bottom teeth were slightly crooked. 'Partridge is used to it.'

'Oh?'

Her grin faded. 'These aren't the first animals I've found.'

He glanced down at Rufus. 'Was he in a sack?'

Lady Isabella's expression became sober. No, not sober— grim. 'I found Rufus on the street. He was only a few weeks old. Half-starved and beaten and—' She bit her lip. Her face softened as she looked at the dog. She reached down to rub his ears. 'By rights he should hate people. But he doesn't. He has a very generous heart.'

As do you. 'He was lucky you found him.'

'Yes.' She continued stroking the dog's head. There was adoration in Rufus's mismatched eyes as he gazed up at her. 'He was so tiny, so frightened, so desperate…' She glanced up at him. 'Sometimes I do not like people at all. They do such terrible things!'

Her words triggered a memory: the fall of Badajoz, the British Army gone mad, soldiers looting, raping, murdering—

Nicholas pushed the memory aside. 'Human beings are capable of great cruelty,' he said, hoping that she would never experience more than she had: kittens drowning in a sack, a puppy starved and beaten. 'But they are also capable of great kindness.'

Lady Isabella looked down at the bundled blanket in her lap. She did not appear to be convinced.

'Do you think they'll live?' he asked.

'I don't know. They're very young.' She lifted her gaze to him again. 'Do you mind, Major, if I don't attend the Fancotts' musicale tonight?'

'Not at all.'

Some of his relief must have made it into his voice. Lady Isabella grinned at him again, giving him a glimpse of crooked white teeth. The imperfection seemed somehow to accentuate her beauty: the flawless skin, the golden hair, the soft, rosy lips. 'You could still go, Major, if you wish…'

'Heaven forbid!'

Lady Isabella laughed. As if in echo, one of the kittens uttered a tiny, muffled squeak. She looked down instantly, her hands curving protectively around the bundle in her lap.

Her animals are like children to her, Nicholas realised suddenly. *She gives them her heart.*

Having made that observation, he hoped very much that the kittens would live.

Chapter Seven

Isabella listened with one ear to the housekeeper. Most of her attention was on the kittens.

'I don't know what to do about young Becky Brown, ma'am. Her mother has taken ill and she's asking for leave—'

'Of course she must go! How much time would she like?'

'She asked for five days, ma'am.'

'Tell her she may have it.'

'Very well, ma'am,' Mrs Early said in a dubious voice, as if the absence of a housemaid would cast the household into chaos.

One of the grey-striped kittens was busily licking its sister's face.

'Is that all?'

'No, ma'am.' The housekeeper's tone was ominous.

Isabella stopped watching the kittens. She shifted her attention to Mrs Early's face.

'I have reason to believe that one of the servants is stealing.'

'What? Surely not!'

'We are going through the wax candlesticks too fast, ma'am.'

Isabella was silent a moment. She didn't need to be told

that wax candles were both expensive and easily sold. 'If your suspicion is true, then it must be dealt with.' *A thief. In this house.* It was a disturbing thought. She paid her servants generously—too generously, some might say. And yet someone was stealing. 'Where are they kept? The dresser between the butler's pantry and the still-room?'

Mrs Early nodded. 'But I can lock them in my parlour, ma'am, if you wish.'

Isabella considered this suggestion, and then shook her head decisively. 'No. I should like to catch whoever is responsible. They have no place in this house. Leave the candles where they are, but keep a close eye on that dresser.'

'I shall, ma'am.' The housekeeper nodded and rose to her feet, an action that required effort given her not inconsiderable bulk.

Isabella's next visitor in the morning room was Harriet.

'The post has arrived, ma'am, and there's no letter from my aunt.' There was a quiver in the girl's voice, and a corresponding quiver to her lower lip. She picked up a black kitten.

'It's been less than a week,' Isabella said calmly. 'It's far too soon to worry.'

Unshed tears filled Harriet's eyes. 'But, ma'am, what shall I do if—?'

Isabella welcomed a footman's entrance into the room. 'Major Reynolds?' she said, glancing at the card he presented on a salver. 'Tell him I shall be down shortly.'

The footman bowed and retreated from the room, taking care not to step on a wandering kitten.

'Major Reynolds!' Harriet put down the kitten she was holding. The colour drained from her face. 'He's here?'

'Don't be afraid, child. He will have come to see about the kittens.' Isabella spoke calmly, but her pulse was beating slightly faster. 'May I suggest that you go to your room?'

'Of course.' Harriet stood. Her eyes were wide and dilated. She looked pale enough to faint.

'Don't be afraid,' Isabella said again. 'He has no idea that you are here.'

'But the footman—'

'The servants all understand that your presence here is not to be mentioned to anyone.'

Harriet looked as if she did not believe these words. She fled the morning room.

'Foolish girl!' Isabella said to the kitten she was holding. 'He's not an ogre!' But the words were for herself, as much as for Harriet.

She placed the kitten in the basket with its siblings and smoothed her gown. 'Come along, Rufus,' she said, holding the door open for him. He preceded her, his tail waving. 'He is not an ogre,' she repeated to herself, under her breath. But her heart beat even faster as she made her way downstairs.

The silent fear faded as Major Reynolds made his bow. There was nothing ogre-ish about him. The green eyes were smiling as he looked at her. 'You look well, madam.'

'As do you.'

His expression changed, becoming faintly derisive. Isabella suddenly saw the scar. She hadn't noticed it—broad and livid across his left cheek—until that slight lifting of his eyebrows.

'Dare I hope that the kittens have survived the night?' He reached down to pat Rufus.

'They most definitely survived,' she said, smiling as Rufus licked the Major's hand. 'Would you like to come upstairs and see them?'

Major Reynolds walked up the stairs alongside her, and she was uneasily aware of Harriet Durham one floor above their heads. Her deception had never seemed so precarious—or so abhorrent. The compulsion to confess all seized her.

Isabella glanced at the Major. She opened her mouth, and then closed it.

Major Reynold's eyebrows rose in enquiry. 'Yes?'

Isabella bit her lip. His eyes smiled at her today, but two days ago in Hyde Park he had declared his desire to find Harriet's benefactress. His eyes hadn't smiled then; they had glittered with cold, hard anger. She had looked at him and been afraid. 'Your boots,' she blurted out. 'Are they ruined?'

'Alas,' the Major said, with a rueful smile.

Isabella looked away from him. *He is smiling now*, she told herself, *but remember your first impression. He's a dangerous man to cross.* She opened the door to the morning room.

'Luxurious quarters,' Major Reynolds said. 'I had thought they'd be in a box in the kitchen.'

The morning room was decorated in shades of yellow. The giltwood armchairs, the pale satinwood side tables, the fanciful ormolu clock on the mantelpiece with its bower of pink and yellow and blue flowers, enhanced the feeling of sunshine, of brightness and light.

'The staff wouldn't be happy with me if I gave them kittens to care for,' Isabella said with a laugh. 'We'll be short a housemaid soon. I couldn't expect them to care for kittens on top of their other duties.' She stepped aside for the Major to enter. 'And besides, I prefer to look after them myself.'

Major Reynolds advanced into the room. 'They're eating?' he asked, with a glance at the saucer of meat broth. 'I confess, I had thought they might be too young.'

'As did I. Major…do you mind if I close the door?'

The Major glanced at her swiftly. He hesitated for a moment, and then said, 'I imagine that we're both of an age where we can be in the same room without being said to have compromised one another.'

Isabella closed the door. 'Precisely my opinion.' She bent to pick up a tiny black kitten that was exploring the room on unsteady legs. Curiosity nibbled at her. She bit her lip, and then asked, 'Major…if you don't mind me asking, how old are you?'

'Six and thirty,' Major Reynolds said. He politely refrained from returning the question.

Not old at all, Isabella thought. Only half-a-dozen years older than herself.

Rufus crossed to the basket. He nosed among the tangle of kittens. The kittens squirmed, squeaking for his attention. The Major watched as the dog licked an upturned grey-striped face. 'Extraordinary,' he said.

'Rufus is very good with kittens,' Isabella said. She stroked the kitten she held. Its purr vibrated in her palm. 'He's had practice.'

'As have you, I see.' He glanced at the accoutrements—the bowls of water and broth, the blanket-lined basket, the box of dry dirt. A laugh came to his lips. 'What does your cousin think of this?'

'My cousin kindly lends me countenance, but the house is mine, Major. If the curtains or the carpet need replacing, I shall do it gladly.'

Major Reynolds crossed to the basket and crouched along-side Rufus. 'I have yet to meet your cousin,' he observed. 'I understand she's in mourning.'

'Mr Westin died more than five years ago.'

The Major glanced up. She saw his surprise.

'My cousin takes her duties as a wife very seriously,' Isabella said.

'Evidently.' The Major reached into the basket and picked up a grey-striped kitten. It mewed piteously for a moment, and then quieted in the shelter of his cupped hands.

'You must have one,' Isabella said, decisively. 'You are their rescuer, after all.'

Major Reynolds put the kitten back in the basket. He stood. 'Thank you, ma'am, but I'm not very fond of cats.'

'You could call it Boots,' she suggested hopefully.

His mouth quirked as if he suppressed a laugh. 'No, madam. But I thank you for the offer.'

Isabella sighed. 'Well, please let me know if you hear of anyone who would like a kitten.'

'Grace Washburne,' the Major said promptly.

'Gussie would never forgive me!'

'I think Gussie and Lucas are quite resigned to another kitten,' he said, turning to examine the room. His gaze lighted briefly on the dainty Louis XV escritoire with its gilded ormolu mounts and floral marquetry, the pianoforte with its gleaming, polished wood and the ivory keys, the low, comfortable sofas upholstered in cream-and-gold damask.

'Oh.' Isabella looked at the basket. A grey-and-black kitten was climbing determinedly over its brothers and sisters. 'Perhaps…'

'Shall you not keep one for yourself?' he asked, turning back to face her.

'I should like to, very much.' The black kitten purred in her hand. 'Every house should have a cat.'

A slight, awkward silence fell. Abruptly Isabella realised that she hadn't offered him refreshments, or even a seat. 'Please be seated, Major.' She sat, flushing slightly at her lack of manners. 'Would you like something to drink?'

'Thank you,' Major Reynolds said, taking a seat across from her. 'But, no. I merely came to see how the kittens fared.'

'Very well, as you can see. My cousin tells me I have a way with strays.'

She was suddenly aware of Harriet in her room upstairs. *Another of my strays.* There was another awkward pause. 'I'm putting together a party for the theatre tomorrow,' she said, rushing to fill the silence. 'I hope you will come?'

The Major inclined his head politely.

'Gussie and Lucas will be there.'

Major Reynolds nodded again.

Isabella bit her lip. She looked down at the kitten in her

hand. 'And the Worthingtons' masquerade is the evening after, out at Islington Spa.' She glanced at him. 'Have you given any thought to a costume?'

'Costume? Is it necessary?'

Isabella lifted one shoulder in a shrug. 'A mask and domino would be acceptable, but for the Worthington masquerade one generally comes in costume.'

'Does one?' The Major looked as if he had swallowed something distasteful. 'What is your costume to be?'

'You will have to wait and see, Major!'

His eyes narrowed on her face for a moment, and then he uttered a laugh. 'Very well,' he said. 'I shall attend the masquerade. But only if I may have two waltzes.'

Isabella was suddenly aware of his maleness, of the closed door to the morning room. 'Then I shall expect you to come in costume,' she countered.

Major Reynolds nodded. 'Very well.'

Another awkward pause fell. She looked for Rufus. He was lying on the floor. Two of the kittens clambered over his outstretched paws.

'Shall you ride in Hyde Park this afternoon?' the Major asked. 'The weather is not particularly clement.'

Isabella glanced at the window and the grey, blustery sky visible above the rooftops. She shook her head. 'No.'

'And what of tonight? The Thorpes' ball, or the Mortons'?'

'I shall be attending both,' Isabella said, looking at him. 'Choose which one you would like to attend, Major, and I shall save two dances for you.'

The Major looked as if he'd like to attend neither. 'Do you enjoy it?' he asked abruptly. 'London. The Season.'

'Yes, immensely.'

His brow furrowed slightly. 'Why?'

Isabella blinked, surprised by the question. She thought for a moment. 'The busyness,' she said. 'The gaiety. My friends.'

She shrugged. 'There are many reasons, Major, but mostly it's because I abhor being idle. In London I'm rarely idle. It suits me.'

Major Reynolds looked at her with a slight frown on his face.

'You do not like it,' she ventured.

'No.' The word was an uncompromising monosyllable.

Guilt made her lower her eyes. 'But if circumstances were different, Major, if…if—' *I had not called you an ogre.*

'I should still dislike it, madam.'

She glanced up. 'Why?'

'The gossip,' he said, a faint, biting note of contempt in his voice. 'The posturing and the pretension. The insincerity.'

'Those things are not confined to London, or to the Season, Major. One may find gossip in any town in England, in any village.'

'Perhaps.' He looked unconvinced.

'And as for posturing and pretension and insincerity, I am persuaded that those are not unique to London either. Where there is society, Major, so too will there be foolishness. It is—unfortunately—part of human nature.'

Major Reynolds smiled. 'Well argued, madam.' But the smile didn't reach his eyes.

Isabella looked down at the kitten she held, aware that the Major's estimation of her had shrunk in the past minute. Was she so vain that she cared? It appeared so.

Major Reynolds stood. 'I have trespassed on your time long enough.'

'Not at all, Major.' But she rose too. The kitten, which had been asleep in her hand, woke with a squeak. Isabella bent and placed the tiny creature on the floor. It shook itself, almost falling over in the process.

Rufus rose when she opened the door. He came down the stairs with them and politely licked the Major's hand goodbye.

'Which ball, Major?'

Major Reynolds accepted his hat and gloves from her butler, Hoban. 'Both.'

Her eyebrows rose. 'Both?'

'If one is to do something, one should do it properly.' The Major's tone was grim, as if he spoke of battle, not dress balls.

Nicholas walked home, deep in thought. Lady Isabella wanted a costume, did she? Inspiration struck as he turned into Albemarle Street. He uttered a laugh as he ran up the steps to the house he had hired for the Season.

'Has Mr Cobb arrived?'

'No, sir,' the butler said, accepting his hat and gloves.

Nicholas glanced at the long clock in the hallway. It still wanted ten minutes to the hour. 'I'll be in my study. Send him in when he arrives, Frye.'

'Very good, sir.'

The house had come furnished, but despite the paintings on the walls and the library full of books it felt more like a hotel than a home. The study was the only room he'd made his own, clearing out much of the heavy and fussily ornate furniture. The wing-backed leather armchair had, in the past few weeks, moulded itself to fit him.

Mr Cobb was punctual to the hour. Nicholas put aside the book he'd been reading and stood. 'Mr Cobb. Thank you for coming.'

'Not at all.' Mr Cobb's hand was dry, his hairline receding, and his grey eyes sharp with intelligence.

'I understand you do some work for Bow Street.'

'On occasion, yes.'

'You have been recommended to me as being both discreet and thorough.'

Mr Cobb made no reply. His expression was as impassive as his person was nondescript.

'I have a commission for you. Please be seated.'

The details were swiftly sorted. Nicholas was conscious of a sense of satisfaction as he watched the man leave. *Soon I'll know.* And when he did—

He turned to look out of the window, watching as Mr Cobb walked down the steps and along Albemarle Street. The man blended in with the other pedestrians, becoming almost invisible, so unremarkable as to be remarkable.

Nicholas lifted a hand to the scar on his cheek and let his fingertips trail over the smoothness and the ridges of hardened flesh. Ogre.

He lowered his hand, clenched it into a fist, and released it. Soon he'd have his revenge.

His next task took him into the snarl of crooked streets around Drury Lane, in search of an establishment recommended to him by his footman, a Londoner born and bred. He spent an hour in conference with a plump gentleman possessing a shock of wiry hair and paint-stained fingers, parted with a not inconsiderable sum of money, and exited whistling.

His next object was his club, where he dined and settled down in a winged armchair in a quiet alcove to read the newspaper and drink a glass of claret. Here, his nephew found him half an hour later.

'Sir! I've been looking everywhere for you.'

Nicholas lowered the newspaper and observed his relative. Charlie's face was flushed and anger was kindled in his eyes—one of which was almost buried in dark and swollen flesh.

'Been brawling, Charlie?'

The colour in Charlie's face heightened. 'Yes!' he said. 'And I will do so again! It's infamous, sir. Infamous!'

Nicholas folded the newspaper and placed it on the

mahogany table beside him. 'You alarm me, Charlie.' He gestured to an empty chair. 'Please be seated. Would you like a glass of claret?'

For a moment Charlie stood, fists clenched, radiating outrage with every line of his body, then he strode to the chair and pulled it closer. Some of the fire seemed to leave him as he sat.

'I haven't seen you for some days,' Nicholas said mildly.

'I've been at a horse race in the country. There was this cracking mare called Winnit— But enough of that, sir!' Charlie's eyes flashed. 'I came back as soon as I heard. It's infamous!'

'So I gather,' Nicholas said, amused. 'Er…what is infamous?'

'What they're calling you, sir. I told Grantham it was a filthy lie!'

Nicholas glanced at his nephew's hands, curled again into fists. 'Is that how you acquired your black eye?'

'Yes! And I shall do so again! I shall make them stop—'

'I thank you for your defence of me,' Nicholas said. 'But I don't need you to fight my battles, Charlie.'

'But, sir—'

Nicholas signalled to a waiter. 'Two glasses of claret,' he said firmly.

He eyed his nephew while they waited. Charlie bore little resemblance to the young man who'd visited him only a few days ago. Gone was the languor, the sullenness, and gone too were the pomaded hair and the absurd shirt points. In their place was animation and anger and a plainly tied neckcloth.

'It's infamous,' Charlie said again, bitterly, once the waiter had brought their claret. 'How can you bear it, sir? It makes me so furious—' His fists clenched.

It was odd, Nicholas thought, sipping his wine, but Charlie's outrage made his own less. 'Ignore it,' he said.

'Ignore it!' cried Charlie. 'How can I? You're not an ogre, sir, and anyone who says so is—'

Nicholas put down his wine glass. 'Charlie, it is nonsense—unpleasant nonsense—and is best ignored.'

Charlie's knuckles whitened. 'But, sir—'

'I beg you not to come to blows with anyone else over this.'

'But—'

'To do so is to set yourself up for London's amusement.' He smiled, tried to make a joke of it. 'One in the family is enough.'

'As if I should care!'

'*I* should care.' Nicholas held his nephew's eyes. 'And your father would too.'

'Father?' Charlie's flush deepened. 'He blames you! Says you've humiliated the whole family!'

The wine suddenly tasted sour in Nicholas's mouth. 'Does he?'

Charlie's lip curled. 'He's talking of leaving town.'

Nicholas put his wine glass down on the table beside the newspaper. He rubbed his forehead.

'I wish he would go!' Charlie said hotly. 'Of all the mean, cowardly—'

'Charles!'

Charlie closed his mouth.

'You will speak of your father with respect. Or not at all. Is that understood?'

Charlie's gaze dropped. 'Yes, sir.' The familiar, sullen note was back in his voice.

The silence between them was awkward for a moment, broken by new arrivals entering the room. 'Hello, Ogre,' one of the men called out cheerfully.

Nicholas returned the greeting with a nod, and glanced at Charlie. His nephew's cheeks were flushed again. 'How can you bear it, sir?'

'There was no malice in that.'

'No, but…'

Nicholas laughed. He reached for his wine glass again. 'So where was this horse race of yours?' he asked, turning the subject.

But Charlie refused to be diverted. 'I wish I knew who had started it! I'd—'

'Don't worry,' Nicholas said. 'I'm handling it.'

Charlie's eyes lit up. The last remnants of sullenness vanished. He leaned forwards. His voice was low and eager. 'You know?'

'I shall very soon.'

Charlie sat back in his chair. His expression was slightly awed. 'What will you do, sir, when you know?'

Nicholas swirled the wine in his glass, considering the question. *What will I do?* It required careful thought.

He swallowed a mouthful of claret and put the glass down firmly on the table. 'A salutary lesson,' he said.

Chapter Eight

Nicholas danced with Lady Isabella at the Thorpes' ball—
a quadrille and a waltz—and then claimed her hand several
hours later at the Mortons', in a ballroom draped in pink silk.
The champagne, when he procured two glasses after a particularly energetic country dance, was also pink.

After handing Lady Isabella to her next partner, Nicholas
retired to the back of the ballroom and leaned his shoulders
against the pink-swathed walls. He took an idle sip of champagne, surveying the dance floor, his eyes sliding from one
débutante to the next. Miss Clarissa Whedon would be acceptable as a wife, as would Miss Agatha Hyde. Miss
Whedon wasn't a beauty, but pulchritude was unimportant
in a bride. A compliant nature, a quiet disposition, youthful-
ness—those were what he required, and Miss Whedon had
all three. Miss Hyde was pretty, in a rather colourless way,
but her air of timidity reminded him strongly of Harriet
Durham.

Nicholas eyed the pink champagne distastefully and took
another sip. His gaze returned to Clarissa Whedon. He tried
to imagine her seated across the breakfast table from him,
plain-faced and quiet. It could work. It could work very well.

He'd settled on his possible choices of bride—Harriet

Durham, Clarissa Whedon, Agatha Hyde—by careful observation over a number of days. He'd finally chosen Harriet because she was the youngest and therefore—or so he'd thought—the most easily moulded into a suitable wife. *And*, he acknowledged wryly, *because she was the prettiest*.

A poor choice, as it had turned out.

Nicholas swallowed the last of the champagne. He would dance with Clarissa Whedon and perhaps take her to supper, to confirm his decision.

He straightened away from the wall, oddly reluctant to solicit Miss Whedon's hand as a dance partner.

The reason for his reluctance—when he paused to think about it—was easy to identify: if he had a choice, he would prefer to dance with Lady Isabella.

Nicholas shook his head, annoyed with himself. He placed his empty glass on a table cluttered with discarded glassware and strolled around the ballroom to where Clarissa Whedon sat with her mother.

Miss Whedon was of middle height, with a round face, brown hair, mild blue eyes and a robust figure. One day she would be as stout as her mother. That was unimportant. What he liked about her was her air of calmness. She didn't blush, as Harriet had used to, when he asked her for the next dance. Her manner was unflustered as he escorted her on to the dance floor.

There was no need to ask Clarissa Whedon to join him for supper; the dance had confirmed what he already knew of her: in temperament and character she was precisely what he was looking for. Nicholas searched for a word to describe Miss Whedon as he led her from the dance floor. The only word he could come up with—stolid—he cast aside. Stolid was not the word he was looking for.

He returned Clarissa Whedon to her mother's care, bowed, and went in search of something to drink. The question now was: when to make his offer?

Nicholas plucked a glass of pink champagne from a tray and swallowed a mouthful. It was flat, like his mood.

He grimaced, and turned the stem of the glass between his fingers. Why not speak to Mrs Whedon tonight? Why not ask if he could call on her and her husband tomorrow morning? He'd spent the past ten months preparing for this moment: selling his commission, taking over the administration of his estate, readying the manse for a wife and children. He should be eager, enthusiastic—

'Nicholas.'

He turned his head. His brother stood before him. Gerald's expression was tight-lipped and distasteful, as if he smelled something unpleasant. Nicholas could only smell lavender water, which fragrance surrounded his brother.

'Gerald,' he said, inclining his head in polite acknowledgement. 'How do you do?'

Gerald's shirt points and neckcloth were so high, so starched, that he was unable to return the gesture. He bowed stiffly from the waist. His person was overloaded with jewellery. Diamonds glittered on his buckles and his fingers, in the folds of his neckcloth. 'I'm leaving town tomorrow.'

Nicholas swallowed another mouthful of champagne and said nothing.

Gerald leaned closer. 'If you had any respect for the family, you would leave town yourself!' His tone was bitter and affronted, each *s* hissed, each *t* hard. 'Instead of forcing me to leave.'

If you had any backbone, you would stay. Nicholas didn't utter the words; he held his temper in check.

Gerald glanced at Lady Isabella, going down the *contredanse* with her partner. 'You're wasting your time,' he said contemptuously. 'She won't have you. She refused two dukes.'

'I have no intention of marrying Isabella Knox,' Nicholas said, stung into replying. *Fool. You let him goad you.* He tightened his grip on the champagne glass and made his voice bored, uninterested. 'We're merely friends.'

Gerald snorted. He turned on his heel and left, taking his outrage—and the scent of Steek's lavender water—with him.

Nicholas sipped the pink champagne, his annoyance diminishing with every mincing step that Gerald took away from him. He watched Lady Isabella dance: golden hair and creamy skin and rosy, laughing lips.

She stood out from among the other dancers, dazzling in a ball gown of forget-me-not blue stitched with seed pearls, but what drew his eyes was more than the gown and the golden hair, more than her height and her beauty. It was something else, something that was purely hers.

Nicholas narrowed his eyes, trying to identify what it was that made Lady Isabella different from every other lady in the ballroom. Not her poise or the easy, graceful confidence. It was something more than that, something indefinable, something—

She had an unselfconsciousness that few people in the room had. *She's happy to be herself*, he realised.

How many people could say that? Could he?

Nicholas half-lifted his hand to the scar, and then clenched his fingers shut. He lowered the hand to his side. The burn was what people saw. *But it's not who I am.*

He scanned the ballroom again, examining the débutantes. Even the prettiest of them was pretending, her confidence superficial, her unselfconsciousness feigned. They were girls, their characters only half-formed. What would they be like as women?

Nicholas returned his gaze to Lady Isabella. Would Clarissa Whedon grow into a woman like her? Would she shine from the inside?

'Good evening, sir.'

Nicholas turned his head, to discover a second member of his family standing alongside him.

'Charlie?' he said, surprised. He surveyed his nephew's clothes. Clearly, Charlie was no longer aping the dandy set. Gone were the extravagances of fashion. The lad was dressed neatly, but quite plainly. Almost like—

Like me.

'Isn't this rather tame for you?' he asked, wondering if Gerald had seen his son's attire.

Charlie flushed faintly. 'Oh, I like balls well enough,' he said in an airy, careless tone.

'I had thought that deep play at a gaming hell was more your thing,' Nicholas said sardonically.

Charlie's flush deepened. 'If you must know, sir, I've...I've decided to not gamble for a while.'

'Pockets to let again, Charlie?'

'No, sir.'

Nicholas glanced at him, his gaze resting on the bruise around the boy's eye. 'Fallen out with your crowd?'

Anger flared in Charlie's face. 'They had no right to call you an ogre! No right at all!'

'All London is doing it,' Nicholas said, drily. He swallowed the last of the pink champagne. It was lukewarm, and even less palatable than it had been before.

'Well, they shouldn't!'

Charlie's loyalty was oddly touching—and if it separated the lad from the wild, expensive crowd he ran with, so much the better. 'I can't recommend the champagne,' Nicholas said, looking for somewhere to put the empty glass.

Charlie continued, as if he hadn't heard him. 'When you find out who's responsible, I hope you horsewhip him!'

'It's a woman,' Nicholas said drily.

'Oh,' Charlie said, his outrage deflating slightly.

Nicholas glanced around the ballroom, at the matrons sitting with their heads bent together in gossip, at the ladies dancing. *Perhaps even a woman in this room.*

* * *

The Major danced well, his hand warm in the small of her back, but he seemed to derive little pleasure from the waltz. His face held a polite smile, but beneath that was an underlying grimness. Isabella knew the reason; she'd heard the excited exclamation as clearly as he had: *Have you seen the Ogre? I hear he's here.* The débutante who'd uttered those incautious words had flushed a vivid red when she'd turned to find Major Reynolds standing almost at her elbow. He had made no sign that he'd heard, had uttered no comment as he escorted Isabella onto the dance floor, but anger had been cold in his eyes.

Isabella danced silently. Her pleasure in the evening was gone. In its place were shame and guilt. *My fault. My tongue that did the damage.* And alongside the shame, the guilt, was anger. She might disagree with Major Reynolds's decision to choose so young a bride, might feel contempt for his reasons, but in all other regards the Major was a man to be admired. He was courageous. He was intelligent. He was honourable. Good qualities, and yet London dared to laugh at him.

'Would you like something to drink?' Major Reynolds asked when the musicians had laid down their bows. 'Champagne?'

Isabella looked up at his face, at the hard green eyes, at the livid scar. 'Thank you. That would be nice.' She laid her hand on the Major's arm, aware of a foolish urge to protect him, to shield him from ridicule.

'Reynolds!'

The Major turned his head swiftly. 'Mayhew! By all that's marvellous!' He extended his hand. Gone was the grimness, the suppressed anger. In its place was a grin that made him look quite startlingly attractive. 'Lady Isabella, may I make Lieutenant Mayhew known to you?'

Lieutenant Mayhew bowed over her hand. He was a loose-limbed man of perhaps her own age, blond-haired and brown-eyed and with the side whiskers of a military officer. His face was tanned above a green Rifleman's uniform, and alive with levity. 'It's a pleasure to meet you, Lady Isabella.' His gaze was openly appreciative. 'May I beg the honour of a dance?'

The Major made a sound beneath his breath that was almost a laugh. He turned to Isabella, still grinning. 'Be warned, my lady. Mayhew is a rackety, ramshackle fellow. A regular here-and-thereian!'

The Lieutenant matched Major Reynolds's grin and made no attempt to deny the charge.

The shame and guilt that had sat so heavily on her, the spark of anger that had burned in her chest, vanished. Isabella laughed and allowed herself to relax. 'Certainly we shall dance, Lieutenant Mayhew.'

She took her place opposite him in the quadrille. 'How un-expected for you to meet Major Reynolds here,' she said, as they waited for the dance to start.

'Unexpected?' The Lieutenant grinned. 'I should have known I'd find him at a ball!'

'Really?' Isabella looked at him from beneath upraised eyebrows. 'I was under the impression that Major Reynolds did not care much for dancing.'

'Reynolds? Not like dancing?' Lieutenant Mayhew laughed and shook his head. 'I've seen him dance the night away on many an occasion!'

'Oh,' said Isabella.

'Why, if you'd seen the lengths he went to in Madrid to procure tickets for himself and his—er…' The Lieutenant hesitated for a moment, and then hurried on. 'It was a grand ball—in Wellington's honour, you know! The tickets were dashed hard to get hold of.'

Isabella glanced across the ballroom to where Major Reynolds stood. She studied his face for a moment, trying to imagine him in Madrid with a Spanish beauty on his arm. It was a difficult image to conjure up; there was nothing of the libertine about Major Reynolds. She couldn't envisage him uttering practised, flowery speeches and whispering sweet nothings in a lady's ear. He was too hard-faced, too disciplined, too stern.

The Lieutenant was another matter. She had no doubt that he'd left a trail of broken hearts behind him, with his easy manners and the light-hearted laughter in his eyes—and the disarming thread of seriousness underlying the levity. 'You served with Major Reynolds?'

'In the Peninsula, and at Waterloo. He was my brigade-major. A regular Come-on!'

'A Come-On?' Isabella said, baffled.

'Officers are either Come-ons or Go-ons,' the Lieutenant explained. 'They lead from the front, or the back. Reynolds led from the front.'

'Oh,' she said, understanding. She turned her head again and observed Major Reynolds, now talking to a young man who bore a marked resemblance to him. 'He was a good officer?'

'The best,' Lieutenant Mayhew said simply. 'There's no one else I'd rather have served under.'

The quadrille claimed their attention and Isabella spent an agreeable half-hour, the Lieutenant's tongue being light and flirtatious and never wanting for words. Their bows made and the musicians' instruments laid down, the Lieutenant escorted her to where Major Reynolds stood. The Major's companion was introduced as his nephew, the Honourable Charles Reynolds, a young man of perhaps two-and-twenty years, with a bruise darkening his face. The young nobleman bowed politely to Isabella and greeted Lieutenant Mayhew most correctly, but his expression as he gazed at the Lieutenant's uniform and his dashing side whiskers approached awe.

'D'you remember the ball at Cuidad Rodrigo?' Lieutenant Mayhew said. 'These draperies remind me of it.'

Major Reynolds grinned. 'How could I forget?' He turned to Isabella. 'Wellington claimed the best house left standing, but there was a hole in the roof where a canon ball had come through, and one in the floor. They hung the ballroom with yellow silk, and as for the hole in the floor—'

'They laid a mat over it,' the Lieutenant took up the tale. 'And posted a man to see that no one fell in!'

Reminiscent laughter lit the Major's eyes. 'Now *that* was a ball!'

On impulse Isabella turned to the Lieutenant. 'I'm hosting a party at the theatre tomorrow night. *The Venetian Outlaw* is playing.' She included young Charles Reynolds in her smile. 'Would you care to join us?'

Both men bowed and expressed pleasure at the invitation, and Isabella was aware of a sense of relief. With the light-hearted Lieutenant Mayhew as one of her party, the Major must enjoy the evening—however much London stared and laughed at him.

The theatre party comprised the Washburnes, himself and Mayhew and Charlie, and Lady Isabella and her cousin. Mrs Westin was a woman of middle years with faded blue eyes and a kindly face. 'It is a pleasure to finally meet you, Major Reynolds,' she said when they were seated. His scar appeared not to disconcert her; she looked fully at his face as she spoke. 'Do you enjoy the theatre?'

'I do.'

Their box was private, and yet the bustle of the theatre surrounded them. The ceiling echoed with the sound of hundreds of voices, with the squawk of instruments being tuned, with laughter and catcalls as the more common members of the audience filled the pit below.

'Major Reynolds is something of a thespian,' Mayhew said, leaning forwards. 'I have seen him tread the boards on a number of occasions.'

Nicholas was aware of Lady Isabella turning her head to look at him, an expression of surprise on her face. Alongside her, Charlie looked equally surprised.

'You act, sir?'

Nicholas shrugged. 'It was a tradition among the Light Division.'

'Is he any good, Lieutenant?' Lady Isabella asked, sounding slightly bemused.

'First rate!' Mayhew answered. 'I wish you could have seen his Romeo, ma'am. It was unsurpassed!'

'Romeo?' Lady Isabella said, sounding even more bemused.

Nicholas shifted in his chair, slightly uncomfortable. 'A comic role.'

'I have never laughed so much in my life!' Mayhew said. 'And as for Wellington, I thought he'd die choking!'

'Wellington?' said Mrs Westin, a note of reverence in her voice.

'We were in winter quarters,' Mayhew explained. 'Fuentes de Oñoro, wasn't it?'

Nicholas nodded.

'We found a disused chapel in Gallegos and put on performances. Wellington rode over sometimes to watch.'

'A chapel,' Mrs Westin said, with a slight frown.

'The Bishop of Ciudad Rodrigo felt just as you do, madam!' Mayhew said. 'He laid a solemn curse on the enterprise!'

His smile, at once apologetic and charming, won an answering smile from Mrs Westin. 'Well, if Wellington didn't disapprove...'

'On the contrary! I have rarely seen him so willing to be pleased. And if you could have seen Reynolds, ma'am, you would understand. His Romeo is the funniest thing I've ever witnessed!'

Fortunately the curtain rose at that moment. The various pairs of eyes that had been fixed on him—Gussie amused, Charlie awed, Lady Isabella with a crease between her eyebrows and an expression of faint astonishment on her face—turned towards the stage, where a picturesque and Gothic grotto was revealed.

A man stepped onstage, a letter in his hand. He paused a moment as the hubbub of the audience subsided, and then read aloud, his voice carrying over the subdued murmur coming from the pit.

"'A man once honoured with your friendship has important secrets to communicate. Repair alone this night, at the hour of eight, to the grotto in the palace gardens.'"

The actor lifted his head and gazed out over the audience, his expression perplexed. 'From whom is this appointment? Its mystery bespeaks an enemy rather than a friend.'

A clock offstage struck eight times, and Nicholas released the breath he'd been holding and settled himself into enjoyment of the play.

After the first act, when the actors had retired from the stage, a box attendant brought refreshments. Lady Isabella had spared no expense; the selection of cakes and beverages was excellent.

Nicholas leaned back in his chair, enjoying the noise rising from the crowd below, the indefinable scent and atmosphere of the theatre. He sipped his burgundy. The wine was velvety on his tongue, slightly spicy.

'I hear that London is calling you an ogre,' Mayhew said in a low, laughing voice.

Nicholas grunted. 'What else have you heard?'

'That you're laying siege to an acknowledged beauty.' Mayhew glanced past him at Lady Isabella. 'You always did have good taste.'

'We're merely friends,' Nicholas said, and ignored Mayhew's expression of disbelief. He had decided on a bride: Clarissa Whedon. She had no beauty, but her nature was quiet and yielding and her mother, with four daughters to dispose of, must be pleased to receive his offer, ogre or not.

He listened with half an ear as Mayhew regaled Charlie

with tales of army life. '…ate acorns for dinner. The commissariat had sent the wagons by the wrong route…'

'A comic actor, Major?' a voice said quietly beside him. 'You have unexpected depths.'

He turned his head. Lady Isabella sat where Mrs Westin had. Her mouth quirked into a smile. 'I must confess that I find it hard to imagine you as Romeo.'

'I mostly took the role of villain.' Nicholas raised a finger to his cheek, tapping the hardened skin lightly.

Her gaze flicked to it. 'Major, if you don't mind me asking…how did you acquire the scar?'

The babble of voices faded. In his ears were shouts, the crackle of flames, the sound of a man screaming. 'The billet I was in caught fire.'

'Ah,' she said. 'How unlucky for you.'

Nicholas met her eyes. 'No,' he said. 'I was lucky.'

She considered the words in silence for a moment. 'There were others in the billet?'

'Four of us.' Crammed into dirt-floored hovel with a tiny, creaking loft beneath the roof.

'I'm sorry,' Lady Isabella said simply.

Nicholas shrugged. 'It was a long time ago.' He raised his glass and took a mouthful, but he tasted smoke on his tongue, smelled the scent of burning flesh. For a moment he experienced nausea, twisting in his belly. Bile climbed up his throat.

Nicholas lowered the glass, his fingers tight around the stem, and forced himself to swallow the wine.

'Forgive me for asking, Major. I apologise.'

He focused on Lady Isabella. Her expression was as contrite as her voice. She had seen his discomfort.

'Not at all.' He forced a smile. 'It was a long time ago, and, as I said, I was lucky.'

Her sober expression did not alter. Was that pity in her eyes?

Nicholas straightened in the chair. The last wisps of memory faded, the whiff of smoke, the nausea. 'I was lucky,' he said firmly. 'Twelve years of soldiering, and no injuries in battle. Few men can say that.'

Her gaze went to the scar again.

'What do you see,' he asked her bluntly, 'when you look at it?'

'Pain.'

He raised his hand to his cheek, to the ridges of melted flesh. 'When I look at myself in the mirror...' he drew his fingertips lightly over the scar, feeling the smoothness, the roughness '...I remember how lucky I am.'

'You do?' Her tone was dubious.

'Yes,' he said firmly. *I survived.*

Lady Isabella's expression relaxed into a smile. She believed him.

Nicholas relaxed too. No more pity.

'Do you know...' Lady Isabella's voice was musing. Her gaze was on the scar again. 'I hardly notice it now. Only when—' She glanced at him, meeting his eyes, and coloured slightly.

'Only when someone calls me an ogre,' he finished the sentence for her.

Her cheeks became pinker. 'Yes.'

I hope my wife will learn to see past it, to ignore it. 'What is your opinion of Clarissa Whedon?' he asked abruptly.

'Clarissa Whedon?' Interest brightened her eyes. 'Do you intend to offer for her—?' She bit her lip. 'Forgive me, Major, that was an impertinent question.'

Nicholas made a gesture of negation with his hand. 'Yes, I do intend.' He tilted his glass and watched the play of light on the wine. 'What do you think of her?'

'She seems a nice girl.'

Nicholas glanced at her. There was a slight frown on her brow, as if she searched for a word. 'Placid,' Lady Isabella said at last, meeting his eyes. 'She seems very placid.'

'Yes,' Nicholas said. That was the word he'd been searching for last night. Not stolid—placid. Calm and unruffled, quiet. And young enough not to be set in her ways. Young enough for a husband to mould her. He smiled and lifted the wine glass to his mouth. Exactly what he wanted in a wife.

After the curtain had fallen, in the bustle of movement and noise, of comments, of cloaks being sought, Gussie turned to Lady Isabella. 'May I bring Grace around tomorrow?'

'Certainly. Would she like to play with the kittens?'

'She would like to have one,' Gussie said wryly. 'The ginger one.'

'Not an hour goes past without her asking after it,' her husband said from behind her, his tone a mix of amusement and resignation. 'She even has a name for it.'

'We gave up,' Gussie said, with a grimace, but there was laughter in her eyes.

Lady Isabella's mouth tucked in at the corners, as if she was trying not to smile. 'Oh, dear,' she said. 'I'm so sorry!'

'Kittens?' Mayhew asked, stepping up alongside Nicholas. 'You have kittens, ma'am?'

'Yes.' Lady Isabella turned to him. 'Do you know someone who would like one?'

'Me,' Mayhew said. 'Would you by any chance have two?'

'Yes,' Lady Isabella said again, looking at the Lieutenant with all the astonishment Nicholas felt.

'Why would you want kittens?' Nicholas asked, putting up his eyebrows.

'To give to my niece and nephew,' Mayhew said promptly. 'They're twins,' he explained to Lady Isabella. 'My sister's children.'

Lady Isabella smiled at him, approval warm in her eyes. 'Certainly you may have two kittens, Lieutenant Mayhew. I would be very pleased to give them to you.'

Nicholas pulled on his gloves. For no reason that he could identify, he was feeling slightly disgruntled.

Chapter Nine

The next day did not start auspiciously. The second house-maid fell down the back stairs and broke her leg.

'Two maids short,' Mrs Early said, stout and agitated. 'It can't be done, ma'am. Not a house of this size, and with Miss Durham staying.'

After Isabella had soothed the housekeeper and sent her off to the registry office to hire a new housemaid, she carried the news upstairs to Mrs Westin's parlour.

'Oh, let me help!' cried Harriet, putting down the handkerchief she was hemming. 'I can dust and make beds and—'

'Thank you, my dear, but it's not necessary.' Isabella smiled at her. A pile of handkerchiefs lay on the sofa alongside the girl. Isabella picked up the top one. It had been hemmed so neatly that the stitches were almost invisible. In each corner a sweet violet unfurled purple petals. 'You did this?'

Harriet nodded.

The next handkerchief had yellow primroses at each corner, and the one underneath pink roses, each petal delicately rendered in thread. Isabella brushed a fingertip over one of the flowers. The needlework was superior to anything she was capable of. 'Beautiful,' she said. 'You're a fine needlewoman.'

Harriet blushed shyly at the praise.

Isabella put down the handkerchiefs and turned to leave the room, holding the door open for Rufus, who followed—as always when she was at home—at her heels.

'Ma'am?'

Isabella turned back. 'Yes, my dear?'

'Has…has the post come this morning?'

'Yes.'

'Was there anything for me?'

'No, my dear.'

Tears filled Harriet's eyes. She twisted her hands in her lap. 'Oh, what shall I do if my aunt doesn't—?'

'There will be time enough for worry if the moment comes.' Mrs Westin didn't pause in her knitting. 'Don't borrow trouble, child.' There was no censure in her voice, just calmness.

Harriet bit her lower lip. She looked down at her lap, tears trembling on her lashes.

'My cousin is right.' Isabella smiled at the girl. 'It's too soon to worry.' But privately she was beginning to worry. It had been a full week. Surely a reply must come soon from the Lake District?

Little Grace Washburne came in the company of her mother, to ecstatically carry off 'Saffron', and after a light luncheon Isabella sat down in the morning room to read the letter she had received from one of her sisters, the remaining kittens curled up in their basket and Rufus warm across her feet.

She was absorbed in a description of her nephew's first venture astride a pony when the butler entered the room, carrying a visiting card on a salver. 'A gentleman to see you, ma'am.'

Isabella put down the letter. She picked up the card. 'Mr Fernyhough? Who is he?'

But the butler didn't know.

'Did he say why he wishes to see me?'

'A matter of business, ma'am.'

Isabella tapped the card with a fingertip. 'I shall see him in the drawing room, Hoban.' She stood and went to the mirror above the fireplace to check that her hair was neatly in place. 'Come along, Rufus.'

She popped her head into Mrs Westin's parlour to warn Harriet that a visitor was in the house, and then walked down one flight of stairs to the drawing room.

Mr Fernyhough was dressed with great plainness and propriety, his bow was punctilious, and his face was pale and earnest. He looked to be not more than three and twenty.

'Forgive me for intruding, ma'am,' he said, upon being invited to sit. 'A complete stranger! But I needed to ascertain…to be sure…' He bit his lip and then blurted, 'Is Miss Durham all right?'

The name shocked Isabella into stillness. 'Miss Durham?' she said cautiously.

'Miss Harriet Durham. I believe she is in your care, ma'am.' Mr Fernyhough leaned forward, his expression even more earnest than it had been. 'Is she all right?'

'I do not perfectly understand you, Mr Fernyhough,' Isabella said, taking refuge in cool hauteur. 'Why would I have a Miss Durham in my care?'

Mr Fernyhough sat back in the crimson-upholstered armchair. His manner became flustered. 'I beg your pardon, ma'am. I was given to understand— The landlady at the Rose and Crown in Stony Stratford told me that…' He fixed beseeching eyes on her face. 'Miss Durham has run away and I am trying to find her, to be certain she is safe and well.'

'What is your relationship to Miss Durham?' Isabella asked carefully.

'We are friends,' Mr Fernyhough said, but colour rose in his cheeks again.

Isabella lifted her eyebrows. 'Friends, Mr Fernyhough?'

Mr Fernyhough's face became scarlet. 'At one time we…we hoped to marry.'

Isabella looked at him with interest. A very different man from Major Reynolds. *Mild, with that puppydog face.* 'May I ask why you didn't?'

'Her grandfather forbade it,' Mr Fernyhough said simply. 'He wanted Harriet to marry a military man, not a country parson.'

'You're a man of the cloth?' Isabella asked, startled.

'Colonel Durham presented me with a living three years ago. I consider myself very fortunate to be distinguished by his patronage.' But Mr Fernyhough didn't look fortunate; he looked miserable.

Isabella abandoned the hauteur. 'Harriet is upstairs. Would you like to see her?'

Mr Fernyhough's face lit up. 'She's here? Oh, yes, I should very much like to see her!' The joy left his face. 'No,' he said, heavily. 'No, I had better not. If the Colonel were to ask me… He has already accused me of harbouring her, of aiding her.' His expression became indignant. 'As if I would do such a thing!'

But if you truly loved her, wouldn't you? She didn't say the words aloud, but perhaps Mr Fernyhough read them on her face, for he flushed again and lowered his eyes. 'I must support my mother and my brothers and sisters, ma'am. I depend upon Colonel Durham's patronage. If he were to withdraw it…'

So it was not backbone Mr Fernyhough lacked, but rather an independent living. Isabella sighed.

'Would you give Miss Durham a letter from me?' Mr Fernyhough's eyes pleaded with her.

'Of course,' Isabella said. 'You may be assured that Harriet is quite well. She is upstairs with my cousin.'

Mr Fernyhough hung on to those few words with painful eagerness.

'We are waiting for a reply to a letter to her aunt,' Isabella continued, slightly disconcerted by the intensity of his gaze. 'As soon as it comes I shall send Harriet to her. By post chaise, of course. I'm certain she will be quite happy there.'

'I'm most grateful to you, madam—as I am persuaded Harriet must be too! Your kindness, your magnanimity—!' Emotion choked Mr Fernyhough's voice. 'Without your aid I do not dare to think what may have happened to my poor Harriet! So sweet, so innocent, so young!'

'I will ensure that no harm comes to her,' Isabella said, uncomfortable at the gratitude shining in his brown eyes. 'Of that you may be certain.'

'Her reputation…'

'Yes,' Isabella said quietly. 'The damage is irrevocable. It is unfortunate.'

Mr Fernyhough lowered his gaze to his clasped hands. His fingers were gripped tightly together. 'I wish…' He swallowed and looked up and attempted a smile. 'But it is of no use!' He unclasped his hands and extracted a sealed letter from his coat pocket. 'I should like to say goodbye to Harriet and…and to wish her happy in the future.' He extended the letter to her. 'If you would, ma'am?'

'Of course.' Isabella took the letter. She turned it over in her hands. 'You are certain you do not wish to see her?'

'I cannot,' Mr Fernyhough said simply. 'If Colonel Durham were to ask me—' He shook his head.

'A hot-tempered man?'

'Very.'

She had a vision of Mr Fernyhough, his widowed mother, and countless brothers and sisters being turned out into the street.

If only—

Mr Fernyhough stood and bowed. 'Thank you, madam. I am more grateful than I can express.'

Inspiration struck as she rose to her feet. 'I shall write to my brother, Mr Fernyhough. He holds a number of livings in his gift. Perhaps, should one become vacant…'

Hope flared in Mr Fernyhough's face.

Isabella bit her lip. *I should not have said that. What if there are none?* She looked down at the letter in her hand. It was addressed to Harriet, care of Lady Isabella Knox, Clarges Street, London.

She glanced up at Mr Fernyhough, suddenly uneasy. 'The landlady, she told you my name and direction?'

Mr Fernyhough nodded.

Isabella bit her lip again. She looked down at the letter. *Miss Harriet Durham, care of Lady Isabella Knox.* 'I had hoped— I sent a man to ensure she would not disclose the connection between Harriet and myself.'

'She did not release the information readily,' Mr Fernyhough assured her. 'It was not until I mentioned my vocation that she revealed she had seen Harriet. Mrs Botham is a very devout woman.'

Isabella pinched the letter tightly between her fingers. Dread crawled up her spine. She inhaled a deep breath and looked up at Mr Fernyhough and smiled brightly. 'I shall give this to Harriet immediately.'

'Thank you.' Mr Fernyhough bowed again.

Isabella opened the door. Voices came from the entrance hall. She recognised Major Reynolds's baritone.

For a moment she stood frozen in panic, Mr Fernyhough at her back, the letter in her hand, evidence of her guilt surrounding her—and then Lieutenant Mayhew's familiar laugh floated down the corridor.

The kittens. They're here for the kittens. Isabella released a shaky breath.

Mr Fernyhough bowed once more, earnest and punctilious, and took his leave. Isabella hurried back into the drawing room. Her fingers trembled slightly as she hid the letter inside a book.

Her heart jerked at a knock on the door. She turned her head. A footman stood on the threshold. 'Major Reynolds and Lieutenant Mayhew to see you, ma'am.'

'Thank you. I'll be along in a minute.' She smiled and tried to speak calmly. 'Can you please tell Miss Durham that we have more guests and that I desire her to stay with my cousin?'

'Certainly, madam.' The footman retreated.

Isabella stood for a few moments, trying to steady her breathing. Then she wiped her damp hands on her gown, arranged her lips into a smile, and went to greet her guests.

Chapter Ten

Lady Isabella came down the corridor, lovely in a gown of deep rose-pink and with her golden hair dressed in ringlets. She greeted them with a smile and an outstretched hand. 'Major Reynolds. Lieutenant Mayhew.'

'I hope we're not intruding.' Nicholas indicated the front door, which had just closed behind Lady Isabella's visitor. 'We can return later if—'

'Not at all. Come upstairs, gentlemen. The kittens are in the morning room.'

She talked lightly of the kittens as they climbed the flight of stairs, Rufus at their heels, and perhaps it was his imagination, but she didn't seem to be quite herself. Nicholas frowned, trying to identify what was different about her.

She's talking too much. Babbling, almost. As if she was nervous.

'Are you all right?' he asked quietly.

Lady Isabella cast him a swift glance. 'Perfectly!' she said, her smile bright and wide.

No, he thought, frowning to himself. *Something is wrong.*

Lady Isabella turned to Mayhew, still smiling brightly. 'They all have different personalities, you know. I can tell you exactly which one will be the first to greet us!'

She opened the door to the sunny morning room. The kittens, asleep in the basket, roused at their entrance. A black one clambered out and came running across the carpet, its tiny tail held high in the air.

Lady Isabella bent to pick the black kitten up. 'This is Boots,' she said. 'And I am afraid you may not have her, Lieutenant!'

'You're keeping one?' Nicholas asked.

'Yes,' she said, stroking the kitten. 'How can I give her away when she comes running to greet me every time I open the door!'

'Boots?' Mayhew asked, walking towards the basket of kittens.

'Major Reynolds ruined a pair of boots rescuing them,' Isabella explained as the black kitten began to purr.

Mayhew cast a laughing glance over his shoulder. 'A hero, no less!'

Nicholas ignored his friend's teasing and closed the door to prevent any escapes.

Rufus trotted over to the basket and stuck his muzzle into the tangle of kittens and began to lick the upturned faces. Mayhew uttered a startled laugh as the kittens squeaked, scrambling over each other, vying for the dog's attention.

'Extraordinary, isn't it?' Nicholas said, walking across to join Mayhew. He patted Rufus. A very nice dog, with his gangly legs and pluming tail and his startling eyes, one blue one brown. *I should like a dog like him.*

'The black and grey is the boldest,' Lady Isabella said, coming to stand alongside them. 'She's a girl. And of the two grey tabbies, one is a boy, and one a girl. Here—' She handed the black kitten to Nicholas, their fingers touching fleetingly, and then bent to pick up a grey-striped kitten. She checked its gender with brief matter of factness and gave it to Mayhew. 'This is the boy. He loves to have his belly rubbed; see, if you hold him like this…'

Mayhew laughed again as the kitten relaxed in his grip, belly up, purring.

'What do you think, Lieutenant?'

Nicholas retired from the conversation, listening with half an ear as he examined the paintings on the walls, Boots cupped in his hand. The grey-and-black kitten set about climbing the curtains while her boldness was discussed and the grey-striped male purred blissfully under Mayhew's ministrations.

When the discussion turned to the logistics of travelling to Southampton with two kittens, Nicholas retired to one of the sofas. The cream-and-gold damask appeared to be untouched, but he thought he discerned some scratches on the lion's claw feet, as if a kitten had tried to climb up them.

Boots settled happily on his lap. Nicholas stroked the kitten idly, listening to her purr. The warmth and softness of her coat, the vibration of her purr beneath his hand, brought back memories of Spain, of campfires and—

'I thought you didn't like cats, Major?'

Nicholas looked up to find two pairs of eyes on him. 'Er…'

'Nonsense!' Mayhew said. 'If he said that, he was gammoning you, ma'am!' His grin widened. 'What was the name of that kitten you picked up after Badajoz? That scruffy, multi-coloured creature?'

'Zoe,' Nicholas said, reluctantly.

'He carried it around with him for months, ma'am,' Mayhew said, speaking to Lady Isabella. 'Said it was too young to fend for itself.'

'Oh,' said Lady Isabella. Her eyes were slightly narrowed, her expression assessing.

Nicholas cleared his throat. He stood and placed Boots on the floor. *Shut up, Mayhew. Or she'll foist the last one off on me.* 'Which ones are you taking?'

'Those two,' Mayhew said, pointing. He turned to Lady

Isabella. 'But I won't take them until next week, ma'am, if that's all right with you?'

Negotiations complete, they exited the morning room, Lady Isabella closing the door in the face of the black-and-grey kitten's attempt to explore.

'What happened to your Spanish kitten?' Lady Isabella asked as they descended the stairs, Rufus preceding them, his tail waving.

'She refused to cross the Huebra.'

She glanced at him. 'Did you miss her?'

'A little,' he admitted.

'Are you sure you wouldn't like—?'

'Quite certain,' he said firmly. Although, truth be told, he had liked the warmth of Boots on his knee, her quiet purr, her soft fur.

In the hallway Mayhew bowed over Lady Isabella's hand and—quite unnecessarily in Nicholas's opinion—kissed it. 'I am in your debt, madam. You have saved my reputation!'

Lady Isabella disclaimed this with a laugh.

'What reputation?' Nicholas said, slightly sourly.

'I always give the *best* presents.'

'Hyde Park this afternoon?' Nicholas asked, while Mayhew accepted his hat and gloves from the butler.

'Oh!' Lady Isabella said, consternation crossing her face. 'Forgive me, Major, but I don't think I can. The masquerade tonight— My costume…' She bit her lip.

'No apology is necessary,' he said, but as he walked down the steps with Mayhew, he wondered whether the costume had been an excuse or a reason. Something was bothering Lady Isabella. She wasn't agitated or flustered, just…not completely at ease.

He couldn't lay the blame at Mayhew's feet—Lady Isabella was no straw damsel to be overset by the Lieutenant's light-hearted flirting.

Nicholas took his leave of Mayhew at the end of Clarges

Street. 'A prime article!' his friend said, with a sly, sideways glance. 'No wonder you're making up to her!'

Nicholas looked at him with exasperation. 'I told you, we're merely friends.'

Mayhew shook his head. 'A word of advice,' he said, leaning close and dropping his voice to a whisper. 'Take that last kitten!'

'Damn it, Mayhew! How many times do I have to tell you? We're merely—'

But Mayhew shook his head, his eyes alight with laughter. 'I must be off!' He raised a hand in a gesture that was very like a salute and swung away.

Nicholas watched him go, torn between annoyance and amusement. Amusement won. He grunted a laugh, and then set his hat more firmly on his head and strode off in the direction of Drury Lane.

Isabella retrieved Mr Fernyhough's letter from its hiding place. Now that the Major was gone, some of her tension eased. She turned the letter over in her fingers. There would be tears when she gave it to Harriet, of that she was certain. Harriet was a sweet child, mild-tempered and eager to oblige, but she was also—as her brother Julian would say—a watering pot.

Although the girl did have good reason to cry.

Isabella sighed and climbed the stairs to Mrs Westin's parlour.

The room was warm with sunlight. Harriet was reading aloud in her soft, child-like voice. Isabella didn't recognise the words, but the tenor of the book was unmistakable: another Improving Work.

Harriet finished the sentence she was reading, in which Duty figured largely, and looked up, marking her place with one finger. 'Your visitors have gone, ma'am?'

'Yes.' Isabella braced herself for tears. 'One of them was

an acquaintance of yours—Mr Fernyhough. He desired me
to give you this.' She advanced across the room as she spoke,
holding the letter out to Harriet, aware of Mrs Westin's head
lifting and the knitting needles stilling, aware of Harriet's
cheeks paling, of the book falling unheeded from her lap.

'Mr Fernyhough?' Harriet spoke the name in a breathless
gasp. 'Here?' She half-rose to her feet.

'He has gone, child,' Isabella said gently. 'He felt it would
be unwise to see you.'

'Oh.' Tears started in Harriet's eyes.

'He was concerned for your well-being. I was able to
assure him that you are safe and well.'

The girl nodded. Her eyes were bright with moisture.

'He left this for you.'

Harriet took the letter with a trembling hand.

'Perhaps you would like to go to your room to read it?'

The girl nodded mutely. 'Thank you, ma'am.' The words
were barely audible. She clutched the letter to her breast,
groping for the door handle as if blinded by tears.

'Mr Fernyhough?' Mrs Westin asked when the door had
closed behind Harriet.

Isabella sighed and sat. 'A clergyman.' She picked up the
book that had tumbled from Harriet's lap, smoothing the
pages. *Duty*, she read. *There is no greater glory than a life
devoted to…* She closed it and glanced at the spine. A book
of sermons. 'An admirer of Harriet's. He withdrew his suit
when Colonel Durham forbade the match.'

'Quite proper.' Mrs Westin nodded her approval. She
resumed her knitting.

Isabella glanced at her. *Proper, yes, but look at the unhap-
piness that has resulted.* She didn't utter the words. Instead
she placed the book to one side and said, 'Lieutenant
Mayhew has agreed to take two of the kittens.'

'That's good,' Mrs Westin said, not looking up from her
knitting.

Isabella bit her lip, wishing she could talk freely with her cousin, and knowing she could not; their views on the subject of familial duty were widely divergent. She stood. 'I have a letter to write, cousin. Please excuse me.'

'Of course, my dear.' Mrs Westin smiled serenely, her needles moving swiftly. A sleeve of sturdy blue wool dangled from one knitting needle.

Isabella let herself out of the parlour. She walked back down the corridor to the morning room and the kittens and sat down at the escritoire to compose a letter to her brother, the Duke of Middlebury. Paper, quill, ink, sealing wax… The words, though, were not easy to find. She stared down at the sheet of hot-pressed paper, aware of an ache growing behind her temples. *What to reveal, and what to hide?*

'How much shall I tell him, Rufus?'

Rufus was no help; he merely wagged his tail.

There was something about a masquerade—a freedom, a loosening of constraints, a slight edge of the *risqué*. One could wear clothing that in other settings, in the same company, would be shocking. Isabella glanced down at her feet, bare in Grecian sandals, with gilded toenails. No, she could not have gilded her toenails on any other occasion—not unless she wished to shock the polite world and draw censure down upon her head.

But hers were not the only painted toenails tonight. A glance around the crowded ballroom showed several other ladies had the audacity to mimic the whores of Paris. One even appeared to be dressed as a whore. *Brave*, thought Isabella. *I would not care to display so much flesh.*

The music fitted the mood of the assembled guests, loud, with a slightly wild edge to it. Beneath it the sound of voices rose, raucous, punctuated with gusts of laughter.

Few débutantes were present. Their mothers had prudently kept them away. The Worthingtons' masquerade did have a reputation, after all.

Isabella scanned the ballroom. The Major's chosen bride—Clarissa Whedon—did not appear to be present. A good thing—this was scarcely the place for a girl just out of the schoolroom.

Isabella found herself frowning. How could the Major wish for so young a bride? And for such a reason? A placid, biddable girl without any opinions of her own. A girl whose character was still unformed.

He'll be bored within a month.

She shrugged. If that was the sort of marriage Major Reynolds wanted, he was welcome to it.

She scanned the room again, searching for him. There were a number of men with his height and breadth of shoulder—she saw a black-bearded pirate, a Roman legionnaire, a knight in armour with a red, perspiring face beneath his visor—*Poor man, not a good choice of costume*—a monk, a sailor with a tarred ponytail, an executioner, and a rather tall Napoleon—but none who had the Major's carriage.

'Isn't this fun!' Gussie said. Her eyes gleamed with merriment behind the concealment of her mask. With her red hooded cloak, pinafore and pigtails and pantalettes, and the basket of strawberries on her arm, there was no doubting who she was.

Isabella laughed. 'Yes!' She reached for another strawberry. Red Riding Hood's basket was almost empty.

A winged fairy flitted past, giggling behind her mask, pursued by a horned satyr. The ballroom boasted half a dozen fairies, in addition to a lavishly feathered peacock, a number of shepherdesses, a mermaid with an awkward tail, a butterfly, several buxom milkmaids, two Marie Antoinettes with powdered hair, a rather clever marionette, and a Cleopatra.

And a Grecian harvest goddess.

Isabella touched the tiny golden corn sheaves that dangled from her earlobes.

'There's another goddess.' Gussie pointed.

Isabella followed the direction of her finger. A Diana stood by the far pillar, boyish in a short Grecian tunic, a bow and a quiver of arrows slung over her shoulder.

'Who's that with her? Good gracious!' Gussie gave a choke of laughter. 'Just look what Sarah Faraday is wearing!'

Isabella had seen. She politely refrained from commenting.

'Oh, and there's Cupid. Look!'

'Yes,' Isabella said. 'But have you seen your cousin? He said he'd be here.'

Perhaps he hadn't realised quite how far the Worthingtons' estate was from town. Seven miles, in the dark, was no slight distance. He could have lost his way, or—

A disturbance near the doorway drew her attention. Voices rose. She heard gasps, laughter.

A man emerged from the crowd near the entrance, dressed in a brown frieze coat. There was no mistaking his height, his soldier's bearing.

Isabella's mouth dropped open.

She was not the only one transfixed. Heads turned as Major Reynolds passed. A stir of conversation rose in his wake.

'Oh,' said Isabella, finding her breath as he walked towards them. 'How perfect!' She held out her hand to him. 'Major! I am truly impressed.'

Major Reynolds bowed over her fingers. 'I'm pleased you approve.'

She could only shake her head and stare at him. An ogre confronted her, grey-skinned, with flaring, red-rimmed nostrils, a jutting, knotted brow, and matted black hair hanging past his shoulders. A livid scar deformed half his face, *papier-mâché* sculpted into scarlet ridges of burned flesh.

'Where did you get it?' Gussie reached out to touch the mask with one finger.

'A costumier near Drury Lane.'

'It's perfect,' Isabella said again. 'Absolutely perfect!' She meant more than the mask. The Major was thumbing his nose at the *ton* and, at the same time, joining them in their laughter.

Very few men would have either the wit or the courage to do that.

'It seemed…apt,' the Major said. His face was hidden behind the mask, all but his mouth and chin.

He had a very nice mouth, Isabella realised. An expressive mouth, with nicely shaped lips. A mouth that, right now, was quirked up at the corners, as if he barely held back laughter.

Bless you for having a sense of humour, Major. There could be no more ridicule after tonight, not after Major Reynolds had invited London to laugh *with* him.

His eyes, green and glittering behind the mask, examined her costume—the elaborately upswept hair bound with gold ribbon, the tiny golden corn sheaves dangling from her earlobes, the gown of cream satin falling to her ankles in long, sheer pleats, its bodice bound with golden cord, the slender Grecian sandals. His eyes lingered a moment on her gilded toenails and then rose to inspect the staff she held, crowned with gold-painted corn sheaves and intricately bound with golden ribbon. 'Demeter,' he said.

'Well done, Major.'

Viscount Washburne emerged from the crowded dance floor, splendid in a huntsman's costume, a wolf skin thrown over his shoulders. 'The quadrille,' he said to Gussie, holding out his hand to her. He glanced at Major Reynolds and his eyes widened. For a moment he stared, and then he uttered a crack of laughter. 'Magnificent!'

Major Reynolds grinned. 'Thank you.'

Gussie put down her basket of strawberries. She took her husband's hand. 'Make sure he has some punch,' she said over her shoulder, as Lucas Washburne pulled her on to the dance floor.

'Punch?'

'A Worthington tradition,' Isabella said. 'You must try it. It's—well, you shall judge for yourself!'

His mouth quirked again in amusement. 'That good?'

'Better!'

'Then I must certainly try it.' He held out his arm to her. 'If you will lead me to it?'

They strolled slowly around the perimeter of the room to the accompaniment of the quadrille. The familiar tune had an edge to it, a slight wildness not found at more formal balls. The dancers caught the mood of the music. Isabella watched them for a moment, enjoying their gaiety, before turning her attention to the guests clustering the edges of the dance floor.

Satisfaction grew in her breast with each indrawn breath, each startled gaze, each delighted choke of laughter, each low-voiced murmur of admiration that Major Reynolds's mask evoked. 'Major,' she said, in a low voice, 'you are a genius!'

'Taken the wind out of their sails,' he murmured, inclining his head to a rather portly Robin Hood.

The table that bore the deep, silver punch bowl was crowded with revellers. It took some minutes before they were able to procure glasses.

Major Reynolds looked at his glass dubiously. Sliced strawberries and oranges floated in the punch. 'It's pink,' he said. 'Are you certain—?'

'Try it!'

His lips twisted in amusement. She thought she saw a gleam in the eyes hidden behind his mask.

The Major's first sip was tentative. His second was not. 'The deuce!' he said, examining the punch more closely. 'What have they put in it?'

'It's probably best if one doesn't know,' Isabella said, raising her own glass to her lips.

The punch was potent, slightly sweet, slightly tart, cool in her mouth and hot in her throat. She swallowed, feeling warmth spread beneath her skin. *Dangerous to drink too much*, she told herself.

After the quadrille came a waltz. Isabella leaned her staff against a wall and allowed Major Reynolds to lead her on to the dance floor. They made their bows and then came together, his hand at her waist, hers on his shoulder. She'd worn no gloves tonight, for the veracity of her costume, and she was aware of the heat of the Major's palm, the strength of his fingers. Their handclasp felt surprisingly intimate.

The Worthingtons' waltz was no staid Almack's dance, but something far more exhilarating and fast-paced. The musicians seemed to ply their bows with ever-increasing speed. Major Reynolds kept time with the music, whirling her around the dance floor until she was breathless and laughing. He retained hold of her hand when they halted, steadying her. 'More punch?' he asked, as he escorted her off the dance floor.

Recklessly she nodded.

Dance followed dance until Isabella lost all track of time. She saw Major Reynolds frequently on the dance floor: the brown coat, the mane of shaggy black hair, the scowling ogre's mask. From the set of his mouth, he was enjoying himself.

The heat in the ballroom rose. The punch bowl was frequently emptied. Eyes glittered behind masks, cheeks were flushed, and mouths were wide with laughter. The knight removed his gauntlets, gorget and breast-plate. Sweat stained his undergarments.

Isabella ate a supper of lobster patties and white soup and returned to the ballroom to dance again.

'Where's your staff, Demeter?'

The voice was familiar: Major Reynolds.

Isabella turned. 'I have no idea!' she said, laughing up at him. 'I have lost it!'

'For shame,' he said.

The mask was grotesque above his grinning mouth. For a moment the wrongness of it almost made her dizzy. Such a strong, well-formed body, such a hideous, deformed head. *Take it off*, she wanted to say, but she bit the words back. *Too much punch*, she scolded herself silently. *I must drink no more.*

'The next dance is to be a waltz,' Major Reynolds said. 'And then I believe fireworks will follow.'

'Isabella!'

Another familiar voice, and this one far from welcome.

Isabella lost her smile. She turned. 'Sarah. Have you met Major Reynolds?'

She made the introductions with cool politeness, but if Sarah Faraday noticed the coolness she made no move to leave. She was well on the way to being intoxicated, her laugh too loud, her words slurring, her face red above the green ruff encircling her neck.

Isabella glanced down at Sarah's dress. What was she? The gown was a profusion of green frills, layer upon layer of them, thickening her already stout figure.

'How charming you look together,' Lady Faraday said. 'Beauty and the Beast!'

Isabella looked up from her perusal of the green gown. 'Demeter and an Ogre, actually,' she said coldly. 'What are you? A cabbage?'

She regretted the words as soon as she'd uttered them, too spiteful, too petty, but Lady Faraday failed to notice the insult.

'A dryad.' She pirouetted, almost falling over in the process, the dozens of frills flaring out, making her look even stouter. 'Dressed in spring leaves.'

'Very…original,' Major Reynolds said, politely.

Very cabbage, Isabella thought.

The musicians struck up the waltz. 'Excuse us,' Major

Reynolds said, holding out his hand to Isabella. 'This is our dance.'

Isabella let him lead her on to the dance floor. 'Beauty and the Beast!' she said, her voice sharp. 'If she starts putting that around London—'

'It's a compliment,' the Major said, sounding amused. 'For you, at least.'

'But you are not a beast! Any more than you are an ogre!' Anger made her tone hot. 'And if she—'

'You sound like my nephew.' Major Reynolds was smiling at her. 'And I shall give you the same answer I gave him: I can fight my own battles.'

'But—'

'Ignore her.'

'Yes, but what if she—?'

'I don't care.' Major Reynolds swept her into the waltz. 'Dance,' he said in her ear. 'Enjoy!'

Isabella pursed her lips. 'Is that an order, Major?'

'Most definitely.'

Her ill humour slid away. 'An autocrat, I perceive.'

He grinned at her, his teeth glinting white beneath the scowling ogre's mask, and tightened his grip on her hand. 'Of the worst kind!' he said, and swept her into a turn.

Chapter Eleven

The music bore no resemblance to the waltzes he was used to dancing in London. It was wild and fast, almost bacchanalian. The musicians' exuberance was infectious. Nicholas heard the music in his ears, *felt* it in his blood. *Dance faster*, it urged. *Faster.* Lady Isabella must have felt the music too; she matched him, step for step, as he led her into one flamboyant spin after another. They were both laughing by the time the musicians laid down their bows. Their hands clung for a moment as they steadied one another. Nicholas dragged air into his lungs and bowed. 'Thank you, Lady Isabella.'

'Not at all,' she said, fanning herself with her hand. 'You are an excellent dancer!'

'As are you.' He offered her his arm. 'A drink, ma'am?'

'Please!'

The line to the punch bowl was long. Lady Isabella fanned her flushed cheeks again with a hand. 'You enjoy dancing,' she said, in her clear, frank way. 'And yet you give the impression of a man who dislikes attending balls.'

'It's not balls I dislike,' Nicholas said, wishing he could remove his mask. He was so damned *hot*. 'It's the Marriage Mart. I feel like a beast up for sale at an auction, being examined by prospective buyers.'

Her face lit with laughter. 'How uncomfortable!'

He shrugged, knowing he'd dislike it less if he didn't have the scar blazoned across his face, but not willing to make that admission aloud.

Lady Isabella's smile faded. 'You are correct, Major. That is precisely what it is: an auction. I'm glad to be out of it.'

I will be too.

They had barely received their glasses when there was a stir of movement behind them, a rise in the babble of voices. Nicholas turned his head and watched as footmen in long-tailed coats trimmed with braid flung open the French windows lining the far side of the ballroom.

Glasses in hand, they joined the drifting crowd out on to the terrace. Flambeaux burned and lamps lit the gardens. The cool night air was welcome on his chin. Nicholas inhaled deeply and wished it was time to unmask. Perspiration trickled down his cheek.

The hell with it.

He put his glass down on the stone balustrade and reached up and pulled the ogre's mask off his head.

The air was cold on his face, refreshing, welcome. He closed his eyes in a moment of enjoyment.

'Much better, isn't it?'

He opened his eyes to see that Lady Isabella had untied her golden mask and was using it to fan her cheeks.

'Yes.' He wiped his face with one hand and ran his fingers through his hair. It was damp with sweat.

'Look!' someone cried behind him. 'They're starting!'

At the sound of the first explosion, the ballroom emptied of guests. The terrace became a jostling mass of people, pressed close to one another, laughing and exclaiming as the fireworks lit up the sky. Nicholas was more conscious of the warmth of Lady Isabella's body alongside him than of the display of pyrotechnics. She felt soft, warm—

Nicholas gave himself a mental shake and drained his

glass of punch. He gazed up at the stars, at the bright cascade of sparks tumbling in the sky. Around him people cried out in delighted awe, clapping their hands.

The fireworks display over, the terrace slowly emptied, the guests drawn back into the ballroom by the light and the warmth and the lilting strains of music. Lady Isabella made no move to leave the terrace. She leaned her forearms on the balustrade and gazed out over the garden. London was several miles distant; the lights and clamour of town did not intrude here. The garden was dark but for a sprinkling of lamps. It was an enchanted fairy landscape of shadows and flickering flames.

Nicholas stayed beside her, breathing the cool air. A few others lingered on the terrace, to converse, to flirt lightly with one another, and in the case of a young buck dressed in striped stockings and a jester's hat, to sit groaning with his head in his hands. Nicholas sympathised with him. Pleasure hummed in his veins. He felt careless, reckless, exuberant. He knew why: the punch. The stuff was lethal.

'Are you enjoying your triumph, Major?'

The ogre's mask sat on the balustrade, alongside his empty glass. Nicholas tapped the *papier-mâché* cheek, sculpted in scarlet whorls, with one finger. 'Yes,' he said. 'I am.'

Lady Isabella laughed softly.

He turned his head to look at her. She shone in the moonlight, pale and golden. *She's beautiful. A goddess in truth.* 'Why Demeter?' he asked. *Why not Venus?*

Lady Isabella touched one of the golden earrings in a reflective gesture. It spun, catching the light of a flambeau, gleaming. 'A suitor of mine once wrote a poem. "To the harvest goddess",' she quoted, '"with her corn-ripe hair."'

Nicholas uttered a crack of laughter. 'Good Lord!' he said.

Lady Isabella was unoffended. She grinned.

'Who was it?' Nicholas asked, before he could catch his tongue.

'Brabington.'

'Brabington?' Nicholas said, startled. 'The Duke?'

Lady Isabella nodded.

'Why—?' He hesitated a moment, aware the question was impertinent, and then plunged onwards, knowing his recklessness was due to the punch, and not caring. It was a night for stepping beyond boundaries. The music streaming from the wide open windows urged it; faerie music, spiralling up into the dark night sky, wild and lilting and as intoxicating as the punch. 'Why have you not married?'

Lady Isabella's eyebrows lifted, but she did not appear to be offended. 'Because I have not wished to.'

'But—' He halted, stuck for words. Didn't every woman want to marry? And then he remembered. 'Your fiancé died,' he said. 'I'm sorry.'

'Roland? Yes. He died a month before we were to be married.' She looked down at the empty glass in her hand.

'That must have been hard,' he said quietly.

'It was,' she said, but he heard no melancholy in her voice, saw none in her downturned face. 'But it was eleven years ago, so do not picture me with a broken heart, Major, for that is not the case!' Her expression grew thoughtful. 'In fact, I have often thought that it was fortunate the wedding did not take place. Not fortunate that Roland died! But…fortunate I didn't marry him.' She glanced at him, and uttered a laugh. 'I've shocked you, Major!'

'Not at all,' Nicholas said, although her words had taken him aback. 'Er…why was it fortunate?'

'Poor Roland had no sense of humour. A necessity, I believe, in a marriage!' She met his eyes, her tone serious, 'Don't mistake me, Major. I was in love with Roland—as much as a child of eighteen can be!—but I'm no longer wearing the willow for him.'

'But you haven't married.'

'No doubt I should have, if my father hadn't died so soon after Roland, and then my mother… She was very ill, and by

the time she passed away I was four-and-twenty and quite used to making my own decisions and I found that I didn't *want* to marry. Fortunately she left me a sizeable fortune, so I didn't have to.'

Nicholas frowned at her. 'Your brothers allowed you to set up house by yourself at four-and-twenty?'

'With Mrs Westin, yes.'

Lady Isabella was looking at him with some amusement. *She thinks me a stick-in-the-mud.*

'And Brabington? What was wrong with him?'

She lifted her smooth shoulders in a light shrug. 'I didn't wish to marry him.'

'But…a duke!'

Her expression became slightly exasperated. 'Pray, what has that to do with it?'

Nicholas stared at her. He shook his head, not understanding.

'"It is a truth universally acknowledged, that a single woman in possession of a good fortune, must be in want of a husband",' Lady Isabella said, her tone ironic.

Nicholas blinked. 'I beg your pardon?'

'A paraphrase.' She put her glass down on the balustrade. It made a dull *clunk* on the stone. 'The world expects me to *want* to marry. Well, I don't! I like my life precisely how it is.'

'Do you dislike men?' he asked, trying to understand, and failing.

'No, not at all! But I have no need for a husband of my own.'

'But—'

'Why should I trade my liberty, my independence, for a husband's name? What would I gain?'

He looked at her, standing pale and golden in the moonlight, the mask with its dark, empty eyes dangling from one finger. 'Children?' he ventured.

'My life isn't empty of children,' Lady Isabella said. 'I have twelve nephews and nieces.'

'Oh,' he said. Her words rang in his ears. *Liberty. Independence.* Perhaps that was what made her shine so much brighter than the other women of the *ton*. She belonged to no one but herself. Within the strict confines of society, she danced to her own tune.

If she were crushed into a mould—wife, mother—would she cease to shine so brightly?

Nicholas turned his head and frowned down at the shadowy, lamp-lit garden. Had Gussie become less of herself when she'd married? Would his own bride—?

A groan drew his attention. The jester staggered to his feet, his hand clapped over his mouth.

Nicholas grabbed his mask, hastily took Lady Isabella's arm, and guided her further down the terrace. The jester reached the balustrade where they had stood and leaned over it, noisily casting up his accounts.

It was quieter here, darker. One of the flambeaux had guttered. They had fewer companions.

Nicholas placed the ogre's head on the balustrade again. The *papier-mâché* mask scowled at him. 'Is marriage wholly repugnant to you?'

'I would not say *repugnant*, Major. Merely…it holds no temptations.'

But what of physical desire? Nicholas held his tongue; it was not a comment he could make.

Lady Isabella turned the golden mask over in her fingers. He watched her frown. 'I will own that there is one drawback to my situation: I must rely on my friends to provide me with an escort.'

He lifted his eyebrows. 'But Mrs Westin—'

'Certainly she will accompany me if I have no other escort, but she has no great liking for balls and rout-parties.'

She leaned against the balustrade again and looked out over the garden at the darkness and the shadows and the flickering lamps. 'Usually one or other of my brothers and sisters are in London for the Season, but this year they are none of them here. Julian has just been presented with his fifth child and poor Marianne is in no state to come to town. Simon has taken his family to the continent, and both Clara and Amabel are expecting.' She turned her face towards him, laughing, moonlight gilding her cheek. 'You see, Major, there is no shortage of children in my family!'

He looked at her for a long moment. 'You truly have no intention of marrying, do you?'

'No.'

'But—'

'I enjoy being a spinster, Major.' He heard the truth clearly in her voice; there was no defensiveness, just a quiet sincerity.

Spinster. An ugly little word. So wrong for her.

Nicholas looked at Lady Isabella in the moonlight. She was golden and silver, beautiful. *Such a waste.*

Lady Isabella looked out over the garden again. 'Legally, a wife belongs to her husband. She is his property.'

He'd never thought of it quite like that, but she was perfectly correct. *I don't think I should like to belong to someone.*

'I have no desire to become another person's possession, Major.'

'But...' He groped for words, trying to articulate his thoughts. 'But if a man truly loved you, he wouldn't try to make you a possession.'

'I have received a number of offers, Major, from men who professed to love me. But what they loved was my face, or my rank, or my fortune—or all three!' There was no bitterness in her voice, just honesty.

'Then you are wise not to have married them.'

She smiled at him. 'We are in agreement, then.'

'But a love match,' he persisted stubbornly. 'If—'

'If it was *me* he was in love with,' she said with irony, 'and not my face!'

'If it was a love match,' he continued doggedly, 'then surely you could have no objection.'

Lady Isabella laughed. The sound had a hard edge to it, matching the glitter in her eyes. 'It is always my face men fall in love with,' she said. 'And I am much more than my face!'

'I am aware of that,' he said with stiff dignity.

The hard glitter left her eyes. Her mouth softened into a smile that was genuine. 'You are a prince among men,' she said, reaching out to touch the back of his hand, resting on the balustrade, with light fingertips. 'Ogre.' The word was said with affection.

She turned to go inside.

'But—'

Lady Isabella looked back over her shoulder. 'I shall never marry, Major. Accept it!'

She was Venus, standing silhouetted in the light streaming from the French windows. Tall and queenly and inordinately beautiful.

Their companions in this corner of the terrace were gone. Some had returned to the dancing; others, judging from the muffled giggles that rose from the gardens, were indulging in more clandestine activities. He and Lady Isabella were alone, apart from the music and the shadows, the moonlight.

She held out her hand to him. 'Come inside, Major. Let us dance some more!'

Nicholas took hold of her fingers. 'You don't know what you're missing.'

She laughed. 'I assure you that I do!'

'No,' he said. 'You don't.'

It was music swirling from the ballroom that made him tighten his clasp on her hand, that made him pull her closer. Faerie music, wild and reckless.

Lady Isabella became very still. 'Major.' There was a note of warning in her voice.

'Don't dismiss something as worthless until you have tried it.'

'Major Reynolds—'

'You have set your heart against marriage, without knowing anything of the pleasures that may attend it.'

'Major—'

'If you were to make a love match, you would find that the…er…physical side of marriage can be extremely enjoyable.'

Lady Isabella pulled her hand free. She folded her arms across her chest, defensive. 'Roland did kiss me once; I didn't like it.'

'He didn't do it right, then.'

Her frown vanished. She laughed. 'And pray, how do you know? You weren't there!'

'How do *you* know if you've only tried it once?'

The question silenced her. She bit her lip.

He looked at her, gilded in music and moonlight. Desire clenched in his belly. Dear God, he *wanted* to kiss her. The music was no help, whispering in his ear, urging, enticing. 'I think you should try it again.'

She stood quite still for a moment, her arms crossed, her face expressionless. 'Just what is it you're proposing, Major?'

He shrugged and tried to keep his tone careless. 'A kiss.'

There was no revulsion in her voice, merely shock. 'You know I dare not!'

He glanced over his shoulder, at the shadowy gardens. 'We wouldn't be the only ones.'

Her brow creased. 'Why, Major?'

Because I want to taste your mouth. 'So that your decision may be more informed.' He leaned against the balustrade. 'It's a very important decision, after all.'

Her lips twisted, as if she tried to hide a smile. 'For my own good?'

'Yes,' he said, striving for a note of piety. 'I feel it is my duty.'

He saw laughter in her eyes; she knew he was teasing her. 'Your duty?'

'Yes. I am a very dutiful man.'

She laughed aloud at this and uncrossed her arms. 'You have a glib tongue, Major. Is this how you won your battles? By sweet-talking your enemies?'

You are not my enemy. Nor was she the woman he wanted to marry. But right now, while the mad, bacchanalian music swirled around him and the night air was cool on his face, he had a burning need to kiss her. 'What do you say?' he asked lightly.

She bit her lip, looking uncertain. 'I don't know.'

It wasn't a *no.* Did the music affect her as it did him? It urged him to take hold of her hand again and stroke his fingers lightly up her arm.

Nicholas gave into the urging. He stepped away from the balustrade and reached for her hand and ran his fingertips up the inside of her arm. *Cool, smooth skin.*

Lady Isabella shivered slightly.

'Aren't you the slightest bit curious?' His voice was low.

'No,' she said. 'I told you that Roland kissed me—and I didn't like it at all!'

He bent his head and whispered in her ear. 'He did it wrong, then.'

She laughed at this. 'Major, you are more conceited than I had thought!'

'Not conceited,' he said, stroking his fingers lightly up her bare arm again, from her wrist to the sensitive hollow of her elbow. 'Merely honest.'

Lady Isabella shivered again. She bit her lip.

Nicholas bent his head closer. 'I dare you,' he whispered in her ear.

'My reputation—'

'Will still be intact. I give you my word of honour.'

Lady Isabella made no demur as he led her down the steps

into the garden, as they followed a barely seen path into the shadows, as he pulled her into the darkness of a gazebo.

'I have drunk too much punch!' she said.

'I know I have.' He pulled her close to him, cupping her face in his hands. 'I should not dare to do this otherwise!'

'Am I so terrifying?' she asked, a tart note in her voice.

Not terrifying—untouchable. He was suddenly, painfully, aware of his ruined cheek. Beauty and the Beast.

And yet I am touching her.

Her skin was cool beneath his fingers, warming to his touch.

'If you dislike it, you must tell me.'

Lady Isabella moistened her lips. 'Yes.' Her voice was barely audible; she was nervous.

She's not the only one.

Nicholas inhaled a slow, steadying breath. He slid his hands from her face to her throat, tilting up her chin with his thumbs. Her eyes stared at him, silver in the night shadows.

'Relax,' he said, smiling at her.

'That's easier said than done, Major!'

He laughed, a slight puff of breath, and angled his head and touched his lips to hers.

Slowly, he told himself, closing his eyes, inhaling the scent of her skin. Orange blossom. *Slowly.*

He started gently, laying soft kisses on her mouth until he felt her begin to relax, then he tasted her lips lightly with his tongue. She tasted of punch, of strawberries and oranges, sweet and tart, delicious.

Heat was building in his body. When her lips parted to his tongue he almost groaned.

Slowly, damn it. Slowly.

He explored her mouth in slight increments, keeping it light and teasing, playful. Arousal jolted through him when her tongue shyly touched his.

Slowly.

But it was impossible when she was kissing him back, her mouth shy and inexperienced, eager.

Nicholas abandoned his caution. He kissed her more deeply, losing himself in pleasure, in heat. His awareness of their surroundings, the gazebo and the shadowy garden, faded. Her mouth was more bewitching than the faerie music, more intoxicating than the punch. He sank into it. His world narrowed to her lips, to her body pressed against his, to the taste and scent of her. This was indulgence, this was bliss, this was—

Madness.

Nicholas forced himself to release her. He opened his eyes and stared at her, struggling to breathe. His heartbeat was loud in his ears. He stepped back a pace.

They stared at each other in silence, in the darkness. He heard her breathing, as ragged as his own, saw the glimmer of moonlight in her eyes.

'Lady Isabella?' he asked softly.

She inhaled a sharp breath. 'I need to return to the ball!' Her voice was low and shaken. 'If my absence has been noted—!'

Nicholas took hold of her hand. 'It will be all right.'

Her fingers clutched his. He saw her nod, heard her try to steady her breathing. 'Yes,' she said. 'Of course it will.' But her hand trembled slightly as he escorted her along the path and up the steps to the terrace. *I shouldn't have kissed her*, he thought as he halted, letting her enter the ballroom alone. She glanced back, framed by the French window, golden in the light streaming from the chandeliers, then moved swiftly from his sight.

Nicholas stayed on the terrace for a full hour, leaning his forearms on the balustrade, frowning down at the garden. There should be exhilaration, reminiscent pleasure; instead there was disquiet. What had happened in the gazebo? A kiss, merely a kiss, spurred on by the punch they had both consumed, by the reckless music. Merely a kiss, and yet...

He was uneasily aware that his world had altered. Something was different. He just wasn't quite sure what.

Chapter Twelve

When dawn seeped in through the chintz curtains, Isabella gave up all pretence of trying to sleep. She had lain awake for what seemed like hours, listening to the clatter of hooves on Clarges Street, to voices raised in song as revellers made their way home, to the nightwatchman's cry: *Four of the clock, and all's well.*

Except that all *wasn't* well.

In the space of a few minutes, everything had changed. Her life had turned upside down.

You have set your heart against marriage, Major Reynolds had said, *without knowing anything of the pleasures that may attend it.*

And he had been correct: she *had* set her heart against marriage. But now, *now*—

Isabella shifted her position again inside the twisted nest of sheets and counterpane. Sleep was impossible; every time she closed her eyes she remembered the Major's kiss, remembered the heat that had washed through her, the spiralling coil of pleasure in her belly—

She hadn't wanted him to stop. That was what appalled her the most—more than her acquiescence to his suggestion, more than her enjoyment of it. She hadn't wanted him to stop. She had wanted more.

Am I so sunk below reproach?

It seemed she was. Every time she closed her eyes she was aware of the heat, the tension, still lingering in her body. *I want more.*

Isabella changed position again. She rearranged a pillow that seemed to have grown lumpier with each hour that passed.

I feel it is my duty, the Major had said, teasing her. And then he'd kissed her. And she'd let him, she'd kissed him back, and now—

I want more.

Isabella closed her eyes and relived Major Reynold's kiss. Warmth flushed inside her at memory of his mouth, the gentleness, the hunger.

It was no longer impossible to imagine the Major with Spanish paramours. If he kissed like that—

Isabella opened her eyes. The curtains shone brighter with suppressed sunlight.

Harriet's grandfather had been correct: the girl was a fool to turn down a man such as Major Reynolds.

And I am a fool for kissing him.

No, not for kissing him, for letting it affect her like this. For allowing a few minutes' pleasure to disorder her mind.

Isabella uttered a muttered exclamation of annoyance. She pushed back the covers and sat up. Across the room, her reflection glimmered ghost-like in the mirror—pale face, shadowed eyes.

Rufus, in his basket at the foot of her bed, sat up and yawned widely.

'Did you sleep, Rufus? I didn't.' She touched a light fingertip to her mouth, watching the movement in the mirror.

Major Reynolds had kissed her, tasted her—

Isabella lowered her hand and briskly got out of bed,

reaching for her dressing gown. She pulled the belt tightly about her waist and stared at herself in the mirror. A stranger met her eyes: a woman who would consider casting aside the tenet she lived her adult life by, a woman who would exchange her liberty for a man's embrace.

Rufus climbed out of his basket, stretched, yawned again, and trotted across the carpet, tail wagging, to greet her with a lick on the hand.

Isabella patted him absently. 'No,' she said under her breath, turning away from the mirror. She was not such a fool. A fool to kiss Major Reynolds, yes, and an even bigger fool to enjoy it—but not such a fool as to fail to realise that it wouldn't be like that with every man. It had, most certainly, not been like that with Roland.

Isabella drew the curtains back. Mild sunlight flooded in.

Why hadn't it been like that with Roland, whom she had loved? Why Major Reynolds? A man who, by his own confession, wanted a bride barely out of childhood. A bride he could mould to suit him. She could not admire him for that. He was either foolish, or arrogant, or perhaps both. And yet—

And yet she wanted him to kiss her again.

When had she come to be so aware of the Major as a man? As an *attractive* man?

She leaned her hip against the windowsill, frowning down at the street without seeing it. Memory of Major Reynolds's kiss still tingled on her lips, but the Major was not a man she wanted to marry. *Any more than he wants to marry me.*

Rufus pushed his nose into her hand.

Isabella laughed suddenly, looking down at him. 'Your mistress is a fool!' she said, loudly. A kiss, one kiss, was no reason for this turmoil of her thoughts.

Rufus pricked his ears, alert. He wagged his tail.

'Yes, you are quite correct, Rufus. It is time for breakfast!' She turned away from the window and reached for the bell-pull.

* * *

They had formed the habit of meeting in Hyde Park between the hours of five and six. Lady Isabella would take him up in her phaeton and drive once around the park and let him down—a flirtation, conducted beneath the *ton*'s interested gaze.

Except that it hadn't been a flirtation; it had been businesslike and friendly.

Until I kissed her.

The question was—would she stop for him today?

Nicholas strolled along the drive. A light breeze ruffled the dark surface of the Serpentine.

'Reynolds!'

Nicholas turned his head.

Lieutenant Mayhew came up alongside him astride a rat-tailed grey. 'Joining the Grand Strut, I see!'

Nicholas lifted one shoulder in a shrug. He glanced at Mayhew's companion and blinked in recognition. 'Charlie?'

'Sir,' his nephew said.

A phaeton swept briskly past with a clatter of hooves and wheels. Perched on the high seat was a dashing young lady with dark ringlets clustered beneath the up-curled brim of her hat. The glance of her dark eyes, the slight smile of her lips as she passed them, were full of coquetry.

Mayhew turned his head to watch her. 'Very nice!' he said. His attention swung back to Nicholas. 'And where's your fair Venus?'

The words brought back vivid memory of the Worthingtons' terrace: Lady Isabella standing framed in the French window, gilded, golden, goddess-like. 'Er…' Nicholas said. He turned to Charlie. 'I didn't see you at the Worthingtons' last night.'

'I dined with Mayhew,' his nephew said. He sounded like a schoolboy trying not to brag: nonchalant, slightly boastful.

Nicholas glanced at the Lieutenant. 'Taken up with this young rattle?' he asked, forcing humour into his tone.

Mayhew gave his easy smile. 'Someone has to tell him about your exploits!'

'My exploits?' Nicholas said, slightly taken aback.

Charlie edged his horse closer. 'You never told me, sir, that during the battle at Badajoz—'

Nicholas stopped listening. Another phaeton was approaching. The lady's elegant posture, her deft handling of the reins, the black-and-brown mongrel at her feet, the middle-aged groom, were all too familiar.

Lady Isabella brought the phaeton to a halt alongside them. 'Mr Reynolds, Lieutenant Mayhew.' She inclined her head in greeting. 'Major Reynolds.' Her eyes met his for a mere instant and then slid away.

Nicholas bowed to her, and wished Mayhew and Charlie gone. He listened to Mayhew's laughing greeting with impatience, to his extravagant praise of Lady Isabella's skill with the reins with something approaching irritation.

'Prime horseflesh, ma'am! You're clearly a capital whip!'

The conversation turned to the kittens, to Mayhew's niece and nephew, to the weather in Southampton, before the Lieutenant bowed in his saddle and took Charlie off, with a grinning backwards glance at Nicholas.

Silence fell between them. Nicholas cleared his throat. 'Lady Isabella—'

'Would you care to drive with me, Major?' It was a familiar question, one she had asked each time she had halted for him, but this time her eyes didn't quite meet his.

'Yes,' he said firmly.

Major Reynolds took the groom's place alongside her. Isabella set the horses in motion. She sat stiffly, aware of an awkwardness between them where there had been no awkwardness before.

'I must apologise for my behaviour last night,' Major Reynolds said. 'It was unforgivable.'

Memory of his fingers sliding up her arm made Isabella's skin tingle with remembered sensation. 'I was at fault too.'

'It was I who offered,' the Major said. His tone was hard to decipher. Grim, with something underlying it that sounded almost like regret.

Does he wish he hadn't kissed me?

She glanced at him. He didn't see. His gaze was frowning, his mouth tight.

Yes, regret.

Mortification flooded her. *I passed a sleepless night wanting more, while he has been wishing it never happened.* She gripped the reins more tightly. 'And it was I who accepted.'

'Yes, but—'

'Shall we argue over who is most at fault, Major?' Isabella asked, her voice sharper than she had intended. 'It seems a pointless exercise to me.'

Major Reynolds was silent for a moment. 'You were gone,' he said quietly. 'When I returned to the ballroom.'

'I generally leave after the fireworks,' Isabella said, encouraging the horses past a slow barouche with a flick of her whip. 'The Worthingtons' masquerade is one of the events of the Season, but it can become a little…a little beyond what is truly respectable.' *Like kisses stolen in a garden.* The mortification had risen to heat her cheeks. She kept her gaze on the horses, on the road. Anywhere but him.

'I feared I had offended you,' Major Reynolds said. 'I thought, when you were gone—'

Isabella glanced at him again. This time he was looking at her. 'You did not offend me, Major.'

'No?'

'No.'

Major Reynolds held her gaze for a moment, his hand resting on Rufus's head, and then nodded. His face relaxed into a smile. 'I'm glad.'

Isabella turned her attention back to the horses. She felt rather more cheerful. *Not regret at kissing me—regret at offending me.*

Memory of his mouth, of his fingers stroking over her skin, brought a shiver and a flush of heat. The Major had been right: kissing him was nothing like kissing Roland. *How ignorant I have been.* 'I didn't realise it could be like that.'

'Neither did I.'

Isabella glanced swiftly at him. 'I beg your pardon?'

'It must have been the punch.'

'What?' she said.

'Last night,' Major Reynolds said. He was no longer smiling. A meditative frown creased his brow. 'The punch, it must have inflamed our senses.'

Isabella stared at him. 'You mean…it shouldn't be like that?'

'Not that good. No.'

She wrenched her attention back to the horses. 'So last night was…it was an aberration?'

'I can think of no other explanation.'

Relief flooded through her. An aberration. The feverish pleasure she had experienced, the sleepless night, the heat, the longing, the disordered thoughts, were due to the punch, not Major Reynolds's kiss. 'And how it was with Roland— *that* is how it should be.'

'Er…what?'

A familiar carriage rounded the bend. 'Lady Sefton, with Princess Esterhazy.'

She slowed the horses. Lady Sefton's barouche, with its matching bays, drew up alongside them. They exchanged bows with Lady Sefton and the round-faced, sharp-tongued Princess Esterhazy.

'Major Reynolds!' Lady Sefton cried, reaching across to give him her hand. 'How clever you were last night! Bravo!'

'Thank you, madam.'

They finished the circuit of Hyde Park, nodding and bowing to acquaintances, stopping to converse with friends. Lady Sefton wasn't the only person to congratulate the Major on his ogre's costume. *Last week they laughed at him; now they laud him.* Isabella's upper lip lifted slightly in contempt as she glanced around her. Beneath the pomaded hair and the glowing ringlets, the bright silks and crisp linens, the silver buckles and the white froth of lace, the *ton* were sheep. *Where one leads, the rest follow.*

For a brief second she saw the *ton* as Major Reynolds must see them: frivolous and shallow, full of pretension and gossip. It was a dizzying, disconcerting moment.

Isabella shook her head, banishing the notion. She drew the phaeton to a halt where her groom waited beside a tree. 'My cousin and I are dining with Gussie and Lucas tonight. I understand we may see you there.'

'Gussie's?' Major Reynolds said. 'Yes. I'll be there.' He leapt lightly down.

The groom scrambled up and took his place. Major Reynolds raised his hand in farewell. A twitch of the reins and the horses moved forwards.

Isabella hummed beneath her breath as the phaeton swung out of the park. The *clop* of hooves and the rattle of wheels on stone were loud as they passed onto the street. *An aberration, because of the punch.*

The anxiety that had ridden beneath her breastbone all day, the twisting doubt, were gone. In their place was knife-sharp relief. She'd felt… Isabella pursed her lips, searching for a metaphor as she slowed the horses' pace. It was as if there was a room inside her head where everything was shelved, where *she* was shelved, all the parts of herself, each neatly in its own place. And Major Reynolds's kiss had turned that room upside down. Everything had tumbled off the shelves, and the shelves themselves had become crooked so that nothing fitted and things kept sliding off to fall on the floor again.

Now everything was back in its place. She was whole, she was herself.

Isabella tilted her chin up for a moment, to the sky, to the sunshine. She felt light enough to float, as if release from doubt had given her wings. The path she had chosen for herself was the right one. *Only an aberration.*

Chapter Thirteen

'We'll be dining *en famille*,' Gussie had said. 'Very informal!' And very informal it was, Nicholas discovered when he arrived. Gussie met him in the doorway to the saloon and stood on tiptoe to kiss his cheek. 'I'm so glad you came,' she said, tucking her hand into his arm and pulling him into the room. 'It's been far too long!'

The saloon was familiar, a room in crimson and mahogany. The occupants were familiar too: Mrs Westin sat beside the fireplace, conversing with Lucas Washburne; his nephew Charlie was good-naturedly teasing a shaggy half-grown dog that clearly had mongrel origins; and Lady Isabella sat on one of the sofas, Grace on her lap and Timothy leaning over the back, both children talking excitedly, and a familiar ginger-striped kitten playing with the ruffled hem of her gown.

Charlie laughed and the dog uttered an answering bark. An adolescent cat with only half a tail mewed plaintively at his feet. Nicholas scooped it up. 'That's Adelei,' Gussie said. 'Her...ah, whiskers are slightly out of kilter due to the arrival of young Saffron.'

Nicholas rubbed beneath Adelei's chin. She was a fluffy creature, wiry beneath her fur, with striking golden eyes and a patchwork coat of black and white and orange. He glanced around the room a second time, taking in the noise, the laughter, the children, the pets. *I want this.*

Adelei began to purr.

'Sir!' Charlie said, noticing him. He came across the room to shake Nicholas's hand. The dog trailed at his heels. It had a rough brown coat, short legs and bright, mischievous eyes.

'Who's this?' Nicholas asked as the dog realised it had a new acquaintance to make and reared up, planting its front paws on one of Nicholas's knees.

'Tam,' said Gussie. 'Down!'

The dog obeyed, sitting on the carpet and beginning to scratch beneath his chin with great determination. His tail hit the floor loudly with each jerk of his paw.

'The, er, flea-ridden puppy?'

'No longer flea-ridden,' said Gussie. She scratched her elbow absently, as if remembering a forgotten itch.

Nicholas laughed. Adelei paid no attention to either the dog or his laugh. She continued to purr.

'Sir,' Charlie said urgently. 'I really must ask you about Badajoz. Mayhew said—'

Badajoz was blood, it was slaughter, it was not what he wanted tonight. 'Later,' Nicholas said.

Gussie clapped her hands. 'Grace, Timothy, time to go upstairs!'

The children clambered eagerly off the sofa. 'I want the story with the bears,' Grace said, tugging at Lady Isabella's hand.

Nicholas stood aside from the doorway as Gussie and Lady Isabella and Timothy and Grace—with Saffron now clasped tightly to her chest—exited the parlour, followed by Tam. The clamour of upraised children's voices faded down the hallway. He looked across the room and met Lucas Washburne's amused gaze.

Nicholas put the cat down and walked across to make his bow to Mrs Westin.

'Claret?' Lucas asked.

Nicholas nodded, and took a chair alongside Mrs Westin. Adelei jumped up on his lap. She turned around once, kneaded his knee briefly, and curled up, purring.

Nicholas accepted a glass of wine from Lucas. 'How are the kittens?' he asked Mrs Westin. 'Getting up to mischief?'

'Mischief? Yes.' Mrs Westin uttered a sigh. Not such an animal lover as Lady Isabella, he deduced. 'One of them made it downstairs this morning. Such a pother! The house was turned upside down, looking for it.'

Nicholas laughed. He glanced down at Adelei, contentedly asleep on his knee. Her purr rumbled faintly. 'I gather they're not the first litter your cousin has raised.'

Mrs Westin shook her head. 'Isabella is forever collecting strays,' she said. Then, to Nicholas's surprise, her thin cheeks flushed and she broke eye contact.

A sudden, awkward silence fell. Nicholas sipped his claret and wondered what in their conversation had embarrassed Mrs Westin. He gave a mental shrug and changed subjects. 'Tell me, Mrs Westin, what is your opinion of Kemble?'

From actors, they moved to playwrights. Mrs Westin had much to say about Shakespeare. She preferred the Bard's tragedies; his comedies, she said with censure in her mild voice, were too vulgar and immoral for today's modern audiences. 'Fornication and deception! Women dressed as men!'

Nicholas, who numbered *Twelfth Night* among his favourites, diplomatically did not disagree with her.

'And as for *A Midsummer Night's Dream*!' Outrage gave Mrs Westin animation, bringing colour to her cheeks. 'Have you read it, Major?'

Nicholas nodded, bemused.

'Such a shocking play! That wicked elixir!' She shuddered. 'Liaisons with beasts! And—' as if this were more dreadful than anything else '—a daughter's disobedience to her father is rewarded!'

Nicholas bit the inside of his lip.

Mrs Westin folded her hands in her lap. 'It is a woman's duty to obey her parents in all matters. Especially marriage!'

Abruptly he remembered Harriet. The urge to laugh deserted him. He glanced down at Adelei, curled up asleep on his knee, and managed—barely—not to frown.

It was with relief that he heard Gussie and Lady Isabella enter the saloon. Dinner couldn't be far away.

When it came time to move into the dining room, Nicholas found himself with Lady Isabella on his arm. He cast Gussie a suspicious, narrow-eyed glance. Was she trying to matchmake?

Gussie met his eyes blandly.

Dinner was an agreeably relaxed and informal affair. With only six at the table they talked freely around it. When the ladies had risen, Nicholas leaned back in his chair and yawned.

'Brandy?' asked Lucas. 'Or port?'

'Brandy,' Nicholas said. He looked across the table at Charlie, also leaning back in his chair now that the ladies were gone. 'What are you doing here, young whelp? I thought you were in Mayhew's pocket.'

'Lieutenant Mayhew has an engagement tonight,' Charlie said, his dignity somewhat stiff.

And Gussie needed another man to even the numbers.

He glanced at Lucas, pouring from a decanter, and debated asking him whether his wife was indeed matchmaking. He decided against it. However hard Gussie tried, she could not succeed. He had settled upon Miss Whedon as his bride, and Lady Isabella was determined in her spinsterhood.

Nicholas accepted the glass Lucas held out to him. He frowned. Spinster. Such an ugly little word, so wrong for her. It conjured up an image of a dried-up stick figure of a woman, withered and shrunken, the exact opposite of Lady Isabella, who was so lush, so—

'Not to your taste?' Lucas asked.

Nicholas looked up. 'Wool-gathering!' he said and swallowed a hurried mouthful of brandy.

'Sir,' Charlie said, leaning forwards, 'I must ask you about Badajoz! Is it true that—?'

'Since when have you been interested in the military?' Nicholas asked, amused.

Charlie flushed slightly. 'Mayhew's been telling me about it.'

'Tales of glory?' Nicholas raised his glass again. This time he sipped slowly, savouring the brandy, letting the heat and the smokiness linger in his mouth. 'There's more mud than glory, you know. And fleas—'

'And blisters and boils and lice. Yes, sir, I know! Mayhew told me all about it.'

Nicholas raised his eyebrows. 'Did he?'

'Yes, sir.' Charlie pushed his brandy glass aside and leaned forwards again. 'But what I particularly wanted to ask you about was Badajoz.'

'Badajoz?' Nicholas repeated, regarding his nephew with something close to surprise. He'd never seen Charlie so animated. His eyes were alight with enthusiasm. 'What about it?'

'All of it, sir!'

Nicholas stroked his cheek thoughtfully, his fingertips sliding over the ridges of the scar. He'd promised his brother to say nothing to encourage Charlie to join the army. Was this breaking his word?

He tapped his cheek, remembering. The battle to take Badajoz had been bloody, the loss of life appalling, and the aftermath, the sacking of the town, the raping and the murder—

No, Badajoz would scarcely encourage Charlie to enlist.

Nicholas lowered his hand. 'Very well,' he said. 'Badajoz.'

* * *

Isabella sipped her tea. 'Have you finished that book I lent you, Gussie?'

'*Pride and Prejudice*? Yes. Very droll! Would you like it back?'

'Please. I have a…a friend who would like to read it. I'm hoping it will raise her spirits.' The tomes Harriet read to Mrs Westin were morally uplifting, but they were scarcely of the sort to cheer up the girl.

She glanced across the drawing room. Major Reynolds stood, leaning against the mantelpiece and talking to Lucas Washburne. About horses, judging from the words she caught.

A good-looking man, taller than Lucas Washburne, broader in the shoulder, leaner. And Harriet thought him ugly? *Foolish girl, to be blinded by a scar.*

'Shoo!'

Isabella's attention was abruptly jerked away from the men. Adelei was on the tea table, sniffing the cream jug.

Mrs Westin clapped her hands. 'Shoo!' she said again. 'Away with you!'

The cat jumped down. She sat for a moment on the carpet, her tail twitching in affront, then stalked across the drawing room, sat down in front of the fireplace, and proceeded to wash herself.

'Wretched creature!' Gussie said, with a laugh. She stood. 'It's in the library. Is there anything you'd like to borrow?'

Isabella rose to her feet, following Gussie from the drawing room. 'What did you think of Mr Collins?'

'Mr Collins? A beautiful combination of pomposity and stupidity!'

'I have to confess, he was my favourite character,' Isabella said as Gussie opened the door to the library.

The library had dark panelling and heavy armchairs upholstered in brown leather. *A man's room*, Isabella thought as they entered. And yet it was Gussie who used it most.

'Here are the first two volumes.' Gussie walked over to one of the tables. 'Now where did I put the third one? Oh, hello, Nicholas. Would you like to borrow a book?'

Isabella turned her head. Major Reynolds stood in the doorway. 'Perhaps,' he said, stepping into the room.

'I can recommend this!' Gussie said, holding out a slim calf-bound volume. 'But it's Isabella's and she's lending it to someone else.'

Major Reynolds took the proffered volume. 'It's good?'

'Extremely!'

He opened the book, turned to the first chapter, and read the first line silently. His eyebrows lifted fractionally. He glanced up at Isabella. She saw in his eyes that he had recognised the passage.

Isabella bit her lip.

Major Reynolds looked down at the page again. '"It is a truth universally acknowledged, that a single man in possession of a good fortune, must be in want of a wife",' he read aloud.

Memory of last night was suddenly vivid in her mind: the terrace and the darkness, their conversation. *And after that you let him kiss you.*

The Major lifted his gaze to meet hers again.

Isabella felt herself blush. She looked down at the carpet, a particularly fine Axminster in red and brown.

'Where did I put the third volume?' Gussie muttered. 'Oh, it's upstairs. Excuse me, I won't be a moment!' Her footsteps hurried out of the room.

Major Reynolds closed the book. 'Good,' he said. 'I had hoped to be able to speak to you alone.'

Isabella looked up from her perusal of the carpet. 'You had?'

'Yes.' Major Reynolds placed the book on the table. 'What I said this afternoon about kissing. I'm afraid you misunderstood me.' His gaze was as direct as his voice.

'I did?'

'What I meant was that, without the punch, it would still have been good. Just not that good.'

Isabella crossed her arms over her chest. 'It would have been like it was with Roland.'

'No,' Major Reynolds said. 'It would have been better than that.'

Isabella shook her head. 'Perhaps kissing is different for men than it is for women. Men enjoy it, and women don't.'

An expression crossed the Major's face. She recognised it belatedly as frustration. 'No,' he said. 'Lady Isabella—' He took a step towards her, and halted abruptly.

It was one step only, but with it everything changed: from awkwardness and embarrassment to a *frisson* of awareness at his proximity crawling over her skin, making her heart beat faster. It was suddenly difficult to breathe.

Major Reynolds felt it too. She saw it in the widening of his eyes, in his stillness.

For long seconds neither of them moved or spoke. Then the Major cleared his throat. 'It should be enjoyable,' he said quietly. 'For both participants. There should be delight and pleasure.'

Delight and pleasure. *Like last night.*

The Major continued, his eyes holding hers, his voice low, the words soft and enticing. 'A kiss should bring heat to one's mind. A kiss should make you want *more*.'

More. It was what she had wanted ever since those moments in the gazebo. She wanted it now. The heat that had spiralled in her belly was there again, the tension and the craving that had made it impossible to sleep.

Isabella dug her fingers more deeply into her arms. *I am not kissing him again.* She was not that weak, that foolish.

But without the punch it would be like it had been with Roland. Not repugnant, but not pleasant either. Something she could live without.

Then prove to yourself that you don't need it. Let him kiss you again.

Isabella moistened her lips. She could hear the sound of her heartbeat in her ears. 'Major—'

'Let me—'

They spoke at the same time.

Major Reynolds opened his hand. 'You first, madam.'

They had been about to ask the same question. She knew it; Major Reynolds knew it too. She saw the knowledge in his eyes, clear green, and yet somehow dark and hot too, saw it in his mouth, in the curve of a smile hovering on his lips.

Her throat was suddenly too dry to speak. Her heart began to beat even faster.

Major Reynolds waited a few, polite seconds, and then spoke. 'Let us try again. Let me *prove* to you...'

No, let me prove to you.

Isabella swallowed. 'Very well.' She uncrossed her arms. 'But only once.'

'Only once,' the Major agreed.

He stepped close and stood for a moment, looking at her, his eyes so dark that they seemed almost black. 'As before,' he said, his voice little more than a whisper, 'tell me if you wish me to stop.'

Isabella nodded, her eyes fixed on his.

Major Reynolds inhaled a deep, slow breath. His hands reached to cup her face. Her skin tingled beneath that light touch. *Such strong hands, so warm.*

Her heart kicked in her chest as the Major bent his head. She closed her eyes.

His lips touched hers, his mouth exquisitely gentle. There was nothing repugnant about it, but nor was there the madness of last night, the pleasure sweeping through her, the sense that she was losing control of herself.

Isabella began to relax. *I was right and he was wrong.*

Major Reynolds licked her lower lip. She shivered, aware

of a prickle of alarm, a prickle of treacherous pleasure. He licked her lips again and murmured something against her mouth. Her ears couldn't make out the words, but she parted her lips instinctively, wanting more, wanting—

No, this is wrong. I don't want—

But he was inside her mouth and she couldn't pull away, she could only kiss him back, leaning into his body, hungry for his mouth. Heat was rising in her, pleasure spiralling, and she'd never felt so *alive*, so filled with urgency, wanting more, *more*.

Chapter Fourteen

There was no punch, no faerie music swirling around them, and yet the intoxication of last night, the arousal clouding Nicholas's mind, were the same. He stifled a groan in his throat and drew Lady Isabella closer, sinking into pleasure, into desire, into bliss. The softness of her skin beneath his hands, the sweetness of her lips, the taste of her mouth—

Her mouth, dear God, her mouth—

Nicholas lifted his head and stepped back, releasing her, dragging air into his lungs, striving for a semblance of control, of sanity.

They stared at each other. Lady Isabella's cheeks were flushed, her eyes dark, her lips rosy. The sight of her mouth arrested his attention. He almost stepped forward again, almost took her mouth again.

'We should stop,' he said. His voice was unaccountably hoarse. 'Gussie will be back any moment.' The words were more for himself than for her. *Stop. Stop now. While I can.*

Lady Isabella didn't answer for a moment. He thought she was trying to catch her breath. Her expression was aghast. 'You said last night was an aberration! You said it wouldn't be like that again!'

He shook his head, trying to deny what had just happened.

But there was no denying it. *And without the punch this time*, a worried voice in his mind pointed out. *Without the music.* 'It shouldn't.'

'Then why—?'

He shook his head again, still staring at her, at the temptation of her mouth. What had just happened? And why her? Why now? 'I don't know.'

Footsteps sounded in the hallway. 'I found it!'

Nicholas turned hastily away from Lady Isabella. He reached for the first volume of *Pride and Prejudice* and fumbled it open. His heart was beating loudly in his ears. He heard Gussie speak again, heard Lady Isabella reply.

He swallowed and tried to slow his breathing, his heartbeat, and to concentrate on the page he was looking at. It was upside down. Hastily he turned the book the right way up.

Gussie plucked the book from his hand and ruthlessly closed it. 'You may read it later!' she said.

Nicholas groped for a suitable retort and failed to find one. His mind was fogged with passion, and not a little panic. What had just happened between himself and Lady Isabella?

Mutely he followed the ladies from the library. An aberration. That's what it was: an aberration. But not caused by the punch. *We are the aberration, the two of us.*

It wasn't love; it was a mindless, physical desire. *Her mouth and mine fit together.* Would their bodies fit together too?

He hastily shoved the thought aside.

An aberration. An anomaly. Something between just the two of them.

Something not to be repeated, he told himself firmly.

Back in the drawing room, Lucas Washburne proposed riding out to Richmond on the morrow.

'A picnic!' Gussie said, clapping her hands together delightedly. She turned to Lady Isabella. 'Do say you'll come!'

Lady Isabella acquiesced. To his ears she still sounded

shaken. Her face, flushed in the library from his kiss, was now pale. She avoided meeting his eyes.

Mrs Westin demurred. So too did Charlie. 'I'm engaged with Lieutenant Mayhew,' he said.

Lucas turned to him. 'Nicholas? Will you join us?'

'Perhaps,' he said, with a glance at Lady Isabella's averted profile. Her hands were clasped tightly in her lap. *Or perhaps not.*

Mrs Westin rose to leave not long after that. He wondered if she'd sensed her cousin's agitation.

Nicholas bowed and bade them a polite goodnight. Lady Isabella murmured something unintelligible in return.

Nicholas resumed his seat. He frowned at the polished toe of his boot.

Gussie came to sit beside him. 'Do say you'll come tomorrow,' she said coaxingly.

Nicholas looked past her to the empty doorway. *I owe Lady Isabella an apology.* He made an abrupt decision. 'Yes,' he said. 'I will.'

The room inside her head, where the parts of herself had been neatly organised, was in chaos. The shelves slanted crookedly. Everything lay on the floor. Some things were broken beyond repair.

Who am I?

On the outside she knew she looked the same—in her slate-blue riding habit with the row of buttons marching militarily down the front and the high-crowned hat with its curling feather—but on the inside everything had changed. She no longer recognised herself.

'Nicholas is joining us too,' Gussie said cheerfully as Isabella placed her foot in the groom's cupped hands and swung up into the saddle.

'I beg your pardon?' The worry that had blanketed everything like a fog evaporated abruptly.

'Nicholas,' Gussie said, as another horse and rider turned into Clarges Street. 'Here he is.'

Clarity returned as she watched the Major approach. He sat on his horse like a soldier, straight-backed and utterly in control. It took no effort of imagination to imagine him commanding in battle.

Isabella let her gaze drop to the horse; it was easier to look at the beast—huge and glossily grey, with strong haunches and a proud neck—than its rider.

'Good morning!' Gussie said cheerfully as horse and rider halted alongside them.

'Gussie,' the Major replied. 'Lucas.' A brief pause, and then, 'Lady Isabella.'

She looked up to acknowledge his greeting. 'Good morning, Major Reynolds.'

The Major's eyes met hers. He gave a nod of acknowledgement, but didn't smile.

No, I don't feel like smiling either. She looked down at her hands, clad in pale Limerick gloves, holding the reins.

'Let's be off!' Gussie said. 'What a beautiful day for a picnic!'

Isabella glanced up at the sky. Blue. She hadn't noticed.

She was heavy with exhaustion, tense with worry, but the fresh air and the exercise seemed to clear her mind. By the time the brick walls surrounding Richmond Park were in sight Isabella had achieved something approaching calmness. She was able to enjoy the opening vista of slopes and woods, avenues and paths.

She glanced at Major Reynolds. He sat easily in the saddle, his posture relaxed. Sunlight fell on his scarred cheek. She saw how smooth the skin was, how distorted, ridges and plains of melted flesh shining in the sunshine.

Something tightened in her chest. She looked away.

Parkland lay before them, scattered with copses of trees. A herd of deer grazed in the distance.

'I have to gallop!' Gussie declared.

'A race?' her husband suggested, a glint in his eyes.

Gussie accepted the challenge.

Isabella declined, shaking her head. Her mood was not light enough for racing. Neither, it appeared, was the Major's. He did, however, play marshal, holding up the white square of his handkerchief. 'Ready?'

The handkerchief descended and the horses leapt forwards.

When the thunder of hooves had died, Major Reynolds turned to the groom, riding a horse burdened with picnic hampers.

'Do you know King Henry's mound?'

The groom nodded. 'Yes, sir.'

'Meet us there.'

The man nodded again, touched his heels to the horse's flanks, and trotted away.

Silence fell. The sound of the leaves rustling in the breeze, the lilt of birdsong, the humming of bees was suddenly loud. Somewhere a squirrel chattered and a woodpecker hammered its beak against a tree trunk, *tat-tat-tat-tat*.

The Major cleared his throat. 'About last night.'

Isabella transferred her gaze from Gussie and Lucas's diminishing forms to his face. His expression was sober, stern even.

The only thing she could think of saying—*You promised me it was the punch!*—was too much like an accusation, so she kept silent.

'I must apologise,' Major Reynolds said, his eyebrows drawing down in a frown as he looked at her. 'I had not quite realised how things stood between us. I thought it was the punch, when really—' the frown deepened, becoming a furrow '—the aberration is *us*.'

Isabella blinked. 'I beg your pardon?'

'It's *us*,' he said, leaning slightly forwards in the saddle, as if closing the distance between them could make her understand. 'Not the punch or the music or anything else. It's something between the two of us.'

Isabella looked at the Major doubtfully. She liked him, but she didn't think she loved him. 'Love?'

'No, no!' Major Reynolds said, lurching backwards in his saddle, his expression so horrified that she almost smiled. *He wants to marry me as little as I want to marry him.* 'Nothing like that! Just…just something purely physical.'

He means lust.

She should be appalled. Instead she was deeply relieved. 'So it will not be like…like *that* with other men.'

'No,' Major Reynolds said firmly, and then a doubtful frown creased his brow again. 'At least…I don't think so.' He met her eyes. 'I've never experienced anything like that and I've, er…' faint colour rose in his lean, unscarred cheek '…I've kissed a number of women.'

I imagine you have, to be so skilled at it. Abruptly, shamefully, Isabella wanted to kiss him again. She wrenched her thoughts in another direction. 'So, if I were to kiss another man…' She searched her mind for one. 'Lieutenant Mayhew, for example. It wouldn't be like that?'

'Mayhew has had a lot of practice,' the Major said, his voice dry. 'I'm sure he'd be good at it.'

'But it wouldn't be as good as—' *kissing you* '—last night.'

'No, I don't believe so.'

Perhaps I should kiss Lieutenant Mayhew, just to see.

Major Reynolds appeared to have the same thought. His eyes narrowed slightly and he opened his mouth to say something, and then closed it, as if he'd thought better of it.

But she didn't want to kiss Lieutenant Mayhew, however blond and laughing he was.

She looked at Major Reynolds, a frank scrutiny: tanned skin and startlingly green eyes, the strong bones of his brow and jaw, cheekbone and nose, the scar.

It was strange, how one's perception of a person could alter so drastically within such a short period of time. Last week she'd seen the Major as hard-faced; now she struggled to remember why she'd ever thought that. Stern, yes, until his face relaxed into a smile, but not hard-faced. His mouth was resolute, his eyes disconcertingly clear, piercing almost, but his face was marked by laughter. The creases at his eyes, his mouth, told of laughter, not anger.

No, that was incorrect. *Half* his face was marked by laughter. The other half was marked by pain. No smile lines radiated from his left eye or bracketed the left side of his mouth. The skin there was smooth, pink, burned.

Maybe that was why she'd thought him hard-faced? When she saw his face, his whole face, with the scar so prominent, all she saw was pain. It gave a false impression of who he was—pain, hardness—instead of a man ready to laugh.

Except that she hardly ever noticed the scar now.

I should learn to see it as he does. Major Reynolds didn't see pain when he looked in the mirror; he saw how lucky he was.

An aberration, he said. Between the two of them.

Memory of his mouth, of his hands on her skin, brought a flush of heat to Isabella's body. *I want to kiss him again.*

She had a label for that sensation now: lust.

The relief she felt was almost exhilaration. The room in her head was no longer in chaos. Almost everything was back on the shelves again. Some things lay broken on the floor, beyond repair. Her ignorance, her innocence—call it what she will—was one of them. *I am still a virgin, but my body knows how to crave physical pleasure.*

She was herself again, only slightly altered. The sun was shining and the birds were singing and everything was in its place again in the world, in *her* world.

Elation bubbled up inside her. 'Shall we race?' She narrowed her eyes against the sun, searching for Gussie and Lucas. They were tiny figures on the hillside.

The Major's eyebrows rose. 'By all means.'

He brought his horse alongside her and flashed a grin. Had he caught her mood, her exhilaration and relief? *Only lust. Nothing as terrible as love. Nothing I can't cope with.*

Isabella grinned back at him.

They were both flushed and laughing, panting, by the time they pulled up. Lady Isabella's mount, a lively blood-bay named Firefly, had proved almost as swift as Douro.

'Congratulations, Major,' she said, laughing, catching her breath. 'You won!'

'Not by much.'

Gussie and Lucas were no longer beneath the clump of trees. Nicholas glanced around, searching for them. They were further down the avenue, their horses ambling side by side.

Nicholas nudged Douro with his knee, bringing himself and the horse around to face Lady Isabella.

'I wish I could have brought Rufus,' she said. 'He would love this.'

'Then let us bring him,' Nicholas said. They were so close that their legs almost brushed. 'And Tam too. And Thomas and Grace. A barouche filled with dogs and children.'

'A splendid idea, Major!'

'But no kittens,' he added firmly.

'No kittens?' Her mouth made a moue of disappointment. 'Don't you think that kittens would add a charming element of chaos to the expedition?'

Her eyes laughed at him and the temptation was suddenly and quite simply too great. Nicholas bent and kissed that laughing mouth.

Her hesitation lasted a mere fraction of a second, and then Lady Isabella kissed him back.

Nicholas reached for her. Her skin was warm beneath his hands, smooth, familiar. He closed his eyes, deepening the kiss, savouring the exquisite pleasure, the softness of her lips, the exciting heat of her mouth. Arousal flared in his belly. He could lose himself in this, in the heat, in the pleasure, in the—

We're in Richmond Park.

With a muttered oath he tore his mouth from hers. At the jerk of his hand, Douro stepped back a pace.

He stared at her, steadying his breathing. She looked as she had last night—dark eyes, flushed cheeks, well-kissed mouth—but not aghast, not dismayed.

'Lady Isabella—'

'Isabella.' Her mouth quirked up at one corner in a wry smile. 'If we are to do *that*, then I think we shouldn't be so formal with each other.'

Her words made hope rise swiftly in his chest. *We'll do it again*, she seemed to be saying.

But not here. Not where we can be seen.

Nicholas cleared his throat. 'Very well, Isabella...I think we had best find Gussie and Lucas.'

'Yes.' The wry smile vanished. 'We had better.' She gathered her reins.

Part of him was disappointed. Had he wanted her to protest? To kiss him again?

Yes. But Lady Isabella—Isabella—knew as well as he did what would happen if they were seen kissing in public. *We would have to marry.* And as much as he enjoyed her company—and her kisses—she was not the bride he wanted.

His thoughts swerved to Clarissa Whedon, the bride he *did* wish for. She was no beauty, but it was her mildness, her youth, that recommended her to him. She would suit him in ways Lady Isabella never would.

And vice versa, whispered a sly voice in his mind.

Nicholas shook his head, banishing the voice. He pressed

his knees against Douro's warm flanks and encouraged the horse into a trot. Clarissa Whedon, he would marry—Isabella Knox, he would kiss.

Douro, at the pressure of his knees, lengthened his stride into a canter. Isabella kept pace beside them.

Nicholas glanced at her. *But I can't kiss Isabella if I'm engaged to another woman.*

He could put off his proposal to Miss Whedon for another week. Or two.

They ate their picnic on King Henry's mound, looking across London to the dome of St Paul's. No opportunity arose to kiss Isabella again. 'Almack's tonight?' Nicholas asked her as they left the green expanse of Richmond, enclosed in its brick wall, behind them.

She shook her head. 'The Peverills' musicale. My cousin particularly desires to attend.'

A musicale. Nicholas managed—barely—not to grimace. Almack's, with its débutantes and its dowagers, its dry cake and tepid lemonade, was almost more appealing. Almost. 'Would you and your cousin like an escort?' he asked.

Isabella glanced at him from beneath her lashes. He thought she suppressed a grin. 'We would be delighted,' she said demurely.

Several hours later, lounging in a very fine Chippendale chair with Chinese-style lattice work, Nicholas found himself regretting his offer. The musicians were superb, the supper superior to anything Almack's could offer, but neither the performance nor the intervals had offered the opportunity for a private word—much less anything else—with Isabella.

He cast a glance around the ballroom. The guests were predominantly female, and predominantly grey-haired. With a sigh he focused his attention on the musicians again: two violinists and a pianist. The pianist was extraordinarily animated. He played with his entire body. His face changed with the mood of the music: dreamy, his eyes half-lidded; exultant, his eyes wide and his mouth open; fierce, a frown furrowing his brow and his lips drawn back from his teeth; melancholy, his mouth pulled down at the corners and his shoulders sagging.

A final trembling chord filled the ballroom. The violinists laid down their bows. The pianist bowed his head.

There was a moment of silence, as if the audience held its collective breath, and then the sound of clapping swelled into the silence. The applause grew until the ceiling seemed to resonate with it. 'Excellent,' said Mrs Westin, seated between him and Isabella, as the musicians stood and bowed. 'Simply excellent!'

They rose, in the clamour of conversation around them.

'Magnificent—'

'—the fingerwork—'

'—such expression!'

They lingered after the crush of guests had thinned, being invited, on the strength of Mrs Westin's friendship with Mrs Peverill, to partake of further refreshments in one of the smaller saloons.

Mrs Westin, almost as animated as the pianist had been, discussed the performance with their hostess. The pianist, when he and his fellow musicians joined the party, was listless and somewhat morose. Or perhaps he was merely exhausted.

From music, Mrs Peverill and Mrs Westin moved on to a discussion of Dresden china figurines. Nicholas stifled a yawn.

'I have just purchased two more pieces,' Mrs Peverill said. 'Would you like to see them?'

Mrs Westin expressed great interest. Nicholas stifled another yawn. He swallowed the last of his wine.

'Isabella, will you join us?'

Nicholas snapped alert as Isabella assented. He placed his wine glass on a convenient table and drifted after the ladies, out of the door, along the hallway. Behind him, from the ballroom, came the scrape of wood on wood as the servants cleared the room of a hundred chairs.

The ladies turned into another saloon. Nicholas strolled slowly after them. 'Exquisite!' he heard Mrs Westin say as he paused in the doorway.

The room was undeniably a lady's parlour, decorated in pink and white. Every surface was covered with figurines. He saw milkmaids and frolicking lambs and goatherds, minstrels and huntresses and harlequins, bright-eyed squirrels and coquettish ponies.

Nicholas blenched slightly.

Mrs Peverill caught sight of him. 'Major! Are you interested in china figurines?'

Lady Isabella glanced up swiftly.

'Er…' He stepped into the parlour. 'In a small way.'

Isabella bit her lip. She picked up a figurine and began to study it.

'The larger pieces are through here.' Mrs Peverill walked across to another door. She opened it. Nicholas caught a glimpse of more pink-tinted walls.

Mrs Westin followed her hostess. Lady Isabella didn't. She was frowning down at the figurine in her hand.

Nicholas stepped closer to her.

'A small interest in china figurines, Major?' Isabella said, still studying the figurine she held. It was a milkmaid with golden curls. 'I would never have guessed.'

'Very small,' he said, glancing at the door through which the older ladies had vanished. 'Minuscule.'

Lady Isabella returned the milkmaid to its place on the giltwood table. 'Minuscule?' she said, turning towards him, a smile on her lips, in her eyes.

'Smaller than minuscule.' He closed the distance between

them and reached for her, capturing her face between his hands, bending his head.

Isabella didn't protest. She leaned towards him. 'Be careful,' she whispered.

The kiss was brief and hurried, scorching. They broke apart at the sound of voices from the adjoining room.

Nicholas turned hastily away from Isabella and picked up a figurine. From the corner of his eye he saw the ladies emerge into the parlour. 'Oh, do you like that piece, Major?' Mrs Peverill asked. 'It's one of my favourites.'

He looked down at the figurine. It was a young man in a puce jacket leaning against a tree, a violin held negligently in his hand. 'Er…' His mind was still caught in the heat of Isabella's mouth.

He glanced at Isabella. Her face was slightly averted; he saw only her profile, the curve of her cheek, faintly flushed, the soft fullness of her lips. Desire clenched in his belly. He wanted to reach for her, to kiss her again, to not stop.

Nicholas cleared his throat. 'Very nice,' he said lamely, and put the figurine down before he could drop it.

Chapter Fifteen

On Thursday morning, the housemaid Becky Brown returned from visiting her mother. She asked to speak to Isabella.

Isabella saw her in the book room. Becky entered with Mrs Early, the housekeeper. They sat at her gesture, Mrs Early solidly, the girl perching nervously on the edge of her seat. One look at Becky's face told Isabella that the news was bad. 'How is your mother?'

Becky shook her head, her hands fisted in her apron. 'Not good, ma'am. She…she can't even get out of bed any more.' The girl swallowed convulsively.

'Has she seen a doctor?' Isabella asked.

The girl nodded.

Had Becky's hard-earned money paid for that bill? 'What did he say?'

'He said…he said that there was something growing inside her. That she wouldn't get better.'

Isabella was silent for a moment, remembering her mother's own illness, remembering the day when she had finally acknowledged that the Dowager Duchess would not recover. 'Would you like to be released from my service?' she asked gently.

Becky nodded. 'Yes, ma'am. Someone needs to look after her and the little ones. My father has to work, you see, and he can't…' She twisted the apron between her hands.

Isabella nodded. She did see. She glanced at Mrs Early. 'You may leave today, if you wish.'

Mrs Early nodded.

Relief flushed the girl's cheeks, but she shook her head. 'Oh, no, ma'am. I thought…a week, if…if it suits you.'

'Are you certain you don't wish to leave today?'

Becky shook her head again. 'One of the neighbours, she said she could stay for a week.' She smiled shyly at Isabella. 'I thought…a week would give you time to hire someone else.'

'Thank you, Becky. That is very thoughtful.'

The girl's flush deepened. 'You've been good to me, ma'am. I didn't want to…to leave sudden like.'

'Thank you, Becky.'

When the girl had curtsied and withdrawn, Isabella turned to Mrs Early. 'Will you please go to the registry office again?'

The housekeeper nodded. 'Yes, ma'am.'

Isabella sighed. 'We seem to be going through house-maids rather fast.' She stared at the square of sunlight that caught the corner of her desk, turning the pale wood golden. 'We will pay her for this month and the next,' she said, looking up. 'And give her references.'

Mrs Early nodded.

'And…please ask Cook to make up a hamper of food for Becky when she leaves. Food for her family. Meat pies, fruit, bread…' She frowned. What else? 'Oh, and some of those plum cakes.' A treat for the children, in the middle of what must be a dark, frightening time for them.

'Yes, ma'am.'

Isabella nodded her dismissal, but halted the housekeeper at the door. 'Mrs Early, are the wax candles still being taken?'

Mrs Early turned to face her. 'Yes, ma'am.'

After the housekeeper had gone, Isabella pulled out her ledgers. She looked back through several months of neat columns, noting how many wax candles had been bought and when. Yes, three months ago. She tapped the page with a fingertip, frowning. A slight increase at first. The following month there was a noticeable jump, as if the thief had gained confidence. And this month—

Her lips pursed. *I should have noticed this.*

When had she added these figures to the ledger? Last week, when her mind had been occupied by Harriet and by Major Reynolds.

Isabella shook her head, unimpressed with herself.

It was fairly easy to determine how many candles had been stolen, using last year's figures as a comparison. She added the numbers on a sheet of parchment. The sum made her eyebrows rise. Wax candles were an expensive luxury. If the thief had sold them for only half their true price he or she had made a tidy little profit.

Isabella laid down her quill. *I don't like this.* It was unsettling to think that there was a thief under her roof. No, it was more than unsettling; it was disturbing.

Major Reynolds kissed her that night at the Tomkin-Smythes' ball, after supper, when the quadrille was announced and the chamber they were in momentarily emptied of dancers. The kiss was as intoxicating as wine, and far too brief.

On Friday he kissed her at Vauxhall, where they managed to part company from Gussie and Lucas as they wandered through the dimly lit gardens. Major Reynolds held her pressed to him. His hands burned on skin, his mouth burned against hers, hungry. She had the sensation she was drowning in heat. When at last he raised his head she clung to him, dazed. Her pulse beat loudly in her ears. *More*, it said. *More, more.*

They stood in silence for a long moment, except for the ragged sound of their breathing. She felt the warmth of Major Reynolds's body pressed against hers, the strength, the solidity. One of his hands stroked lightly down her back.

Isabella trembled with the pleasure of it. She clutched his lapel and closed her eyes. *Is this truly me? Have I gone mad?*

'I like to kiss you,' Major Reynolds whispered against her cheek.

'I like to kiss you too.' And she turned her head, her mouth seeking his, kissing him. *Yes, I have gone mad.*

On Saturday she looked at herself in the mirror and scarcely recognised herself. Had her eyes always been this bright, her cheeks this rosy? *This is what lust looks like.*

Isabella accompanied her cousin and the Peverills to the opera that evening. She searched the boxes with her eyes. Mrs Westin's voice, the voices of Mr and Mrs Peverill, were a meaningless blur of sound. Major Reynolds had said that he might—

There he was, on the other side of the chamber, scanning the boxes, swiftly examining each set of occupants before dismissing them.

Isabella's heart suddenly began to beat faster. She held her breath as their eyes caught across the auditorium. For long seconds they looked at each other, and then the Major smiled at her, a smile that made her blush with her whole body. A smile that *promised*.

Isabella tore her gaze away from him. She looked down at her hands, clasped in her lap. Anticipation hummed in her veins. She barely heard a word her companions said. The music, when it started, was a vague noise.

During the first interval their box filled with friends and acquaintances paying their respects. Major Reynolds didn't visit. She glanced once across at him—leaning back in his chair, watching her, an ironic twist to his mouth—before firmly turning her attention away.

When the curtain lowered for the second interval, her cousin and the Peverills expressed the intention to visit the Seftons, in a box opposite. 'I shall stay here,' Isabella said, as the others rose.

'Are you feeling unwell?' Mrs Westin asked, her brow creasing with concern.

'No, no,' Isabella said. 'I just want to sit here and be quiet.'

'Shall I stay with you?' her cousin asked, half-lowering into her seat.

'Oh, no! I shall just sit and watch people.'

Mrs Westin looked dubious, but allowed herself to be persuaded. She followed the Peverills, glancing back once from the doorway.

Isabella looked across at Major Reynolds's box. It was empty.

She looked down at her hands. *I was untruthful.* How had this happened? How had she become someone who told lies, who stole secret kisses from a man she had no intention of marrying?

I should stop this. Before I can no longer stand myself.

'Isabella.'

The sound of her name, quietly spoken, made her heart lurch in her chest. She turned her head swiftly.

Major Reynolds stood in the shadows at the back of the box.

'Nicholas!' She rose.

The clandestine kisses were wrong. Why then did it feel so *right* when the Major took hold of her hands and drew her back into the shadows? When he smiled at her, his eyes dark? When he bent his head and kissed her?

His hands were at her waist, strong, holding her closely against him. Their lips clung together. There was heat and dizzying delight, and then Major Reynolds bowed and was gone.

Isabella stood alone in the back of the box. She touched a trembling finger to her lips. *I have gone mad.*

* * *

On Sunday Isabella accompanied her cousin to the Chapel Royal, as was her habit when in London. The day stretched ahead unbearably—no ride in Hyde Park with the Major, no dancing tonight. *No kiss.*

Isabella looked down at her hymn book. It wasn't just Major Reynolds's kisses she would miss today, it was his company, his conversation.

When had the Major come to be such an important part of her life?

Isabella opened the hymn book and stared blindly at the text. *And when did I become so infatuated with his kisses that I became blind to the risks?* Last night had been the height of foolishness. To steal a kiss in so public a place!

And yet she had kissed him quite willingly; had, in fact, *lied* to facilitate it.

Isabella frowned down at the hymn book. The lines of text were like centipede tracks across the pages, unreadable. The Rector's voice droned unheard in her ears.

What she was doing was profoundly wrong. *I should stop it, all of it: meeting him, kissing him.*

And yet the thought of no longer seeing Major Reynolds brought something like panic to her chest.

When had she come to like him so much?

At the Worthingtons' masquerade. When he had made everyone laugh *with* him instead of *at* him. When he had kissed her for the first time.

The Rector's voice was rising, the sermon coming to its climax. Isabella heard none of the words; they were noise in her ears. *How much do I like him?*

The answer was terrifying. She looked up blankly and stared at the pulpit, at the Rector, without seeing them.

There was a rustle of sound and movement as the congregation stood. Isabella scrambled to her feet belatedly. She had no idea what hymn was to be sung.

The organ music, when it started, made no sense. The words were unfamiliar. Isabella gripped the hymn book tightly, her fingers crumpling the pages. Was it more than lust? *Am I in love with him?*

How could she be in love with a man she'd known such a short time? And, equally as important—or perhaps even more important—how could she love a man who had admitted that he wanted to mould his wife to suit him?

The organ music stopped. Pages turned with a rustle of paper. Isabella thumbed through the hymn book at random, opening it to a new page. She stared down at it blindly. What did she know about Major Reynolds?

He'd been a good soldier, a good leader of men. *The best*, Lieutenant Mayhew had said.

He had a sense of humour.

When he looked at himself in the mirror, at the scar, he saw how lucky he was.

He was proud. He was intelligent. He was courageous.

Was that enough? *Do I want to marry him?*

By his own admission Major Reynolds was an autocrat— although surely he'd been joking? But still, joking or not, he was a man used to command, to giving orders and having them obeyed.

What would it be like to be such a man's wife?

The singing stopped. The congregation sat. Isabella followed, half a second later. She tried to recall her first impression of Major Reynolds: a dangerous man. It was difficult to think of him like that now. When she thought of him, she thought of laughter, of kisses.

Don't let the kisses fool you; he is still a dangerous man. How many men had he killed in his twelve years as a soldier?

Isabella shivered. She stared down at the hymn book, gripped tightly in her hands. The Rector was talking again. The words blurred together in her ears. *What do I want?*

'Isabella?'

Isabella looked up blankly. Everyone else was standing, talking, moving. The service was over.

'Isabella?' Mrs Westin said again. 'Are you all right?'

'Yes,' she said hurriedly, rising. 'I was just, er…thinking.' *What do I want?*

She tried to focus on her cousin, on the conversations around her, on anything but the answer. But the answer refused to go away as she gathered her hymn book and bible, as she donned her wrap, as she stepped out into the sunlight.

If Major Reynolds is the man I think he is, then I would like to marry him.

To acknowledge the words, to say them in her head—if not aloud—was shocking. For a moment she stood frozen. People brushed past her, their voices a babble of sound in her ears.

'Isabella?'

With effort she focused on her cousin's face.

'Are you certain you're all right?' Concern furrowed Mrs Westin's brow. 'You're looking…'

Lost. In the past week I have become someone I don't know. I no longer recognise myself.

'…very pale.'

Isabella attempted a smile. She swallowed and spoke. 'I'm perfectly all right, cousin.'

She might not recognise who she was, but she recognised the emotion rising in her breast. Not dismay, but hope.

I want to marry Major Reynolds.

Isabella blinked and looked around her. The world seemed somehow different, unfamiliar—a world in which she might have a husband, children, a family.

It was a dizzying thought.

Isabella walked carefully down the steps, holding on to the railing.

The route home seemed much shorter than usual. Isabella listened with half an ear as her cousin discussed the

morning's sermon. In her mind she built dreams of a husband
with a scarred face and green eyes, of children, of laughter
and love. Reality returned as she stepped into the cool foyer
of her house in Clarges Street.

Would Major Reynolds want to marry her? She bore no
resemblance to the bride he had described, youthful and
biddable. *Perhaps he thinks me too old, too odd.*

Would he want to mould her into someone else? He liked
her, that much she knew. And he wanted her. But to want
someone and to love someone—to love someone as they
were, unchanged, unmoulded—were two completely different things.

Isabella climbed the stairs beside her cousin, her brow
creased in thought. Was it merely lust that Major Reynolds
was experiencing—his hungry kisses, the way he held her
pressed so close to his body—or was it something more?

The only way to know was to ask him.

Dare I?

Rufus bounded down the second flight of stairs, his tail
wagging. Isabella bent to greet him, patting him, ruffling his
fur. She glanced up at the sound of footsteps. Harriet.

Isabella straightened slowly.

And dare I tell him the truth about Harriet?

How would Major Reynolds react?

If he was the man she thought him to be, a man of calm
good sense, then he wouldn't judge her too harshly.

If he wasn't—

Isabella shivered, suddenly cold.

On Monday Isabella paid a morning call on Gussie, ostensibly to see how Saffron was. 'I still have one kitten left
unhomed,' she said, as ginger-striped Saffron purred in her
cupped hands. They sat in Gussie's morning room, with
sunlight streaming in through the lace curtains. 'I was wondering…perhaps your cousin might take her.'

'Which cousin? Nicholas?' Gussie said, looking up from her cross-stitch. 'Why don't you ask him?'

'I thought I'd ask you first what kind of man he is,' Isabella said, avoiding Gussie's eyes.

'What kind of man?' Gussie laid down her needle. 'You ask me, after you've been in each other's pockets the past two weeks?'

Isabella felt a blush rise in her cheeks. 'I know his…his *social* face,' she said, focusing on the gilded urn clock on the mantelpiece. *And I know the lover.* 'But you know him so much better than I. I just wondered…what your opinion of him is?'

'My opinion of him?' Gussie repeated in an amused voice. 'You want to know my opinion of Nicholas before you bestow a kitten on him?'

Put like that, it did sound odd. Isabella studied the ornate metal fire guard. 'Er, yes.'

There was a moment of silence. Gussie cleared her throat. Her voice, when she spoke, was uninflected and businesslike. 'Nicholas is one of my favourite cousins. My opinion of him is very high.'

'But…but *why*?'

'Because…' Gussie's voice trailed off as she thought. 'Because I trust him. Because he makes me laugh. Because he's *nice.*'

'Nice?' Isabella repeated doubtfully. A bland word, a word that told her nothing. 'Would you say he's domineering?'

'Domineering?'

Gussie was silent a moment. Isabella risked a glance at her. Her friend's brow was creased in thought. She was chewing her lower lip.

'No,' Gussie said finally. 'I wouldn't call Nicholas domineering. He is very *decided*, and he has a great deal of determination, but he is not domineering. At least—' she qualified this '—he has never been so to me.' She put her embroidery frame aside. 'Nicholas is a very capable man. He has a reputation for getting things done.'

'He does?'

Gussie nodded. 'When I was a child we used to spend our summers together, and even then, when I was…' she shrugged '…six years old, maybe seven, I knew that if I needed something *done*, it was Nicholas I should go to, not Gerald.' Her smile was wry. 'That's why Gerald dislikes him so much. Nicholas is so much more competent than he is.'

'Oh.'

Gussie leaned forwards. She clasped her hands together on her knees. Her expression was serious. 'The Nicholas I knew was a schoolboy—kind to me and patient—but that was many years ago. The man…' She shrugged with her face, with her mouth. 'I am learning to know him again. He was gone a long time.'

'At war,' Isabella said. Twelve years of soldiering, of fighting, of leading men into battle, of killing. Twelve years of blood and death. Her gaze dropped to Saffron, sleeping peacefully, a warm bundle in her hands. 'Such an experience must change a person. Harden them.'

'Yes,' Gussie said. 'But I *think* Nicholas is still the person he was. I think he has not become…too hard. Although I have to admit that he is more restrained than he was, quieter, more controlled.'

Yes, Major Reynolds was a very self-controlled man. A disciplined man. *Except when he is kissing me.*

Isabella glanced up and met Gussie's eyes.

After a long moment of silence, while tiny motes of dust spun in the sunlight, Gussie said softly, 'I think he would make a fine husband.'

Heat scorched Isabella's face. Her gaze skittered to the silver teapot, the dainty porcelain cups, the plate of cakes. 'I wasn't—I didn't mean—I was only asking because—' She bit her tongue, stopping the babble of words. She met

Gussie's eyes and said, with what she hoped was dignity, 'I was only asking because of the kitten.'

Even to her own ears it sounded ridiculous.

Gussie raised her eyebrows. 'Oh,' she said blandly. 'I see.' Her lips pursed, as if she tried not to smile. 'More tea?'

Lady Isabella halted the phaeton. Her groom leaped down. Nicholas stepped up into the carriage, fending off Rufus's eager tongue, and greeted her. 'Good afternoon.'

'Good afternoon, Major.'

He settled back on the silk-lined seat as the horses moved into a slow trot. How many times had they done this? A dozen?

Rufus nudged his knee. Reminded, Nicholas rubbed his warm flank. The dog leaned against his booted legs and closed his eyes in pleasure.

The weather was mild, the temperature warm and the sun bright. Only the faintest breeze stirred the air. Hyde Park was busier than he'd yet seen it. Curricles and phaetons, barouches and landaulets, thronged the drive.

Isabella wore a carriage dress of Clarence blue trimmed with braided ribbon. The colour made her eyes seem bluer, her hair more golden. He glanced at her smooth cheek, her soft lips. *I must kiss her tonight.*

He looked ahead, not seeing the busy drive, absently pulling one of Rufus's ears between his fingers. Where would they be tonight? Oh, that was it: the Middletons' ball.

The phaeton stopped.

Nicholas focused his gaze. The roadway ahead was blocked. A curricle had clipped the wheels of an elegant barouche. The curricle's driver had lost his horses' reins. A red-faced young gentleman was enduring the scathing commentary of the barouche's coachman while his tiger attempted to gather the reins.

Isabella ignored the commotion. She turned to face him.

'You know why I do not wish to marry, Major,' she said, in her clear, frank way. 'May I ask, why do you *want* to marry?'

The question drew his attention most effectively from the disturbance ahead. He studied her for a moment, the direct grey-blue gaze, the hair gleaming golden beneath the jaunty hat, the serious set of her mouth.

'Why?'

She nodded. 'Yes.'

Nicholas glanced down at Rufus, leaning against his legs. He could brush off the question, give an answer that was flippant or vague, one that told her nothing…but she had answered his questions honestly on the Worthingtons' terrace; he owed her the truth.

'Soldiering is about death,' he said slowly, pulling Rufus's ear between his fingers. 'I knew that. I'd always known it. But at Waterloo…' His surroundings faded as memory flooded over him: the sound of gun and cannon fire, of horses and men screaming; the smell of gunpowder, of blood; death all around him.

Rufus nudged his hand. Nicholas realised he'd fallen silent, become motionless. He cleared his throat. 'Waterloo was a slaughter. I watched so many men fall—' Memory intruded again: a welter of blood, of torn flesh and shattered limbs, of death, death everywhere, the smell of death, the taste of it on his tongue, the sound—

He swallowed. 'It seemed that no one could survive. It seemed…impossible.' He glanced at Isabella. She was staring at him, her face pale. Was he shocking her? 'I remember a moment, when I stood on the battlefield. My horse had been shot from under me, and all around me were dead men. Dozens of them, hundreds, thousands. The French cavalry were attacking again and…and to survive seemed impossible.' He'd touched his cheek. *I am lucky*, he'd told himself, but he hadn't believed it.

Nicholas drew Rufus's ear slowly between his fingers. 'I

vowed that if I lived, if I survived that day, I would sell my commission, that I'd have nothing more to do with death.' He met her eyes, held them. 'I want *life*. I want children. I want to see them grow. I want to watch them go out into the world and have their own children. *Life*, not death.'

Isabella swallowed. He saw the muscles move in her throat. 'I had heard Waterloo was bad,' she said in a low voice. Her face was almost—but not quite—expressionless.

I did shock her. 'It was,' he said simply.

She looked away and moistened her lips. 'Thank you for telling me.'

This was too dark a conversation for Hyde Park, for the frivolity of the Grand Strut, the ladies with curling feathers in their hats and the gentlemen with absurdly high neck-cloths, the prancing horses and the silk-lined carriages, the sunshine and birdsong. 'It was a long time ago,' Nicholas said, his voice hearty and cheerful.

Isabella cast him a narrow-eyed glance. *You do not need to treat me like a child*, he read in it. 'Major, why did you decide to become a soldier?'

So she refused to be diverted, did she? Part of him respected her for it. No milk-and-water miss, Lady Isabella.

'Why?' He had to think back. It was hard to remember the young man he'd been, fresh out of Cambridge and eager to make his mark on the world. 'I had intended on a diplomatic career, but…I decided I wanted more of a challenge.'

'And was it a challenge?'

'Oh, yes.' The challenges of soldiering had been many. He'd learned how to scout terrain and assess enemy positions, how to command men, how to lead them into battle even when the odds seemed stacked against them. He'd learned how to kill, how to lose one's friends, how to survive. And then there had been the purely physical challenges: the forced marches, the filth, the bitter cold and the searing heat, the scarcity of food, the boils and the lice and the fleas, the fevers. 'It was everything I'd thought it would be, and more. It was extremely challenging. But I enjoyed it—for the most part.'

Isabella nodded. She glanced ahead. The offending curricle was gone. The barouche was almost alongside them, the coachman sitting erect on the driving block, his chest puffed out, proud victor of the moment.

With a deft flick of her whip, Isabella encouraged the horses into motion. 'Thank you for telling me,' she said again.

'You're welcome,' Nicholas said. He looked past her, towards Kensington Gardens. Trees, sunlight, water.

He experienced a moment of disorientation, as if the world tilted slightly on its axis. His fingers stilled, pulling Rufus's ear. How could this greenness, this sunshine, this safety, exist in the same world as the mud and blood and carnage of Waterloo? How could that battle, that slaughter, have been less than a year ago? How was it possible?

He blinked and shook his head slightly.

Isabella caught the movement. She glanced at him. Her eyebrows rose inquiringly. 'Major?'

Nicholas shook his head again, more firmly this time. 'Are you going to the Middletons' ball tonight?'

'Yes,' she said. 'Shall you be there?'

'Most definitely,' Nicholas said. *I have to kiss you.*

Colonel and Lady Middleton's ball was well under way when Nicholas arrived. He gave his hat and gloves to a footman and climbed the stairs to the ballroom. It reminded him of Gussie's ball, two weeks ago: the hubbub of music and laughter and conversation, the mingled scents of perfume and perspiration, the almost-suffocating warmth.

But tonight there would be no sly laughter, no sideways glances, no whispers. *I am* passé. *London has moved on.*

Nicholas accepted champagne from a servant. He sipped it as he strolled around the perimeter of the ballroom, nodding to acquaintances, pausing to talk with friends, all the while scanning the room for a glimpse of wheat-gold hair. The ballroom was colourful with the dress uniforms of various regiments: the blue, scarlet and gold of the Royal Horse Guard; the green of his own Rifle Brigade, with its black facings and silver lace; the red jacket of the Lifeguards, trimmed with rich gold lace. Lieutenant Mayhew wasn't present; Lady Isabella was. He found her going down a set with Lucas Washburne. She was tall and cool in a white satin slip under a robe of celestial blue crêpe, but her mouth was laughing and her eyes were bright. *A queen*, was his first, inadvertent thought. And then he corrected it: *a goddess*.

Nicholas watched her, his shoulders propped against the wall, sipping his champagne. When the cotillion had finished he pushed away from the wall and strolled across the dance floor. 'Lady Isabella,' he said with an inclination of his head. 'Lucas.'

He observed with satisfaction as Isabella's cheeks flushed faintly. *I am going to kiss you tonight*, he promised her silently. Anticipation twisted in his gut, a quicksilver flicker of desire.

'Would you like something to drink?' Lucas asked Isabella. 'Lemonade? Champagne?'

'Champagne, please.'

She watched Lucas stride away, glanced at him, coloured faintly again and fixed her attention on the dance floor, where a quadrille was preparing to start.

Nicholas followed her gaze. 'You know him?'

'Lord Riles? Yes.'

Something about her tone made him study her more closely. 'Another of your suitors?'

Isabella nodded.

Nicholas looked at the dance floor again. Riles was moderately tall, moderately handsome, and possessed of impeccable breeding and a large fortune. 'Why didn't you marry him?' From what he knew of the man, he had a sense of humour.

'I felt that his personality was…too compliant.'

Nicholas swallowed a laugh. *You would have led him by the nose.*

'We shouldn't have suited.'

'No,' he said, voicing his thoughts aloud. 'You would need a strong husband.'

Isabella looked sharply at him. 'To dominate me?'

'To match you.'

'Oh.' Her gaze fell. She turned her attention to the dance floor again, watching as the partners made their bows to one another.

Clarissa Whedon was in the same set as Riles. Nicholas observed her for a moment in silence. *My bride*, he thought, sipping his champagne. It tasted slightly sour in his mouth.

Isabella glanced sideways at him. 'A strong wife would suit you too.'

Nicholas looked at her. 'No.'

'Not wilful and obstinate,' she said. 'But strong-minded. To match you.'

Nicholas shook his head. 'I want a peaceful marriage. A marriage without arguments. For that, a young bride is best.'

'Do you not think you could have a…a peaceful marriage with a slightly older wife?' Her tone was diffident. 'Someone whose character is formed?'

'No.' Young soldiers lacked experience, but they were more tractable, less likely to complain, to question orders, to argue. It stood to reason that a young wife would be similarly tractable.

Isabella made no reply. She bit her lip and looked at the dance floor again.

Nicholas followed the direction of her gaze. He watched as Clarissa Whedon stood placidly waiting for the quadrille to begin.

That is what I want.

But the wife he'd imagined—quiet and biddable, agreeing with everything he said—no longer seemed quite as ideal as he'd once thought. 'You think I'm wrong.'

Isabella glanced at him. 'I think that you are…misguided.'

Misguided? What did she mean by that? Was she telling him—politely—that she thought him a fool? He opened his mouth to ask her, but at that moment Lucas returned. 'Colonel Durham's here,' he said as he handed Isabella her champagne glass. 'Have you seen him?'

'No.' Nicholas pushed semantics to the back of his mind. He scanned the ballroom. *I shall take care to avoid him.*

'Colonel Durham?' Isabella said. 'I should like to meet him.'

Nicholas turned his head to stare at her. 'You would?'

'From what I've heard, he's an unpleasant man.'

Very, he thought drily. He raised his glass and paused, looking past her shoulder. *Damn.* He took a long swallow and said, 'You're in luck, Lady Isabella. You are about to meet him.'

'I am?' She turned her head, following the direction of his gaze. 'Is that him?'

He wondered what she saw—the lines of bad temper etched into Colonel Durham's face, the sour mouth, or the erect carriage, the forceful footsteps, the bristling and almost aggressive energy of the man?

Colonel Durham halted. 'Major Reynolds.'

Nicholas bowed. 'Colonel Durham. May I present Lady Isabella Knox and Viscount Washburne?'

Colonel Durham favoured Isabella with a bow and a glance, both equally brief, and then turned to Lucas Washburne. *He doesn't see her,* Nicholas realised in disbelief.

The conversation was not protracted—the Colonel invited him to dine at his club the following evening and spoke a few words about the weather and London traffic. Harriet was not mentioned. Another bow and he was gone.

Nicholas glanced at Isabella. Had she noticed the Colonel's dismissive manner towards her? 'Well? What is your opinion of Colonel Durham?'

She glanced at him. 'Truthfully? I think him a man who places no value on women.'

Lucas Washburne blinked. 'You do?'

'He addressed himself entirely to you both. I may as well have not existed.'

'Oh?' said Lucas blankly, turning to stare after Colonel Durham. 'I didn't notice.'

Nicholas raised his glass and drained it. 'The Colonel is not the brightest of men,' he said drily.

Lucas Washburne turned back to face Isabella. His expression was faintly perplexed. 'Are you certain that's what he did? Because I didn't notice anything.'

Isabella laughed. 'You are a man, Lucas. Of course you wouldn't notice!'

Lucas Washburne didn't venture a reply to that; he grinned sheepishly and bowed and went in search of his wife.

'You were perfectly correct,' Nicholas said, his eyes on Isabella's face. 'Colonel Durham places no value on women.'

She grimaced slightly. 'Poor H—Miss Durham.'

The words were an unwelcome reminder. Nicholas frowned down at his empty glass. 'Yes. Poor Miss Durham.'

'You are nothing like the Colonel,' Isabella said.

'I should hope not.'

Her brow creased. 'Then how could Harriet Durham have thought—?'

He tapped his left cheek with one finger. 'Don't forget this.'

Isabella's eyes fastened on the scar for a moment, and then she shook her head. Her lips thinned. 'Foolish girl!'

'Yes, I agree.' He looked at the dance floor, at the lines of dancers, at Clarissa Whedon. She didn't appear to hold him in aversion. But then, he hadn't noticed that Harriet had, either. He'd mistaken her dislike of him for shyness.

Isabella was silent.

Nicholas glanced at her. She was watching Miss Whedon. Her expression was unreadable. 'May I have the next waltz?' he asked.

'Do you even need to ask, Major?' Her glance, her smile, her tone, were wry.

Nicholas looked down at his empty glass again. He turned the stem between his fingers. Soon there would be no more waltzes, no more kisses. He glanced again at Miss Whedon.

Boring, whispered a voice in the back of his head.

He ignored it.

The waltz came after the quadrille. Nicholas enjoyed the familiar pleasure of dancing with Isabella—the curve of her waist beneath his palm, the warmth of her gloved hand on his shoulder, the ease with which their steps matched. Her height too was a pleasure. Isabella's chin was level with his shoulder; he didn't have to bend his head to speak to her. It was easy to meet her eyes. Easy to kiss her.

Later, he told himself, sternly quashing a flicker of desire.

If there was a later. The Middletons' house seemed to be depressingly without concealed corners in which to kiss.

The music finished with a flourishing final note. Nicholas escorted Isabella from the dance floor, cool and elegant in the white slip and blue robe, queenly in her height. Diamonds sparkled at her ears and around her throat.

She was the perfect society lady, polished and glittering, graceful and poised, untouchable, unkissable—until she grinned at him and he caught a glimpse of her teeth, white and charmingly crooked. 'Thank you for the dance, Major Reynolds.'

Desire kicked in his stomach. 'The library,' he said. 'In five minutes.'

Isabella's grin faded. Her eyes caught in his. Blue-grey eyes. Beautiful eyes.

I want her.

Nicholas clenched his hands. He was *not* going to kiss her in the Middletons' ballroom in front of everyone. 'The library,' he said again, his voice slightly hoarse, and then he bowed and turned on his heel and walked away from her.

He knew she would come. This thing that held them both, this lust, was mutual. It twisted in her gut, the same as it twisted in his. *We are in the grip of madness.*

He studied the volumes on the shelves. Poetry. Wordsworth and Coleridge and Byron's *The Corsair*.

The door opened.

Nicholas swung around. He watched as Isabella closed the door behind her.

'Dare we?' she asked in a low voice as she came towards him.

He held out his hand. 'We shall be very careful,' he said, drawing her with him to the furthest shadowy corner of the large room. A wing-backed leather armchair loomed, the bronze studs gleaming faintly in the light of the two lamps that were lit.

'If anyone sees us—'

He took her face between his hands. 'They won't.'

She stared up at him, her eyes dark and unreadable.

'Kiss me,' he whispered.

Isabella lifted her mouth to him.

Chapter Sixteen

Isabella lost all track of time. The warmth of Nicholas's body, the strength of his arms, the urgency of his mouth, the sheer magic of kissing him, of being held by him, drove all thought from her mind.

Heat rose in her until she burned with it. She needed more, ached for more. This—his mouth on hers, his arms around her—wasn't enough. *I need more than this.* She broke their kiss. 'Nicholas…'

He rested his cheek against her temple. His breath was ragged. 'What?'

A sound at the door made them break apart.

'Down!' Nicholas whispered fiercely, pushing her behind the wing chair.

Isabella crouched as the door opened. She pressed her forehead against the cool leather and closed her eyes. Her heart beat rapidly. *If we are discovered—*

Nicholas knelt alongside her. His arm came around her shoulders, pulling her close. She felt the pressure of his thigh against hers.

The door shut with a *snick*. There was a moment of silence, when she strained to hear past the beating of her heart, and then she heard a man's low voice and an answering feminine whisper.

The minutes passed slowly. She leaned into Nicholas's warmth, her eyes closed, trying not to listen to the giggles and low murmurs. *Is that what we sounded like?*

No. She and Nicholas had kissed silently. There'd been no coquetry between them, no teasing, no muffled laughter.

Because ours is not a flirtation. It was something much more intense, exhilarating beyond anything she had ever imagined—and quite terrifying.

I could lose myself in him.

She knelt with her head bowed and her eyes closed while the lovers kissed, while they murmured farewells, while the door opened again and then shut.

Nicholas uttered a deep sigh. His arm tightened briefly and then he released her. 'We're not the only ones to use the library as a rendezvous.'

Isabella opened her eyes and looked at him. His face was in shadow, the scar hidden.

Her heart clenched in her chest. *I love you.*

'I apologise,' he said. 'This was not a good idea.'

Isabella shook her head mutely.

Nicholas was silent a moment, looking at her, his eyes a dark gleam. He uttered a shaky laugh. 'My lady, don't look at me like that, or I shall have to kiss you again.'

Then kiss me.

He sat very still, staring at her, and then as if he'd heard her he reached for her, pulling her towards him. His mouth was hot and hungry.

Isabella closed her eyes and kissed him back fiercely. *I love you.*

The rows of books with their leather spines, the carpet beneath her knees, the armchair casting its shadow over them, ceased to exist. Her awareness narrowed to Nicholas's mouth, to the grip of his hands. She was drowning in sensation, drowning in *him*, in the scent and taste of him, in his heat, in the sound of his breathing, his heartbeat.

This time it was Nicholas who broke their kiss. He pulled back, putting distance between them. His face was flushed, his eyes so dark they looked black. His breath was ragged, panting.

He stared at her for a long moment, and then rubbed his hands over his face. He leaned his head back against the wall and squeezed his eyes shut. 'This is madness!' he said. 'We're insane.'

'Yes.'

He turned his head to look at her. 'If we are discovered…'

'It would be a scandal,' Isabella said quietly. She clasped her hands in her lap. 'A scandal of such proportions that—'

'We would have to marry.' His words were as quiet as her own had been. His eyes held hers, his stare intense, as if he looked inside her. He wasn't offering, she knew he wasn't offering, and yet, dear God, she was mad enough to *want* him to.

'I'm not the sort of woman you would like to marry.' The words blurted from her. 'Am I?'

She knew she was not; he'd told her precisely what he wanted—youth, a yielding nature. *And I have neither of those.*

Isabella felt a stab of jealousy for Clarissa Whedon, as sudden and intense as it was shameful. She looked down again, at her lap, at the crumpled fabric of her gown, at her hands clasped tightly together. *Tell me I am not what you want.*

'I…uh—'

The door to the library opened again.

Nicholas ducked his head. He slid sideways towards the shelter of the armchair and reached for her, pulling her close, shielding her.

Footsteps entered the room. She heard the stealthy *clink* of decanters, furtive male voices, laughter. Servants, stealing a little brandy.

The servants were quicker than the lovers had been. Barely two minutes passed, while she leaned into Nicholas's warmth and listened to his heartbeat.

More laughter came, then the sound of the door opening and closing. They were alone again.

Nicholas released her. He stood.

Answer my question, Major. Am I someone you could marry?

Nicholas held out his hand. 'We've got to get out of here.'

She let him pull her to her feet. 'Nicholas—'

But he wasn't listening to her. His mouth was grim. 'This was one of my more stupid ideas.' He tightened his grip on her hand and drew her with him across the library.

He released her hand, opened the door a few inches, and glanced out. 'It's clear,' he said, turning to her.

'Nicholas…'

His hand reached out to touch her cheek, freezing the words on her tongue. His mouth twisted wryly. 'We must stop this,' he said, as his thumb moved across her skin, stroking, caressing.

Stop it?

His head dipped, his lips touched hers, and then he turned to the door, glanced out again, and opened it more widely. 'You first,' he said. 'I'll follow in a few minutes.'

Isabella hesitated. *You haven't answered my question.*

'Quickly,' Nicholas said.

The urgency in his low voice made her obey. She slipped through the opening.

The door closed behind her with a quiet *snick*.

Isabella stood for a moment in the hallway. Absurdly, she wanted to cry. She turned away from the ballroom, heading for the ladies' dressing room.

Damn you, Major Reynolds. You didn't answer my question.

Nicholas collected his hat and gloves and walked down the steps to the street. He stood for a moment in the light of the flambeaux. *In the library.* He winced, disgusted by the depth of his stupidity. *I should have known better than to take such a risk.* He *did* know better.

Except that when it came to Lady Isabella, it appeared that he didn't.

I look at her and my wits dribble out of my ears, he thought sourly, hunching his shoulders against the cold night air and beginning to stride in the direction of Albemarle Street. The sound of his footsteps echoed flatly, thrown back at him by the tall stone façades of the houses.

No more. He shook his head. No more risks. No more kisses at balls. No more kisses at the opera.

At the opera.

He winced again in memory. He'd kissed Isabella at *the opera* of all places, in the back of a box, where anybody could have walked in and seen them. 'I'm mad,' he muttered. 'Mad!'

A pedestrian, approaching, shied away, giving him a wide berth.

Nicholas scowled at him.

I am a fool. A smitten, besotted fool, taking appalling risks for a few kisses, a few seconds holding her.

The scowl faded as he recalled the softness of Isabella's lips, the warmth of her mouth, the smoothness of her skin beneath his hands. Memory looped through his head: the leather-and-paper scent of the library, the dark shadows, the glimmer of diamonds in her hair, the way her lips had parted for him.

Nicholas turned into Albemarle Street. He halted outside his house and closed his eyes a moment, savouring the memory of Isabella's kiss and the wash of heat that came with it. *Kiss me,* he'd said. And she had.

And then, afterwards, she had said, *I'm not the sort of woman you would like to marry. Am I?*

Nicholas's eyes came open.

He stood for a moment, frowning, and then he climbed the steps slowly and let himself into the house.

It was silent inside; he'd told the servants not to wait up for him. He stood for a moment in the dimness of the entrance hall. The silence, the shadows, suited his mood.

I'm not the sort of woman you would like to marry. Am I?

Nicholas grunted. Did she expect an answer?

He lit a candle from the lamp in the hall and walked up the stairs, shielding the flame with his hand. In his bedchamber he shrugged out of his coat and sat to remove his shoes. Her question ran in his head, endlessly repeating itself, as he untied his neckcloth and pulled his shirt over his head. *I'm not the sort of woman you would like to marry. Am I?*

How the hell was he supposed to answer a question like that?

He had fallen asleep to the sound of her voice and woke several hours later with her question still turning in his head. *I'm not the sort of woman you would like to marry. Am I?*

Nicholas stared up in the darkness. Clarissa Whedon was the bride he wanted. He could mould her into the perfect wife.

Isabella was merely—

Epiphany came then, so bright that it seemed to light up the room. The flash of it seared across his retinas, making him blink. Isabella was merely *perfect*.

The perfect friend, the perfect lover, the perfect wife.

I've been so blind.

Nicholas sat up abruptly and threw back the covers. He strode across to the window and jerked the curtains back. Moonlight streamed in.

The answer to her question was *yes*.

He stared down at the empty street, frowning at the pool of light cast by the gas lamp. What made him think she'd say yes if he asked her? Isabella Knox didn't want to marry; she had told him why, quite plainly, at the Worthingtons' masquerade. She had turned down many offers, from men far wealthier and more highly born than he was. Why would she choose to marry a scarred ex-soldier with a modest fortune?

Nicholas chewed thoughtfully on his lower lip. Her question turned in his mind. *I'm not the sort of woman you would like to marry. Am I?*

Why had she asked it? Did it mean what he thought it did? And what would Isabella's answer be if he asked *her* that question? *Am I the sort of man you would want to marry?*

Nicholas woke to sunlight slanting in through the window— and with the sunlight, doubts. Was Isabella really perfect? She was a society lady, a darling of the *ton*. She enjoyed the whirl of the Season. Would she be happy on a country estate with no more excitement than being a wife and mother?

It seemed extremely unlikely.

Pushing back the covers, Nicholas climbed out of bed and walked over to the window. He stared out at Albemarle Street, at the tall houses, at the blank windows, the grey stone, the steep roofs, at the smudge-coloured smear of chimney smoke across the glimpse of sky. Noise drifted up to him: the rattle of a hackney's wheels, the shrill shout of a street sweeper.

We could live here, in London.

His reaction was deep and instinctive: a shudder, a *no* in his chest. He wanted expanses of blue sky, he wanted hills and valleys, meadows and woods. He wanted to inhale air that was rich with the scents of the countryside. He wanted his children to grow up climbing trees and fishing in the stream. He wanted them to know the smell of grass, of leaf mould, of hay drying in the sun.

Nicholas turned away from the window. *If I could have Isabella, how much would I give up?*

Major Reynolds was frowning when Isabella stopped the phaeton for him that afternoon. The frown faded when he saw her, but his expression was unsmiling and almost stern as he stepped up into the carriage.

'Major,' she said, in greeting, 'how are you?'

'Very well.' But the faint crease between his eyebrows and the set of his mouth belied the words.

Isabella set the horses in motion and bent her mind, for what must be the hundredth time today, to how to get him to answer her question.

Should she be blunt? *Major, do you remember I asked you a question last night? Well, I should like to know the answer.*

Or should she try to turn it into a joke? *You never answered my question last night, Major.* And then a little laugh. *I should like to know the answer!*

She glanced sideways at him. He was patting Rufus.

Oh, for heaven's sake, just ask him!

Major Reynolds looked up and met her eyes. The frown still sat on his brow. 'Lady Isabella,' he said abruptly. 'You enjoy town life.'

Isabella blinked. 'Er, yes. Yes, I do.'

'Would you…would you ever consider living in the countryside?'

Isabella blinked again. She transferred her attention to the horses. What an odd question. 'The countryside? Well, of course!'

'But…you said that you like being in London, that you like the Season.'

'So I do. But if you recall, Major, what I said was that I dislike being idle. One can be busy equally well in the country as in town.' She glanced at him. His brow was no longer creased into a frown. If anything, he looked slightly taken aback. 'I spend quite half the year in the country, you know!'

He shook his head. 'No, I didn't know.' His fingers rubbed Rufus's head. 'Ah…you enjoy it?'

'Yes.' A barouche had halted by the side of the drive. Isabella guided her team neatly between it and the curricle coming in the opposite direction. 'Very much! My eldest brother Julian lives in Derbyshire. I visit him often. In fact, I've only just returned.' And on her journey home, she had encountered Harriet Durham. Isabella bit her lip. She glanced at Major Reynolds. *Should I tell him now?*

No. Privacy would be best for that disclosure. To tell him now, under the gaze of the *ton*, would be the height of folly.

Isabella smiled brightly. 'My other brother has a home in Kent, and of my sisters, one lives in Suffolk and the other in Somerset. You may believe that I spend a lot of time in the country!'

'Somerset?' Major Reynolds said, a note of interest in his voice. 'My estate is in Devon.'

'Not far from my sister Amabel, then.'

'No.' His gaze was intent. He seemed on the verge of saying more.

Isabella glanced ahead. The landaulet approaching was a familiar one. 'Lady Jersey.'

An expression of frustration crossed Major Reynolds's face. He shifted slightly, so that they weren't sitting quite so closely together.

Lady Jersey had a lot—and very little—to say, as was her custom. It was quite ten minutes before they were able to part from her.

Isabella glanced at Major Reynolds. The polite smile he'd favoured Lady Jersey with was gone. In its place was a small frown.

'Major—'

'Lady Isabella—'

Major Reynolds opened his hand. 'After you.'

'Will you tell me about your estate?'

The frown vanished from his brow. His eyes seemed to brighten with pleasure. 'It's called Elmwood,' he said, reaching down to pat Rufus. 'I had it from my maternal grandparents. It's not large, but…'

Isabella drove slowly, nodding and bowing to acquaintances, enjoying the timbre of Major Reynolds's voice, the enthusiasm with which he described Elmwood. He loved his estate, that was very clear. She listened to his description of a lake and woods, the cliffs of the coast, the salt tang of the breeze, hayricks in rolling fields, the red-brick Jacobean manse with its high ceilings and light-filled rooms. *I could be happy there.*

'It sounds very beautiful.'

'It is. I hope…I hope my wife will love it as much as I do.'

'How could she not?' Isabella said lightly. 'Your wife will be very happy.'

'I should try to be a good husband.' His voice was diffident, and when she glanced at him she saw that he was looking at Rufus, not at her. 'To, er…not treat my wife as if I own her.' Major Reynold's gaze lifted. His eyes met hers.

The intensity of his stare was unnerving. *Is there more to this conversation than I realise?*

Isabella moistened her lips and glanced ahead. Her groom stood beside the drive. She drew the horses to a halt several yards distant from him. 'Major Reynolds,' she said, fingering the reins, 'you are, by your own confession, an autocrat.'

His eyebrows rose slightly. 'I am?'

'Yes. At the Worthingtons' masquerade you said—'

'Ah…' Major Reynolds grinned. 'So I did.' As he looked at her, his grin slowly faded. His eyes were green and very intense. 'I was joking. My wife will be free to be herself.'

'But…you said that you would mould her—'

'I have changed my mind.'

Is he saying what I think he is?

Isabella swallowed. 'Major Reynolds—Nicholas…last night—'

She glanced down. Her groom was standing beside the phaeton.

'Yes,' Major Reynolds said.

Her eyes flew to his. 'Yes?'

'The answer to your question.' Major Reynolds looked down at the groom, standing at his feet, and then back at her. 'I have a question for you too, but now is neither the time nor the place.'

Isabella clutched the reins more tightly. Her heart began to beat loudly in her chest.

'Tonight I dine with Colonel Durham.' The Major grimaced briefly. 'Tomorrow…may I call on you?'

Isabella nodded, unable to speak.

'Two o'clock?'

She nodded again.

Major Reynolds made a slight movement, as if to lean over and kiss her cheek, caught himself, nodded briefly to her and descended.

Isabella watched him walk away. She felt dizzy, breathless, euphoric.

The groom climbed up into the phaeton and settled himself in the place Major Reynolds had just vacated.

'You drive, Coate,' Isabella said, handing him the reins. 'I'm feeling…' *Quite light-headed.* 'A little unwell.'

She sat back in the seat and clasped her hands tightly together. *Nicholas said yes.*

But mingled with the euphoria, the dizzy breathlessness, was dread. Tomorrow…tomorrow she had to tell him about Harriet.

Chapter Seventeen

It was one of the less enjoyable meals of Nicholas's experience. The food was good—almost as good as White's—and the wine excellent, but Colonel Durham was not the most pleasant of dining companions. His conversation consisted almost entirely of reminiscences about campaigns he had fought. In his minute and pedantic dissections of the errors of each battle, Colonel Durham never acknowledged any mistakes of his own—the blunders were always someone else's.

Everyone makes mistakes, Nicholas thought as he chewed on buttered lobster. *It is part of what makes us human.* He reached for his glass, swallowed a mouthful of wine and looked sourly at the Colonel. He'd had a commanding officer like Colonel Durham once. It had been an unpleasant experience. A good officer should acknowledge his errors, not push them off on someone else.

Interspersed with the reminiscences were heated animadversions about the slyness and dishonesty of his granddaughter. 'I have nursed a viper in my bosom!' Colonel Durham declaimed, his face red with rage and alcohol, spittle forming at the corners of his mouth.

No blame, of course, attached to the Colonel in his

dealings with his granddaughter. He was guilty neither of bullying her into marriage, nor of refusing to listen to her pleas. The blame was all hers. 'A viper!'

By the end of the evening Nicholas had conceived a deep and profound pity for Harriet Durham. He wished the girl well, wherever she was. He couldn't even whip up any animosity towards her benefactress; Harriet had needed rescuing, and whoever the woman was, and whatever she had said regarding ogres, he no longer cared. Sometime in the past week his rancour had faded.

It was because of Isabella, he thought, a smile playing lightly on his lips as he stepped out from under the portico of the Colonel's club. How could he be angry when he was so foolishly and fatuously in love?

A misting drizzle was falling, smearing the light of the gas lamps. Nicholas scarcely noticed. He began to stroll back in the direction of Albemarle Street, whistling softly under his breath. Mr Cobb had requested an interview tomorrow to report his findings. He would call the man off.

Let it rest, he thought as he turned the corner.

Mr Cobb arrived punctually at one o'clock. He entered the study, bowed and bade Nicholas good day. 'I have had some success,' he said, 'in the matter of locating Miss Durham.'

'You have?' Nicholas said, not much interested. 'Good, good.' He opened one of the drawers in his desk and drew out a roll of guineas. 'However, I have decided that the matter is of less importance than I had thought. If you tell me what your expenses were, I can settle your account now.' He gestured the man to a chair.

Mr Cobb drew an envelope from his breast pocket, handed it to Nicholas, and sat. 'Here is an itemised list of my expenses,' he said. 'And a report detailing my findings.'

'Thank you,' Nicholas said, picking up the envelope and

sliding his thumb under the seal. He glanced quickly through
the sheets of paper. The list of expenses was short, neatly
written in copperplate, and came to a rather high total. He
read through it. Ah, the man had taken the stage to Stony
Stratford and stayed two nights.

The report was surprisingly long. Nicholas flicked to the
last page. His eyebrows rose. An address in London.

He glanced at Mr Cobb, sitting quiet and nondescript on
the chair in front of him. 'She's here? At this address?'

Mr Cobb nodded.

Nicholas leaned back in his chair. Some success? Modesty
was clearly one of Mr Cobb's virtues, along with efficiency
and punctuality. 'Tell me,' he said, laying the report on the
desk. 'The brief version.' As opposed to the pages of closely
written parchment.

Mr Cobb did so, succinctly. 'I determined that Miss
Durham took the stagecoach north and alighted at Stony
Stratford, where she attempted to stay at the Rose and Crown,
but having insufficient funds was turned away. However, a
lady who was already residing at that establishment came to
her aid, offering her a bed, and taking Miss Durham with her
to London the next day.'

Nicholas nodded. 'Go on.'

'I spoke to one of her ladyship's servants yesterday. Miss
Durham is still in residence with her in London.'

Nicholas picked up the report again and turned to the back
page. Clarges Street. That was where Isabella lived.

His eyes narrowed suddenly. The street number—

Hastily he turned to the previous page. *Lady Isabella
Knox*, he read. *Travelling with her servants and two outriders provided by her brother, the Duke of Middlebury.* 'No,'
he said aloud. 'You've made a mistake. This is wrong.'

Mr Cobb was unruffled. 'I assure you, Major Reynolds,
that my information is correct. Lady Isabella Knox is the person you seek.'

Nicholas shook his head. 'No.'

'Lady Isabella was staying at the Rose and Crown on the night in question. She provided accommodation for Miss Durham and took the girl to London with her.' Mr Cobb's voice was light and dry and precisely inflected. 'Miss Durham is presently residing with her, on Clarges Street.'

'No,' Nicholas said again, putting down the report and leaning forward across the desk. 'I've *been* to her house. I tell you, Harriet is not there!'

'The cook assures me she is. Staying in the blue chamber on the third floor.'

They matched stares, Nicholas's fierce, furious, and Mr Cobb's impassive.

He's wrong.

Wrong or not, Mr Cobb had spent twelve days—and not a little money—coming to his conclusions. Nicholas reached for the guineas, counted out what he owed the man and handed them over. 'Here,' he said curtly. 'Thank you for your work, Mr Cobb.'

Mr Cobb accepted the money. He stood. 'Read my report, Major Reynolds. It will all be quite clear.'

Nicholas thinned his lips.

Mr Cobb bowed and exited the room.

Nicholas sat for a long moment after the door had quietly closed, staring at the report. *Lies. It's all lies.*

But the problem was that it was entirely like Isabella to rescue a penniless runaway. He could *imagine* her doing it.

No, he told himself firmly. It wasn't Isabella. She'd said she didn't know where Harriet was and he believed her, he *trusted* her.

Nicholas reached for the report, determined to read through it and find Mr Cobb wrong.

The first few pages detailed Mr Cobb's efforts to determine what mode of transport Harriet had taken in her flight from London, and where she had alighted: in Stony Stratford.

Mr Cobb's interview with the landlady of the Rose and Crown was brief and uninformative. In his opinion the woman had been bribed not to reveal any information concerning Harriet Durham—her manner had been adamant and defensive.

His subsequent interview with one of the porters, lubricated by several tankards of ale and a guinea, was much more interesting.

He showed Miss Durham into the taproom and fetched his mistress, Mr Cobb wrote. *Upon ascertaining that Miss Durham had insufficient funds for a room for the night, Mrs Botham refused her accommodation, unswayed by the girl's tears and entreaties.*

At this point, another lady had entered the taproom. The porter had only heard the conversation through a partly closed door, but in his words the newcomer was *'awful polite'* and in less than a minute had *'routed the old besom'*. Mrs Botham had been, in the porter's opinion, spitting mad, but far too afraid of offending the lady to cross her.

The porter's description of Harriet's benefactress was detailed. Mr Cobb produced it verbatim. Nicholas could almost hear the porter's voice in his head: *A prime 'un. A real beauty. Tall, with yeller hair, and so elegant you wouldn't believe.*

The porter knew her name too: Lady Isabella Knox, a frequent guest on her way to and from Derbyshire. *A duke's daughter, but she looks like a princess*, the man had said.

No, Nicholas thought. *Not a princess—a goddess.*

The porter had also described the lady's dog: black and tan, with one blue eye and one brown, and a curling tail. *A mongrel if ever I saw one, but real well behaved. Never bites anyone.*

Nicholas closed his eyes. He rubbed a hand over his face. Clearly Isabella had been in Stony Stratford. And why shouldn't she? It was on her route south to London.

But she wasn't the lady who had rescued Harriet. He *knew* she wasn't. The porter had made a mistake.

Nicholas opened his eyes and turned the page, reading further.

Mr Cobb, not content with the porter's word, had interviewed an ostler. This man, similarly plied with ale and a guinea, had confirmed the identity of Harriet's benefactress, on account of her *'bang-up horses'* and the liveried outriders. Both men had agreed that Lady Isabella Knox took up the girl into her carriage the next morning.

Nicholas put down the report. He pushed his chair back and strode across the study to the cluster of decanters standing on the sideboard. He poured himself a glass of brandy and stood for a moment, breathing deeply. *Calm*, he told himself. But anger was rising inside him and the brandy, cool, burning down his throat when he gulped it, didn't help.

He strode back to the desk and sat and read the rest of the report. Mr Cobb had spoken to a number of Lady Isabella's servants, both casually at the local tavern, and more formally with the offer of money. All had refused to speak about any guests their mistress might or might not have had staying with her.

But yesterday Mr Cobb's luck had changed; he had managed a few words with the cook, a Mrs Shepherd, who had been quite happy to accept a few guineas in exchange for information concerning Lady Isabella's houseguest. Miss Durham, she confirmed, had inhabited the Blue Room for the past two weeks. Yes, she had arrived with Lady Isabella when she returned from Derbyshire. No, she had not left the house.

Nicholas closed his eyes. He pinched the bridge of his nose, hard. Isabella's image wavered behind his closed eyelids. *I trusted you.*

She had been playing him. For two whole weeks she had been playing him.

Where once there had been faith and trust, there was now

anger. The taste of it, black and bitter, mingled with the taste of brandy on his tongue.

Nicholas opened his eyes. Mr Cobb concluded the report with a note concerning a Mr Fernyhough, who, he said, had been in Stony Stratford several days before himself enquiring as to Harriet's whereabouts.

Who the devil was Mr Fernyhough?

Nicholas put the report down. He rubbed his face. The ridges of the scar were hard beneath his fingers, smooth and rough.

Ogre.

He made a sound of disgust and lowered his hands and turned to the final page of the report. For a full minute he stared bleakly at the address, at each flourishing *s* and neatly looped *e*. Clarges Street.

Nicholas glanced across at the clock above the fireplace. It was nearly time to visit Isabella.

I have been such a fool.

Rage flared inside him. He pushed back the chair and stood. On the way to the door he paused and looked at himself in the mirror, looked at the scar.

Ogre.

Lady Isabella had coined that sobriquet.

Nicholas turned his back on his reflection. He jerked the door open and strode into the hall.

Chapter Eighteen

Isabella blew out a shaky breath. 'How do I look?' she asked her maid, Partridge. She studied herself in the mirror. Did the yellow of the gown make her hair look dull? 'Perhaps I should wear the blue after all—'

'If you wish,' Partridge said, her voice carefully neutral.

Five gowns lay on the bed. Isabella had tried them all on. The pink had been too girlish, she'd decided, the blue too plain, the white too formal, the green too severe, the cinnamon brown too matronly.

The yellow had seemed hopeful, joyful.

Isabella glanced at the clock. She was trembling with a mix of apprehension and anticipation. It lacked ten minutes to two. This gown would do—it would have to do—there was no more time.

But I want to look perfect for him.

'Perhaps I should try the blue again.'

'Miss Isabella,' Partridge said, with something approaching frustration in her voice, 'you look lovely.'

Isabella swallowed and looked at the clock again. Nine minutes. And she still had to speak to her cousin and Harriet.

'Very well,' she said. 'Yellow it is.'

She took a deep breath. She'd never imagined this moment

would come: waiting for a man, wanting to marry him. It was exhilarating. It was terrifying.

She smoothed her gown with damp palms and turned towards the door. There was no more time.

'Are you all right, Miss Isabella?' Partridge asked, with the perspicacity of one who had known her from her girlhood.

Or perhaps it's not perspicacity. Perhaps I look as nervous as I feel.

'Perfectly,' Isabella replied. She blew out another shaky breath. First Elinor and Harriet, and then Nicholas. She squared her shoulders, crossed the bedchamber and opened the door. Rufus scrambled up from a sunny square of carpet and followed her, his tail wagging.

Isabella's steps were firm and purposeful as she walked along the corridor and down one flight of stairs. Her knock on the door of Mrs Westin's parlour was firm and purposeful too.

Mrs Westin looked up from her knitting. 'Yes, my dear?'

'Major Reynolds will be here shortly. I am going to tell him about Harriet.'

For a moment there was silence. Harriet stared at her, frozen, over the handkerchief she was embroidering.

Mrs Westin nodded and laid down her knitting. 'Very wise, my dear. Honesty is always the best course. As the good Lord said, *Thou shalt not lie.*'

'Tell him?' said Harriet. The blood had drained from her face. 'But he will find me!'

'He is not an ogre,' Isabella said. 'However much you imagine him to be.'

Harriet shook her head.

Exasperation rose in Isabella's breast. How could the girl be so foolish? So blind? 'You have nothing to fear from Major Reynolds. He's a good man. A kind man.' *The best of men.*

Harriet put down the embroidery frame. And then, predictably, she began to cry.

Mrs Westin tutted.

Isabella considered trying to convince Harriet of the Major's good qualities. A few seconds' thought made her give up the notion as hopeless. The picture Harriet had painted in her head of Nicholas was as inaccurate as it was ridiculous, but it would take more than a few words to persuade the girl she was wrong. *She needs to meet him, to see him as he truly is, not as the ogre she has imagined.*

She gave her cousin a look of apology and left her to deal with the weeping Harriet. In the corridor she smoothed her gown again and took a steadying breath. A glance at her watch told her it lacked five minutes to the hour. Would Nicholas be on time?

Rufus took a step forward. His head cocked slightly and his ears pricked.

Isabella walked to the head of the stairs. She heard the sound of men's voices in the foyer below: her butler Hoban saying something in welcome, Nicholas replying.

Early.

Isabella received him in the library. The morning room was sunnier and more pleasant, but the kittens were in residence. She left Rufus there too. She wanted no distractions, no witnesses. *Just him and me.*

The apprehension, the anticipation, were a hard knot beneath her breastbone as she stood beside the fireplace. She concentrated on breathing, on not fidgeting, but even so, her heart began to beat much faster as the door opened and the butler ushered Nicholas into the library.

She was conscious of him—the green of his eyes, the weight of his presence in the room. And she was conscious of herself in a way she'd never been before, of her appearance, of her nervousness.

Isabella swallowed. 'Nicholas.'

'Isabella.' His voice gave nothing away, nor did his face.

No smile, no softening of his expression. Was he as nervous as she? As awkward?

'Please be seated.'

He didn't. He walked past her to the window. He stood looking out for a moment, his figure silhouetted against the daylight, and then turned to face her. His features were in shadow.

Now.

Isabella took hold of her courage. She clasped her hands together and inhaled a deep breath. 'Nicholas,' she said. 'There is something I must tell you. About Harriet Durham.'

'I know,' he said.

'You do?' Isabella began to walk towards him. Relief swelled inside her.

'Yes.' Nicholas laughed. It was a hard, ugly sound. He stepped away from the window.

Isabella halted. She could see his face, the hard glitter in his eyes, the tight line of his mouth, the anger. 'Nicholas…'

His mouth tightened still further. 'I *trusted* you.'

The apprehension, the anticipation, were gone. In their place was something close to panic. 'Nicholas—'

'Keep your friends close and your enemies closer.' His voice made her flinch. 'Congratulations, Lady Isabella. You succeeded admirably.'

'No!' she said. 'It wasn't at all like that, Nicholas!'

His mouth twisted. 'Wasn't it?' There was a derisive edge to his words, a mocking note.

'No!' Isabella cried. 'Of course not! I was trying to make it better, to…to stop people laughing at you!' *To atone for my mistake.*

Nicholas's mouth tightened. His hand lifted to touch his left cheek. 'I had forgotten to thank you for my new name.' He bowed, a sardonic movement. 'Thank you for reminding me.'

Shame flushed her cheeks. 'It was a *mistake*, Nicholas. I

never meant for any of that to happen!' She clutched her hands more tightly together. 'I only said it once. Once! But Sarah Faraday heard me, and you know what her tongue is like! She—' Isabella bit her lip. *Stop. It sounds like excuses.*

Nicholas said nothing, he merely shook his head. Anger was etched on his face. His mouth was tight and bitter, his eyes flat with disbelief. He turned away from her to look out of the window again.

Isabella took a hesitant step towards him. She moistened her lips and spoke quietly. 'I never intended to harm you, Nicholas. And once…once it had happened I did my very best to undo it!'

He didn't look at her. 'You lied to me.' His voice was as quiet as hers had been.

'I'm sorry. I didn't mean to! But you were so angry. I was afraid to tell you—'

He turned to face her. His expression almost made her flinch. He was as angry now as he'd been then. Angrier.

'It wasn't deliberate, Nicholas,' she said desperately. 'None of it was! I didn't mean for any of it to happen!'

'You lied to me,' he said again.

Isabella stared at him, trying to see past the anger and the bitterness to the Nicholas she knew. 'Yes,' she said. 'I lied to you. I am very sorry, Nicholas.'

He turned his head, looking past her at the fireplace. 'You named me an ogre, and then kept me in your pocket like a pet. Was it amusing, ma'am?'

The words, the tone of his voice, were like a slap across the face. Isabella flinched. 'Nicholas, you know it wasn't like that.'

His gaze came back to her. 'Do I?' His rage seemed to bloom. His lean, unscarred cheek flushed with it, his eyes grew brighter, colder, harder. He inhaled as if to speak, then closed his mouth tightly, clenching his jaw as if he held the words back with his teeth. He bowed stiffly and stepped past her. 'Good day, madam.'

'Wait! Nicholas!' *I love you.*

He halted at the door and turned to face her. 'I have nothing more to say to you, madam.' His voice was flat and distant, but his eyes—

Anger, so hot it scorched her.

'Nicholas, please…'

He looked through her, past her, his face expressionless, his eyes burning, and then turned away and opened the door. It shut behind him with a quiet *snick*.

Isabella was left standing in the empty library. The silence seemed to resonate with an echo of Nicholas's anger, like a bell ringing soundlessly.

She turned away from the door and walked to the fireplace. She was cold, as cold as ice. Dimly she was aware that she was shaking.

Thou shalt not lie.

She had lied, and this was her punishment.

Isabella smoothed her gown with trembling hands. The gown she had chosen so carefully, with such hope. Yellow.

The clock on the mantelpiece, the Sèvres figurines, the candlesticks, blurred. *I am not going to cry*, she told herself fiercely.

It was too late. She already was.

Nicholas had never been so *seethingly* angry in all his life. Anger roiled in his belly and burned in his chest; it smouldered inside his head until he couldn't think clearly, the hot red-black smoke of his rage clouding everything. The afternoon passed in a blur: striding back to the hired house on Albemarle Street, ordering his horse brought around, riding the poor beast as hard as he could, out of London. Vaguely he noticed that paved streets had given way to winding dirt lanes, that tall buildings had been replaced by trees and hedgerows and paddocks where sheep grazed. His thoughts were turned inwards.

He chose the inn at random and shouldered his way into the busy taproom. A tankard of ale quenched his thirst; the second began to quench his anger. By the third, the fog of rage in his head had begun to disperse. His anger, he realised, was mostly directed at himself. For being such a fool. For trusting Lady Isabella. For being duped for so long.

This fury is for my pride.

The anger returned, tiredly, when he remembered his defence of her to Mr Cobb. *Such a damned fool.* But he couldn't whip himself up into rage again. He stared at the empty tankard and rubbed his face wearily.

The shroud of rage that had cloaked him had kept the other patrons away from his end of the taproom. They clustered at the counter, leaning against the scarred wood, their voices loud. Farmers in patched smocks, a blacksmith, a couple of coal-haulers with soot-stained clothes. *Where am I?*

It didn't matter. Nor did it matter, when he hauled himself lurching out of his chair and asked the publican if a bedchamber was available, that the chamber he was escorted to was small and smelled of stale sweat. The mattress was lumpy, the pillow thin, and he had no idea whether the linen was clean or not, but it didn't matter. None of it mattered.

Nicholas had a headache when he woke the next morning. A profound one. His rage was gone. It had dissipated in the night, leaking away, leaving him with a feeling of extreme weariness.

I should go back to London.

But it was easier to stay here—wherever that was. The taproom was dirty, but the ale was good, and he didn't have to think about Lady Isabella or his stupidity at all. He could just sit on the rough wooden bench in front of the inn, with the sign creaking above his head, and watch the world slowly pass by, sipping his ale. And when the sun went down, he could sit in the corner of the taproom that had become his, and order another tankard.

And not think about anything.

The postman in his scarlet coat and cockaded hat delivered a letter for Harriet while they were still in the breakfast parlour. It was postmarked from Penrith, in the Lake District.

Finally, thought Isabella. But there was no relief, just numbness. How long would the numbness last? Would she be trapped for ever in this empty, echoing place?

I hope so. Because under the numbness was pain. She was aware of it, aware that it would *hurt*, that it would hurt more than she could bear if only she wasn't numb.

She watched without interest as Harriet broke open the seal and almost ripped the letter in her haste to open it. Another letter fell out from the folded paper, falling to lie on the tablecloth. Harriet's original letter. The one she'd sent to her aunt more than two weeks ago. Unopened.

Isabella's numbness faltered slightly. *That does not look good.*

'It's from…it's from a Mrs Jayne. She says—' Tears suspended Harriet's voice entirely. She thrust the letter at Mrs Westin and ran out of the room.

Mrs Westin read the letter calmly. 'Oh, dear,' she said, and then held it out to Isabella.

I don't think I want to read it.

She put down her knife and fork and took the proffered letter.

Mrs Jayne wrote briefly. Lavinia Mortlock had remarried two years ago and emigrated with her new husband to America. Mrs Jayne had an address for her in Baltimore, which she enclosed. She apologised for the delay in replying; she had been laid up with the influenza.

Isabella refolded the letter and placed it neatly on the tablecloth. She closed her eyes. *What am I going to do with Harriet?*

She opened her eyes and picked up the knife and fork and began to eat her breakfast again.

'What shall we do?' Mrs Westin asked.

'I don't know.' *I don't care.*

But the numbness was beginning to fracture. Dear God, what *was* she going to do with the girl?

And beneath the worry, pushing determinedly through the cracks, was pain, loss and grief, so intense that her throat closed.

Isabella reached for her tea cup. She swallowed to clear her throat, not tasting the tea.

'You never said yesterday… How did Major Reynolds take the news?'

Her throat tightened again. She drank another mouthful of tea. 'Not as well as I had hoped.'

'Ah,' Mrs Westin said. 'A shame.'

Isabella looked down at her plate. She had no appetite. She placed her knife and fork neatly alongside one another and folded her napkin.

'And how are you, my dear? Has your headache gone?'

'Gone?' Isabella said, staring at the congealing egg yolk on her plate. *What am I going to do about Nicholas? About Harriet?*

'You still look rather pale.'

Isabella looked up at her cousin. She forced a smile. 'A slight headache still, cousin. I believe I shall stay at home today.' *And tomorrow. And the next day. I shall hide forever.*

She pushed back her chair and stood. The door was slightly open from Harriet's flight.

Harriet.

Dear God, what am I going to do about her?

Harriet wept in her bedchamber all day. Isabella's brain was working too slowly to come up with a solution to the problem of the girl's future. The inside of her head seemed filled with an echoing emptiness, as the library had been after Major Reynolds's abrupt departure.

She spent most of her day at the pianoforte, labouring over Beethoven's Sonata No. 14. There was no beauty in the music. The soft lamenting first movement, the stormy third, sounded equally flat and lifeless, the notes sliding from beneath her fingertips with one dull *clunk* after another, the ivory and wood, hammers and strings, making noise, not music.

The numbness was steadily disintegrating, crumbling away as each slow hour passed. Her chest, her throat, were tight and aching. Isabella tried to ignore it, to concentrate on the movement of her fingers over the keys, to not acknowledge the pain, to pretend that the ache in her skull, the pressure of unshed tears did not exist.

The next morning Harriet joined them at the breakfast table. She wept quietly over her eggs. The sound grated on Isabella's nerves. Even Mrs Westin seemed weary of the girl's tears. A gently worded admonishment was uttered: one should not allow one's emotions mastery of oneself; one should bear one's misfortunes with fortitude.

'The Lord helps those who help themselves,' Mrs Westin concluded, with a gentle smile.

Harriet appeared to take Mrs Westin's words to heart. Her expression was wan, but if she wept again that morning, she wept in private.

In the afternoon, Lieutenant Mayhew came to fetch the kittens. His sunny good humour was painful, as was his cheerful enquiry about Major Reynolds.

'I haven't seen him for a few days,' Isabella said. The smile felt stiff on her lips, but it fooled the Lieutenant.

For a few minutes they were busy, capturing the two kittens, installing them in the wicker basket lined with strips of blanket that Lieutenant Mayhew had brought with him.

'Wonderful!' the Lieutenant said. 'Thank you so much, ma'am. I am indebted to you!' He bowed over her hand with a flourish, his eyes laughing at her.

'I hope they don't give you any trouble on your journey, Lieutenant.'

Lieutenant Mayhew had no such fears. He laughed and left, running lightly down the stairs, carrying the kittens. Their mews came indignantly from the basket.

Isabella stood at the top of the staircase, Rufus beside her, long after the Lieutenant was gone. The conversation with her cousin looped in her head.

How did Major Reynolds take it?

Not as well as I had hoped.

Rufus sat down with a thump. He began to scratch himself vigorously.

'I should have told Nicholas earlier,' she said to him. 'He would not have been so angry.'

Rufus continued scratching, a strained grimace on his face.

Isabella sighed. 'I should have never lied.'

So many 'should haves'. But she had done what she had done—and the result was this aching, unbearable sense of loss.

So what do I do about it?

Isabella came to an abrupt decision. She turned and headed for her bedchamber. Rufus scrambled to his feet and bounded after her. 'Partridge?' she said, opening the door to her chamber. 'I'm going out. I should like you to accompany me.'

They walked to Albemarle Street. She told herself that it was because she needed the fresh air, but, truthfully, it was because she needed to muster her courage. Partridge walked silently beside her and Rufus trotted ahead, his ears pricked and his plumy tail wagging.

Isabella halted outside Major Reynolds's house. It seemed

very tall, very stern. She took a deep breath and trod up the stone steps.

A butler with thinning grey hair and rather startlingly bushy eyebrows answered the door.

'My name is Lady Isabella Knox,' she said. 'I would like to see Major Reynolds.'

'I regret that Major Reynolds is not in town, ma'am.'

'Not?' Her momentum, her courage, faltered. 'Do you know when he will return?'

The butler shook his head. 'No, ma'am.'

Had he left London permanently? Gone to Devon? No, the house would be closed then, the knocker off the door, the servants gone. *Unless the servants are packing up the house now.* Panic tightened in her chest. 'Do you expect him back?'

'Yes, ma'am.'

Isabella expelled a shaky breath. 'Where is he? Do you know?'

'No, ma'am. He did not inform us of his destination.'

Is he gone because of me?

'When did Major Reynolds leave?'

'Two days ago, ma'am,' the butler said. 'In something of a hurry.'

Yes, he left because of me.

'Thank you,' Isabella said. She turned away from the door. Her footsteps were slow with defeat as she walked down Albemarle Street.

'Lady Isabella?'

Isabella looked up from her listless observation of the last two kittens, sprawled on the floor with Rufus. 'Yes, Mrs Early?'

'I know who the thief is.' The housekeeper's mouth was pinched, her expression grim.

Not now. 'Who?'

'Mrs Shepherd.'

Isabella straightened on the sofa. 'Cook?'

'Yes, ma'am.'

'But—' Mrs Shepherd had been in her employ for three years. 'There must be some mistake.'

Mrs Early shook her head firmly. 'No mistake, ma'am. I counted the wax candles this afternoon, and not five minutes later I saw Mrs Shepherd go down to the stillroom and come back with something in her apron pocket. I checked again and two candles were gone—the best beeswax!'

Isabella bit her lower lip. 'You're certain? You didn't miscount?'

'I checked twice, ma'am.'

Isabella sighed.

'Mrs Shepherd went to her bedchamber not long after that—to tidy her hair, she said—and when she returned, her pocket was quite clearly empty.'

'But…' Isabella said again. *But why?* The woman earned a generous wage. She closed her mouth and struggled to think clearly. 'Please ask her to attend me in my book room. I wish for you to be present too, Mrs Early.'

The housekeeper nodded and withdrew.

Mrs Shepherd?

Isabella made her way purposefully downstairs. She sat behind the desk and folded her hands together on its smooth maplewood surface. She didn't have to wait long. A tap sounded on the door. 'Come in.'

Mrs Shepherd entered, followed by the housekeeper.

'Please be seated,' Isabella said.

She watched as Mrs Shepherd sat. The woman was rawboned, with a gaunt, ruddy face. Her hands were large, their backs knotted with veins. *Such clumsy-looking hands to create such dainty delicacies*, Isabella thought, not for the first time.

The cook looked at her. Her expression was politely enquiring, not defensive, not afraid.

'Mrs Shepherd,' Isabella said. 'We have a problem.' She unfolded her hands and reached for the current ledger. 'For some months now someone in this household has been stealing.'

Mrs Shepherd's polite smile froze on her face.

'Beeswax candles,' Isabella said, turning to the latest month's columns of figures. She glanced up at the woman. 'And perhaps other things as well.'

Mrs Shepherd said nothing. She sat stiffly in the wooden chair. A plain woman, hard-working. *And honest, I had thought.*

Isabella sat with her hands resting gently on the open page. 'Is there anything you would like to tell me, Mrs Shepherd?'

'Me, ma'am?' But there was a flat, false note to Mrs Shepherd's outrage. 'Surely you don't think that *I* would steal anything!'

Isabella looked at her gravely. 'You were observed taking two wax candles this afternoon.'

'Wax candles? Me?' The cook's voice was affronted, but her expression was scared. Her cheeks, instead of flushing with indignation, had paled.

'I should like to check your room, please,' Isabella said calmly, with no accusation in her voice.

Mrs Shepherd swallowed convulsively. Her hands were tightly clenched in her lap.

Isabella stood. 'Shall we do it now?'

'But my pastries! I should get them out of the oven. I'm too busy for this now! Surely it can wait…' The woman's voice ran down as Isabella shook her head.

Mrs Shepherd's room was downstairs, near the kitchen. The woman's manner became more flustered when they halted outside the door to her bedchamber. 'Lady Isabella,' she said, 'I can explain!'

Almost a confession. Isabella looked at her sadly. 'Open the door, please, Mrs Shepherd.'

The cook began to sob as she unlocked the door to her bed-chamber. It was a large room, as befitted her status, with a half-canopy bedstead, a fireplace and an armchair.

They stepped inside. Isabella glanced around the chamber, taking in the chest of drawers, the washstand, the sturdy pinewood trunk. 'Can you open your trunk, please, Mrs Shepherd?'

The cook began to cry in earnest. She made no move to open the trunk.

Isabella turned to Mrs Early. The housekeeper's plump face was sombre. *She's enjoying this no more than I am.* 'Mrs Early? If you wouldn't mind?'

The housekeeper stepped forwards and lifted the lid of the trunk. Blankets lay neatly folded inside. Mrs Early rummaged with her hand, her mouth tight, as if she found the task distasteful. Her hand stilled. She looked up. 'Ma'am?'

Isabella made herself step forward, made herself look. The beeswax candles were tucked down one side of the trunk. She turned to face the cook, but found herself unable to look at the woman. *I trusted you.*

She turned away. 'Mrs Shepherd, you are dismissed. Please gather your belongings and depart this house within the hour.'

'But, ma'am, please…'

Isabella turned back to her. 'You stole from me,' she said quietly.

Mrs Shepherd's face was red and tear-stained. 'But, ma'am…'

Isabella stared at her. Was this how Major Reynolds had felt? This sense of disbelief, of disappointment so intense that it felt as if someone had kicked her in the stomach.

No, he had been angry. She wasn't angry. She was just sad. 'Why, Mrs Shepherd?'

Mrs Shepherd gulped and sniffed back her tears. 'My daughter's getting married soon. I wanted…I wanted to give her everything.'

Isabella sighed. She turned away again. 'One hour, Mrs Shepherd.'

'You won't…you won't press charges?'

Isabella turned back to face her. She met the woman's eyes, saw the fear in them. No, not fear, terror.

She understood the terror: people had been sent to the penal colonies for stealing less. 'No, Mrs Shepherd.'

The cook subsided weakly on her bed. She began to sob again, noisily.

Isabella met the housekeeper's eyes. She made a slight beckoning gesture with her hand. The woman followed her outside into the corridor. 'Stay with her, Mrs Early, and see that she does as I have asked.'

The housekeeper nodded.

'Would you like me to send for one of the footmen, just in case…?'

'I don't think it will be necessary, ma'am.'

No, Isabella didn't think the cook would create trouble, either. But then she hadn't thought the woman would steal. 'After Mrs Shepherd has gone, can you please go to the registry office and see about engaging a new cook?'

Mrs Early nodded again. 'Yes, ma'am.'

'I'll speak to the kitchen maids, explain to them what has happened.' Isabella rubbed her brow. 'We shall dine plainly until there's a new cook. I think they'll cope for a few days. They're competent girls.'

The housekeeper nodded her agreement.

'Thank you, Mrs Early.'

The housekeeper nodded, then stepped back into the bed-chamber and shut the door.

Isabella sighed. She needed to thank the housekeeper with more than words. A bonus, perhaps? A week's leave? She turned away. *I hate this.* To have one's faith in someone destroyed so suddenly, so utterly, to know that one's trust had been misplaced. It made her feel slightly sick.

She had done this to Major Reynolds, only worse.

Would he ever forgive her? *Could* he?

Isabella sighed and rubbed her face with both hands and walked back towards the kitchen.

Chapter Nineteen

Harriet was studying the newspapers. 'A companion,' she said, looking up from the pages. 'It says here that a position is available in Sussex.' Her lip trembled and she blinked away tears.

Mrs Westin smiled kindly upon this new bravery, but Isabella found that two hours of it was as much as she could bear. She sought the solitude of the morning room, sitting at the pianoforte, turning to the beginning of the sonata.

But the music refused to flow. Nicholas's words kept coming back to her—*You lied to me*. The discordance of the notes she produced matched the discordance inside her, the disjointed pain and grief, the incoherence of her thoughts.

After half an hour Isabella gave up. She bowed her head, resting her forehead on the pianoforte, and closed her eyes. *What am I to do?*

A knock on the door jerked her upright. Rufus woke abruptly, scrambling to his feet, shedding the two kittens who had been dozing on his flank.

'Yes?'

'The Duke of Middlebury,' her butler said.

'Julian?' She stood as abruptly as Rufus. 'Here?'

'I took the liberty of showing him to the library, madam.'

'Thank you, Hoban,' She hurried to the door. The butler stood back to let her pass. 'Fetch up a bottle of the best claret, please.'

Julian was standing by the window in the library, as Nicholas had done. He turned at her entrance and came towards her, blond and tall, thickening slightly now that he had reached forty, and engulfed her in a hug.

Isabella clung to him. *I am not going to cry.*

Julian released her. He looked down at her, smiling. 'I had thought you'd be in Hyde Park, showing off that phaeton of yours.'

'Not today.' Nor yesterday either. She hadn't driven out since—

Firmly she pushed thoughts of Nicholas away. 'Come,' she said, taking hold of his hand and drawing him to the sofa. 'Sit. Tell me how Marianne and the children are.'

Julian sat down beside her, sinking back into the cushions and stretching his legs out with a sigh. 'They're well.' He rolled his head sideways on the green brocade and looked towards the door as it opened. At the sight of the butler bearing a tray with a bottle and two glasses, he straightened slightly. 'Claret?'

'Of course.'

Julian examined the bottle and poured with careful reverence.

'I didn't know you were coming to town,' Isabella said, as her brother took a first, savouring mouthful. His eyebrows rose in silent appreciation of the claret. 'How long shall you be here?'

'Just tonight,' Julian said, lowering his glass. 'I've put up at Grillon's.'

'Grillon's? But you can stay here—' Abruptly she remembered that she had no cook. And that she had a secret guest upstairs.

'You'll be out anyway, if I know you. What is it tonight?' His voice held a teasing note. 'A masked ball? The opera?'

'Nothing,' Isabella said, looking down at the glass in her hand. 'I…I'm rather tired. I shall be staying in tonight.'

Julian said nothing. She glanced up to find his eyes on her face.

Isabella forced a smile. 'Are you here on business?'

'No,' he said. 'I came to town because of you.'

'Me,' she said blankly. 'Oh, about the letter I sent you!' Hope rose sharply inside her. Here was a solution for Harriet. 'You have a vacant living?'

Her brother shook his head.

'Oh.' Isabella tried not to show her disappointment. She bit her lip and looked down at the wine glass again.

Julian laid his arm along the back of the sofa. His hand almost touched her shoulder. 'I came because a number of people have mentioned your name in connection with a Major Reynolds.'

Isabella's head jerked up. The wine slopped in her glass, almost spilling.

'In more than ten years I've not known you to show interest in any man, let alone make one your beau.' Julian's expression was serious, but his eyes were smiling. 'I would like to meet this Major Reynolds for myself.'

'He has left town.' *Because of me.*

'Ah.' The smile faded from her brother's eyes. 'A shame. I had hoped to make his acquaintance.'

Isabella bit her lip again. She looked down at the dark wine. 'Tell me about him.'

Her gaze jerked to his. 'About Nicholas?'

Julian's eyebrows rose slightly. His expression sharpened with interest. Too late, Isabella realised what that slip of the tongue told her brother. *Yes, I call him by his Christian name.* Faint heat flushed her face.

On the heels of that first realisation, came a second. *If I speak of Nicholas, I will cry.* She prevaricated. 'What do you know of him?'

'Major Reynolds?' Julian swirled the wine in his glass. He looked at her a moment and then seemed to come to a decision. He put the wine glass down. 'You're not in the habit of indulging in flirtations, so when I heard about this man I was curious. Very curious.' He shrugged slightly. 'So I asked a few people about him.'

Isabella moistened her lips. 'You did?'

Her brother nodded.

'What did they say?' she asked, clutching the stem of her glass more tightly.

'Everyone I spoke to thought highly of him. He was respected by the men he commanded, and by the men who commanded him. Respected and liked.'

Isabella relaxed her grip on the glass. 'Yes,' she said. 'He is a…a good man.' *The best of men.*

'I also heard that he would be a colonel, if he hadn't chosen to sell his commission.'

'I didn't know that,' she said, surprised.

Her brother's fingers tapped on the back of the sofa. He was frowning now. 'He turned down a colonelcy—which is not something most men would do.' The frown deepened. 'War can do things to a man, can unbalance—'

'Nicholas is not unbalanced,' Isabella said firmly. 'He left the military because he had had enough of death. He wants children. He wants a family.'

Her brother's fingers stilled their tapping. He observed her face for a long moment and then asked softly, 'And are those things that you want?'

Isabella flushed. 'I—' *Yes.* But she couldn't utter the word. Her throat had closed. Tears threatened. She swallowed and held tightly to her composure. *I am not Harriet. I am not going to cry.*

Julian waited for her to answer. When she didn't, he continued. 'He has a reputation for fairness, your Major, and a reputation for getting things done. A very competent man, by all accounts.'

Isabella nodded. Very competent. She'd witnessed that. And then she frowned slightly. How *had* Nicholas discovered that she was sheltering Harriet?

'So, what I want to know is: is he worthy of you?'

Isabella swallowed again. 'He is…the best of men.' Her voice was only slightly unsteady.

Julian surveyed her thoughtfully. One of his fingers moved, *tap tap,* on the back of the couch. 'May I ask what your intentions are with this Major? Your name has been…rather closely linked with his.' There was no censure in his voice, in his expression. Instead she saw his concern, heard how much he cared for her. *He loves me. He's worried about me.*

'My intentions—' Her voice broke. Hastily she averted her face. She put down her wine glass with a shaking hand. *Don't let me cry in front of him.*

'Bella,' Julian said softly. His hand was on her shoulder, warm and comforting. 'Is everything all right?'

She squeezed her eyes shut. *No. No, it's not.*

Julian shifted on the sofa. His arm came around her. 'Bella,' he said again.

The composure she had held on to so tightly fractured into tiny pieces. She began to cry, and, as she had feared, she couldn't stop. There was too much pain, too much grief.

'Hush,' Julian said, holding her, one hand smoothing her hair as the sobs tore in her chest, endless. 'Hush.'

The storm of grief passed finally, leaving her limp. Julian didn't release her. She leaned against him, her face pressed against his waistcoat. Tears seeped from beneath her eyelids. 'I love him,' she whispered. 'And he…and he—' *He hates me.*

Julian's hand, stroking warm, comforting circles on her back, stilled. She felt him stiffen. 'Has he done anything to you? Has he—?'

'It was me,' she said, into his waistcoat. 'I was the one who did something wrong. I…I lied to him.'

'You? Lied to him?' But Julian didn't push her away; instead his arm tightened around her shoulders. His hand resumed its slow, stroking circles. 'I've never known you to lie, Bella. You must have had good reason.'

Isabella sighed. The sound was ragged, almost hiccupping. 'I didn't mean to, but everything…it all…' She paused and inhaled a shaky breath. 'It started in Stony Stratford, when I was on my way back from visiting you.'

She told him the whole story: finding Harriet, her slip of the tongue in front of Sarah Faraday, the attempt she'd made to stop the ridicule, her growing friendship with Nicholas. She left out only the kisses. Everything else—the lies, the little deceits—she recounted in a halting voice. Julian listened silently.

'I don't know what to do,' she said, at the end of her recitation. 'Nicholas has left town. I don't know if he'll come back. He was so *angry*—' Tears threatened again. She bit her lip, holding them back.

'If Major Reynolds truly loves you—' Julian's voice was low and serious '—he'll come back.'

Isabella gulped a breath. 'You think so?'

If he loves me.

'Yes.' Julian stopped rubbing her back. He groped in his pocket and handed her a linen handkerchief.

Isabella blew her nose. 'I'm sorry,' she said into his waistcoat. 'I didn't mean to cry.'

Julian tightened his arm around her. 'I haven't seen you cry since you were a child. Not like that.'

'No.'

They were silent a long moment, and then Julian said, 'He means a lot to you, this Major Reynolds.'

'Yes.' *He means everything.* Isabella straightened and sat up. She wiped her face. 'Would you like to meet Harriet?'

Julian reached for his wine glass again. 'Yes.' He didn't drink, though. 'You did the right thing, helping her. If Felicity was ever in such straits—' His mouth tightened.

But his daughter never would be in such straits. She had parents who loved her, whereas Harriet did not.

Isabella sighed. 'Yes, it was the right thing. But I did everything wrong after that.'

Julian didn't deny it. His mouth twisted in a wry grimace. He tilted the glass and swallowed a mouthful of claret.

Isabella reached for her own wine glass.

'Should I take her home with me? A companion for Felicity? They're the same age, you said.'

Isabella paused, glass in hand. For a moment she felt lighter, as if a weight had lifted from her shoulders, then the weight settled again. She shook her head. 'Thank you, but it's best if Harriet remains here. The fewer people who know, the easier it will be to keep this a secret.'

If the *ton* found out—

Isabella sipped her wine slowly. Nicholas's parting words echoed clearly in her head: *You named me for an ogre, and then made a pet of me.*

The *ton* would think that too. She could see it in her mind's eye: the sly amusement, the laughing whispers, the ridicule.

Her hand tightened on the glass. *I will not let that happen again. Not to Nicholas. Not ever.*

Julian stayed to eat dinner with them, a fricassee of rabbit and onions and a raised giblet pie. With a seventeen-year-old daughter of his own, he managed—with no apparent effort— to put Harriet at ease. After they had drunk tea together in the drawing room and discussed in detail the appetite and sleeping habits of his youngest son, three-month-old William, he took his leave. 'I shan't see you again, Bella,' he said cheerfully. 'I'm off early tomorrow morning.'

He bowed to Harriet and to Mrs Westin. Mrs Westin bade

him a polite farewell and forbore to comment on his travelling on the Sabbath.

Isabella accompanied her brother to the door. 'I don't like this responsibility you've taken upon yourself,' Julian said. The cheerfulness was gone. His face was serious.

'You don't like Harriet?'

'No, not that. What I meant was…' He frowned. 'You've taken trouble upon your shoulders, and I can't see how it will turn out.'

Neither can I.

'If you need help, you must tell me. Promise?'

'I promise.'

Julian continued to frown. 'If this Major of yours is still angry when he gets back to town, if he's…difficult, I'll come at once.'

If he wants revenge, you mean. If he tries to punish me. She remembered the moment in Hyde Park when Nicholas had asked after Harriet's benefactress, the expression on his face—implacable, hard, cold—and repressed a shiver. 'Don't worry.'

'Promise me,' Julian said again.

Isabella bit her lip, looking at him. He was as tall as Nicholas, broader, but older too. *Nicholas is more dangerous than Julian.* If it came to a duel—

'Promise me,' Julian repeated, and his expression was as implacable as Nicholas's had been.

Isabella sighed. 'All right, I promise. But he won't be difficult. He's not that kind of man.' *I think. I hope.* And if she was wrong…well, she had earned whatever punishment Nicholas chose.

Julian wished aloud that he had a vacant living to bestow on Mr Fernyhough, kissed her cheek and departed.

Sunday dawned cloudy and rather colder than they had been used to. Isabella accompanied her cousin to church. She sat in the pew, her hands clasped, her thoughts turned inwards. The sermon flowed around her, words and fragments of sentences drifting and twisting in her head, making no sense. When the service was over, she followed her cousin outside and stood blinking in the grey daylight, with no memory of what the sermon had been about.

Harriet had been busy while they were away. She presented Isabella with a sheet of paper.

'What's this?' Isabella read the first two items on the list.

Invalid's companion.

Nursemaid.

She glanced at Harriet. *The Lord helps those who help themselves*, Mrs Westin had told the girl. Clearly Harriet had taken those words to heart. 'Milkmaid?'

Harriet blushed and twisted her hands together. 'I like cows. They look so…so gentle.'

'Have you ever milked one?'

Harriet shook her head.

And probably never touched one, either. Would Harriet think that cows looked gentle when she was close to one? Isabella doubted it. The girl was still wary of Rufus—stretched out now in a strip of sunlight with the two remaining kittens asleep between his front paws—and Rufus was much smaller than a cow.

She read further. 'Seamstress.'

'Yes,' Harriet said. 'I'm good at needlework. I enjoy it.'

That, undeniably, was true. Harriet was neat and quick with a needle. Isabella had lost count of the number of sheets and handkerchiefs the girl had hemmed in the past three weeks—tasks that would have bored Isabella to tears but that Harriet apparently enjoyed.

The girl certainly had the skills to be a seamstress, but… Isabella shook her head. She read the next item—*Trimming hats*—and shook her head again. Yes, Harriet had the skill, and the temperament, too, not to mind being indoors all day, sitting and sewing, but—

Not an easy way to earn a living, bent over a needle and thread.

Lady's maid was the next item on the list. And after that, *Kitchenmaid* and *Housemaid*.

Isabella rejected those careers. She read back up the list again. 'Nursemaid? You have skill with small children?'

Harriet hesitated, and then shook her head. 'But I *like* them, ma'am. They look so small and soft and…and *darling.*'

'Hmmm,' Isabella said, thinking of soiled napkins and the screams of thwarted toddlers. She looked at the first item on the list. It was the most promising. *Invalid's companion.* But such a position would be more arduous than the tasks the girl performed here: reading aloud to Mrs Westin, hemming handkerchiefs and embroidering sweet violets and primroses at the corners. There'd be fetching and carrying, perhaps nursing her employer. *And she's only seventeen, far too young. A child still, not a woman.*

She put down the list and looked at Harriet. The girl looked back at her, anxiously. At least there were no tears in those soft brown eyes. Not yet.

Isabella sighed. *What am I going to do with her?* Harriet had been raised to be a gentlewoman, not a servant. Although that meant nothing in these days of economic crisis; many an indigent gentlewoman eked out an existence as a governess or paid companion, or even a seamstress.

As if Harriet had read her thoughts, she said, 'I didn't put down governess because…' She flushed. 'Because my grandfather didn't think that girls need education.'

Of course he didn't.

Isabella looked down at the list again, reread it. The best solution, of course, was marriage. The girl needed someone to look after her.

I need to find a vacant living for Mr Fernyhough.

And until then…could the girl stay as Mrs Westin's companion? But openly, without any of the secrecy of the past few weeks.

When Nicholas comes back, I will ask him. He deserved a say in Harriet's future. He had cared enough about the girl to want to marry her.

Harriet was still watching her, her expression anxious. Did she think she was in danger of being thrown out?

'Thank you,' Isabella said, folding the sheet of paper. She gave the girl a reassuring smile. 'I shall bear these in mind. But you mustn't worry, my dear. You shall stay with us for as long as is necessary.'

Grateful tears filled the girl's eyes. Her mouth trembled. 'Thank you, ma'am.' She bobbed a curtsy and left the morning room, quietly shutting the door behind her.

Isabella sighed. She looked down at the folded piece of paper in her hand. *Damn you, Nicholas. Where are you?*

Chapter Twenty

Nicholas lay awake, staring up at the ceiling. The small window with its cracked panes of glass was open, letting in fresh air and moonlight and the sound of crickets. It was time to think about Isabella again. He had distance. The distance of days spent doing nothing more than sitting in the sunshine with a tankard in his hand, the distance of evenings spent in the noisy taproom. The distance of not thinking, of not remembering, of not being angry.

Cautiously he allowed himself to remember, pulling out the memories, turning them over in his head, examining them, waiting for the anger to resurface.

It didn't.

Nicholas blew out a breath. He interlaced his fingers above his head and stared up at the elongated square of moonlight on the ceiling. *So what now?*

It was time to make decisions, without the heat of rage clouding his judgement. Time to decide what to do.

So, what were the facts? He laid them out in his mind.

Firstly, she sheltered Harriet.

For that, he could only thank her.

Secondly, she named me for an ogre.

He grimaced at memory of Gussie's ball, the whispers and

the sniggers, the sideways glances, his rage on discovering what he was being called. Ogre.

He waited for fury to resurface. It didn't.

So, Isabella had named him for an ogre. But it hadn't been intentional. She'd said so, and he believed her. Isabella was someone who rescued kittens from streams; she would never deliberately harm anyone. A mistake, then. One that he could forgive.

Thirdly, she lied to me.

That was the most painful memory. Isabella had lied to his face. He could recall the moment, the time and place: late afternoon in Hyde Park, with the sun low in the sky and a breeze lifting the leaves on the trees. He'd sat alongside her in the phaeton and spoken of his intention to find Harriet's benefactress. Isabella had been beautiful. And tense.

I was angry. And she was afraid.

And so she had lied to him.

It was understandable. It was forgivable.

Nicholas sighed.

Isabella had planned to tell him, to reveal her lie. *Nicholas,* she had said. *There's something I must tell you. About Harriet Durham.*

But he had been too furious to listen, too hurt by her deceit of him, too hurt in his pride.

Nicholas grunted. *Idiot.* Isabella had made a mistake, several mistakes, but her intent had never been to harm him.

Everyone makes mistakes. It's part of what makes us human.

And he'd made a mistake, too, calling on her immediately after Mr Cobb's visit, allowing his rage to rule him, accusing Isabella of using him, of amusing herself at his expense.

He could hear her voice in his ears, see the tears shining in her eyes: *Nicholas, you know it wasn't like that.*

And he *had* known, even when he'd thrown the accusation at her. What had grown between them, the friendship,

the laughter, the kisses—that had been genuine, it had been
real, it hadn't been a game.

I think she loves me.

No, he corrected himself. *I think she loved me.*

Now…

Nicholas stared up bleakly at the ceiling. Everyone made
mistakes. He just wished he hadn't made this particular one.

Isabella called at Nicholas's house in Albemarle Street on
Tuesday. He was still out of town.

'Would you like to leave a message, madam?' the butler
asked.

'No,' Isabella said, as she had said yesterday, and as, no
doubt, she would say tomorrow. No messages, no ink on
paper.

She turned away and walked down the steps. Partridge said
nothing. She was wearing her expressionless servant's face.
What did she think of these daily treks to Albemarle Street?

Rufus was easy to read. He didn't care. He lifted his leg
against one of the steps—fortunately the butler had closed
the door—and then pranced ahead of her, sniffing the fence
railings in passing.

When they reached Clarges Street, Isabella's steps slowed.
She halted outside her house. It had begun to feel like a
prison.

Partridge halted too, silent. Rufus sat on the doorstep and
began to scratch himself.

Isabella stared up at the house, at the blank windows. She
didn't want to go inside, to sit with her regrets and her grief,
her helplessness.

I need to face the world again. She needed to *do*. Anything. Something.

Accordingly, at five o'clock, she drove to Hyde Park in her
phaeton. Her appearance caused a slight stir. Had she been

unwell? the solicitous asked, stopping their carriages to greet her.

Isabella smiled and kept her replies vague.

No one enquired whether her disappearance from the ballrooms had anything to do with Major Reynolds's departure from London, but she was certain some of them were thinking it.

Isabella found that she didn't care. The fresh air, the sunlight, the breeze on her face, lifted her spirits.

No more hiding, Isabella told herself when she returned home. She climbed the stairs to her bedchamber. *From now on I face the world.*

She unbuttoned her gloves and pulled them off. 'I shall be going out tonight, Partridge. The Griffiths' ball. I shall wear...the cream slip and the Turkish red robe.' *Red for courage.*

'Very good, ma'am.'

Isabella dined with her cousin and Harriet, and then went upstairs to change her gown. She surveyed herself in the mirror once she was dressed—the cool folds of cream silk falling to her ankles, the rich red robe fastened over her bosom with rosettes of pearls, the long gloves, the satin dancing slippers, the pearl-and-ruby earrings dangling from her earlobes.

She took a deep breath—*courage*—and picked up her reticule and fan. She was ready to face the *ton*.

It was easier than she'd expected, to lock her emotions away and fix a smile on her face. Gussie greeted her with delight as the footman handed her up into the Washburnes' carriage. 'You're better?'

'Yes,' Isabella said, and her smile, at that moment, felt genuine.

'Good,' Gussie said. She reached out and took Isabella's gloved hand and squeezed her fingers slightly.

She has guessed.

Isabella's smile felt suddenly stiff and unnatural. She busied herself with settling her skirts neatly, smoothing the cream silk, the red crepe, so that no creases might form.

Of course Gussie had guessed. Half of London probably had.

But I don't care.

Tonight she was going to enjoy herself. She was going to show London a smiling face. And she would start right now, by laughing at the joke Lucas Washburne was relating.

The Griffiths' ball was one of the larger events of the Season, and the mood of the evening—gay, hectic—caught her up almost as soon as they trod up the stairs to the brightly lit ballroom. She enjoyed it all: the babble of conversation almost drowning out the music, the laughter, the dancing. Particularly the dancing. If people were glancing at her, Isabella chose not to notice, not to care. She was *enjoying* herself.

After a particularly energetic *contredanse*, Isabella retired to the side of the ballroom to drink a glass of cold champagne and fan herself. Gussie and Lucas joined her. Lucas was red-faced and panting. 'I'm too old for this,' he said. 'If you have any compassion, Isabella, you will lend me your fan.'

Isabella laughed and handed it to him. 'Where's yours?' she asked Gussie.

'Lucas stepped on it,' Gussie said, pulling a face. 'And it was made of ivory!'

'Not my night,' Lucas Washburne said ruefully, fanning himself.

Gussie reached out and took his hand.

The glance that they exchanged—loving, amused—made Isabella's throat close. She looked hastily away and swallowed a mouthful of champagne.

The dance floor was empty. Guests milled around the edges, talking and drinking and laughing. At the far end of the ballroom, a man paused beneath the arch of the doorway. His face was in shadow but he had a soldier's bearing, a soldier's way of standing quietly and observing, watching.

He could almost have been Nicholas, except that Nicholas wasn't in town.

Isabella averted her gaze. She took another hasty swallow of champagne. Her pleasure in the evening had evaporated. *I want to go home.*

'Oh,' said Gussie. 'Look!'

Isabella raised her head and followed the direction of her friend's gaze.

The man had stepped into the blaze of light from the crystal chandeliers. He was walking towards them. His hair was brown, his face tanned. A scar was livid across his left cheek.

Nicholas.

Lady Isabella stood tensely, watching him approach. She was dressed in rich cream and deep, flowing red. Pearl-and-ruby earrings hung from her earlobes. A sybaritic outfit, if she hadn't been so pale, so tense.

The musicians struck the opening notes to a new dance as he bowed over her gloved hand. A waltz.

'Where have you been?' Gussie asked.

Nicholas ignored the question. 'May I have this dance, Lady Isabella?'

She seemed to grow even tenser, even paler. She swallowed. Her eyes meeting his were…what? *Scared*, he realised. *She thinks I'm still angry.*

He smiled to reassure her and repeated the question. 'May I have this dance?'

Isabella hesitated. He watched her inhale a shallow breath, watched her swallow again. She nodded.

Nicholas held out his arm. After another hesitation she laid her hand on it.

They walked out onto the dance floor, something they'd done dozens of times before. Tonight it was different. Isabella was a queen in that gown, the cream and the red, the rubies and the pearls, and yet she had shrunk into herself. She was tense, uncertain.

A bow, a curtsy, and her hand was in his, but their dancing was awkward tonight. Isabella's grace, the ease with which they'd matched steps, were gone. *This was a foolish idea.* He should have waited until tomorrow, waited to speak to her alone.

'Isabella,' he said softly.

Her head was bowed. She didn't look up at him.

Words gathered on his tongue. *Isabella, I love you. Isabella, I forgive you. Isabella, I haven't come to punish you, I've come to ask you to marry me.*

Nicholas opened his mouth, looked up and met the gaze of Lady Faraday. She was dressed in a frilled ball gown of jonquil yellow. The yellow made her look sallow, the frills old. Beneath a tall headdress of dyed ostrich feathers her eyes were bright and interested.

Nicholas shut his mouth. He steered himself and Isabella in the opposite direction.

'Nicholas.' Her voice was low, so low he barely heard it.

He bent his head.

'Nicholas, I—' Isabella's voice broke. Her hand shook faintly in his. *She's trying not to cry*, he realised suddenly.

His throat tightened. Something clenched in his chest. He drew her more closely to him and guided her to the edge of the dance floor.

Isabella didn't look up when he halted, releasing her. 'Nicholas,' she said again. He heard tears trembling in her voice, as the ruby-and-pearl drops trembled from her ear-lobes.

'Not now,' he said, placing a hand in the small of her back and guiding her with gentle pressure towards the nearest open door. It was the refreshment room, empty except for a liveried servant replenishing the lemonade.

'Forgive me,' he said, lifting a hand to touch her cheek and then halting the gesture, aware of the servant. 'I didn't mean to—'

'No.' Her voice was low, rushed, barely audible above the strains of the waltz. 'I'm sorry, Nicholas. For everything that happened.'

Behind them, the servant bustled, collecting used glasses on a tray.

'Nicholas—' She raised her head and looked at him.

Isabella had looked at him like that once before, with tears shining in her eyes. Then he had walked away; now he had to clench his hands to stop from reaching for her.

'It was a mistake. I only ever said it once. Ask Gussie, she was there—'

The servant departed with a full tray of dirty glasses.

Nicholas unclenched his hands. He reached for her, pulling her towards him. 'I don't need to ask Gussie,' he said, speaking the words against her temple. His lips brushed her skin. Her hair was soft against his cheek. 'I believe you.'

She inhaled a quick, shaky breath. He felt her tension, the faint shaking of her body. She was close to tears, close to the humiliation of being seen crying in public. *My fault. I should have waited until tomorrow.*

'Did you come with Gussie?'

'Yes,' she whispered.

'Go get your wrap,' he said. 'I'm taking you home.' He released her, stepping back, away from her. 'I'll tell Gussie.'

Isabella nodded. Her head was bowed, gloved fingertips pressed to her mouth.

Nicholas clenched his hands again. He wanted to take her in his arms, to hold her tightly, as tightly as he could. 'Go,' he said. 'I'll meet you in the vestibule.'

Isabella lifted her head. She looked at him. 'Nicholas…'

Tears, shining in those grey-blue eyes.

Nicholas cleared his throat. 'Go,' he said again, his voice hoarse, and he reached for her, cupping the nape of her neck with one hand, bending his head and kissing her brow—*the smoothness of her skin, its scent*—before turning on his heel and striding out of the refreshment room. A servant stepped back to let him pass, bearing a tray of fresh glasses. The waltz was still playing.

Isabella was waiting for him in the vestibule. She stood pale and silent beside him as a linkboy hailed a hackney. Nicholas took her hand as soon as they were inside. The interior was musty and smelled faintly of onions.

'I apologise,' he said. 'I shouldn't have come tonight. It was…ill judged of me.'

'I thought you were out of town.' Her voice was a whisper. Her fingers lay limply in his hand. 'Your butler said—'

His butler said that she had called three times, asking to speak to him.

Nicholas tightened his grip on her hand. 'I'm sorry. I should have come back sooner.'

'Where were you?' A diffident whisper, as if she had no right to ask him.

'Mastering my temper.' Nicholas stared bleakly across the carriage. Its age, the wear and tear, were invisible in the dark. He could smell it, though. Years of use. 'I must apologise for leaving so abruptly the other day.' He'd been afraid he would say something unforgivable, had in fact come very close to it in his rage, in his hurt pride. 'The things I said to you were—' *Unpardonable, inexcusable.* 'I allowed my anger to rule me. I must beg your forgiveness.'

He was dimly aware of Isabella shaking her head in the darkness—the pale blur of her face, the faint gleam of her earrings.

'I accused you of using me, of finding amusement in our

situation.' An ugly accusation, thrown at her in anger, with even uglier words crowding on his tongue, words that he had held back with his teeth. 'Isabella…' He turned to face her on the narrow seat, gripping her hand tightly. 'Can you ever forgive me?'

Silence filled the carriage. He was acutely aware of its sway, of the rattle of wheels on stone, of the *clop* of the horse's hooves, of Isabella's hand lying limp in his grip. *She's going to say no.*

And then he realised that her head was bent, that her free hand was pressed to her face. 'Isabella?' he said, reaching out to touch her cheek.

She was weeping.

'Isabella,' he said again, softly. 'What is it? Please tell me.'

Silence again, and the swaying of the carriage, the sound of the wheels, of the horse.

Nicholas released her hand. He moved closer to her on the lumpy seat, putting an arm around her. 'What is it?' he asked again.

She didn't lean into him, as he'd hoped. She stayed stiff and tense, miserable.

'Please,' he said. 'Isabella…tell me.'

For a long moment she was silent, then she inhaled a shuddering breath. 'You're asking me to forgive you, when it's all my *fault*—'

'Ah,' Nicholas said, finally understanding.

'I called you an ogre,' she sobbed.

'Yes,' he said, stroking the nape of her neck lightly with his thumb. 'That you did.'

'I wish I had cut out my tongue before I said such a thing!' She was crying in earnest now.

Nicholas drew her close. He put both his arms around her. 'As I understand it, it was a mistake.'

'And then I *lied* to you.' Isabella was crying so hard that the words were hard to decipher.

Nicholas rested his cheek on her hair. 'That was my fault,' he said. 'You were afraid of me.'

She shook her head against his chest. Her sobs were deep and wrenching.

Nicholas held her, rocking her gently, his face pressed into her hair. *Have you been this miserable, my lady, my goddess?* 'Shh,' he whispered. 'It's all right.'

Her head moved again, a shake, a negation.

'Yes,' he said. 'It's in the past. Forgotten. And one day…' He drew in a deep breath—*Listen to me, Isabella. Hear what I am saying.* 'And one day, we will laugh about this. When we're married.'

She heard. She became very still. Her sobbing shuddered to a halt.

'Isabella,' he said softly, 'will you marry me?'

He held his breath, waiting for her answer, hoping.

For a moment Isabella stayed stiff and tense in his arms, silent, and then the tension seemed to melt from her. She began to weep again.

'Is that a yes?' Nicholas asked.

She nodded against his shoulder.

Nicholas released his breath. He leaned back into the corner of the hackney, drawing her with him. 'Hush,' he said, and laid a kiss on her soft hair.

'I *never* cry,' Isabella sobbed, her face pressed against his waistcoat, her fingers clutching the lapel of his coat.

Nicholas uttered a shaky laugh. 'You are now, my love.'

She drew a deep, shuddering breath and stopped crying. He felt the effort it took her.

Nicholas tightened his grip on her. He glanced out of the window. They were turning into Clarges Street. 'I think…your servants had better not see you like this. We can go to my house. There's no one there. I gave everyone the night off.' *Because I didn't know what you would do when I found you. You might have turned your back on me. You might have hated me.* And he'd wanted no witnesses to the man he would have been if she'd done that.

Isabella nodded. He released her reluctantly as she sat up.

'We've changed our minds,' Nicholas said to the jarvey as the man opened the door. 'Take us to Albemarle Street.'

Isabella was groping in her reticule. Nicholas handed her his own handkerchief. She took it with a quiet word of thanks. In the dark, malodorous carriage he dimly saw her wipe her eyes, blow her nose, fold the handkerchief and place it neatly in her reticule.

Nicholas held out his hand to her. Isabella hesitated a moment, then took it, allowing him to draw her into his embrace again. She relaxed against him, her head leaning on his shoulder. 'I apologise,' she said. 'I do not normally cry.'

Nicholas stroked his fingertips lightly down her upper arm. *Mine.* 'No more apologies,' he said. 'Let us agree to forget what has happened.'

Isabella sighed. He heard the vestige of tears in the sound, shaky. 'Yes.'

They sat in the dark, swaying silence for several minutes, then Isabella said, 'Are you certain? I'm much older than you wanted—'

'I don't care how old you are,' Nicholas said firmly.

'But I'm almost thirty—'

'I don't care if you're almost forty.' He shifted on the seat, tightening his grip, pulling her closer, bending his head to kiss her.

Their lips clung for a moment. *Such a soft mouth.* She tasted of tears.

The hackney jolted to a halt. Nicholas raised his head. Albemarle Street.

Nicholas didn't let go of her hand as he unlocked the front door. He drew her inside. Isabella glanced around her. The house was silent, dark except for a lamp flickering on the

marble-topped table in the entrance hall. A candle stood in a
holder alongside the lamp. Nicholas lit it one-handed.

Ahead, a corridor vanished into darkness. To the right
loomed the staircase. His bedchamber was up there, somewhere. She was suddenly nervous. Did Nicholas think that
they—?

'This way,' he said, and the gentle pressure of his hand
pulled her down the corridor after him.

Isabella relaxed. Not the bedchamber.

Nicholas opened the door to what was clearly a library.
The walls were dark with books, the writing on their spines
gleaming slightly in the candlelight. 'There should be a fire
laid,' he said. 'Ah, yes…' He released her hand with what
seemed like reluctance, touching his knuckles to her cheek
in a light caress. 'Have a seat while I light the fire.'

Isabella chose a sofa. It was upholstered in a soft fabric.
Damask? She rubbed her fingers over it.

He asked me to marry him.

The rush of emotion was so strong she had to close her
eyes, squeezing back tears. *He came back. He forgave me.*
Elation might come tomorrow; tonight there was just wonder.
Wonder, and a relief so intense that it took all her effort not
to cry.

Isabella let out a shaky breath. She opened her eyes and
watched as Nicholas lit the fire. He was in silhouette against
the feeble candlelight. She saw the breadth of his shoulders,
saw the muscled length of his thighs as he crouched, saw his
profile. *The best of men.*

'Brandy?' he asked, straightening and turning to her. 'I
know it's not a lady's drink, but—'

'Yes,' she said. 'Please.'

Nicholas poured them both generous portions. He handed
her a glass and stood looking down at her. Firelight flickered
on his unscarred cheek. 'Drink,' he said.

She did, no sip but a mouthful, and then a second one. The

brandy was cool on her tongue, but warm in her chest. As the warmth spread, the urge to cry faded.

Isabella released a deep breath. She felt herself relax. 'Thank you,' she said. 'I needed that.'

Nicholas sat beside her, so close that their thighs touched. He took her free hand and interlaced his fingers with hers. 'When would you like to marry? I confess that my preference would be for sooner, rather than later.'

Isabella leaned her cheek against his shoulder. 'There is the problem of Harriet.'

Nicholas sighed. 'Ah, yes. Harriet. I had forgotten about her. Is she still with you? Has she not gone to her aunt?'

'Harriet's aunt has emigrated to America.'

'Ah…'

She did not need to elucidate; he understood the problem. Harriet was penniless and homeless. *And my responsibility.*

Nicholas swirled the brandy in his glass. 'What would you suggest?'

'Well…there is a Mr Fernyhough—'

Nicholas uttered a sound that was halfway between a grunt and a laugh. 'Fernyhough,' he said.

'What?'

'His name came up last week. I wondered who he was.'

Isabella told him, while Nicholas's thumb traced light circles on the back of her hand. She explained about the affection that existed between Harriet and Mr Fernyhough, and about Colonel Durham's refusal to countenance such a marriage. 'If Mr Fernyhough were not obligated to the Colonel, he would marry Harriet,' Isabella said. 'But he's supporting a widowed mother and a number of brothers and sisters.'

'I see,' Nicholas said. His voice was thoughtful.

'I asked my brother if he had a vacant living, but he doesn't.' She nestled her cheek on Nicholas's shoulder. Such a nice solid shoulder. 'We must find Mr Fernyhough a new living. A good one.'

'And if he were to get one…?'

'Then the problem of Harriet is solved.'

Nicholas was silent for a moment. When she looked at him she saw that his brow was furrowed in thought. 'I have a feeling there's a vacant living on one of my brother's estates,' he said slowly. 'I wish I could remember…'

'We will find one,' Isabella said, with certainty in her voice. 'Whether your brother has one or not.'

'We will?' Nicholas glanced at her. She saw a glimmer of amusement in his eyes.

'Yes,' she said firmly.

'And how can you be so certain?'

'Because…' She paused, struggling to find the words to describe how she felt, the certainty, the knowledge that everything was going to work out. 'Because a month ago I would have said this was impossible.'

'This?'

'Us.' *Being together like this, loving each other.* 'And last week I would have said it was even more impossible.'

'Ah.' The sound was almost a sigh. 'Yes.' His fingers flexed around hers.

'If *this* can happen—us—then anything is possible. We will find Mr Fernyhough a living.'

Nicholas uttered a soft laugh. 'Yes,' he said. 'I believe we will.' He put down his glass and turned to face her. 'Isabella…' One of his hands still held hers in a tight clasp, the other reached to touch her cheek lightly.

Isabella caught her breath. That half-smile on his mouth, the dark intensity in his eyes, were familiar. *He's going to kiss me.*

He did, dipping his head, touching his lips to the corner of her mouth.

Isabella reached out blindly, trying to find somewhere to put her glass. Nicholas took it without lifting his head. She heard a faint *clunk* as he placed it on the table.

His mouth moved against hers, his tongue touched her lips lightly, a question.

Yes. Isabella kissed him back.

It started slowly, but became something else, something intense, almost urgent. He tasted of brandy, he tasted male, he tasted of Nicholas. Isabella clutched him, her fingers digging into his arms. *Don't leave me ever again.*

She was trembling, panting, when at last they broke apart. Nicholas's eyes glittered blackly. 'Isabella…' His breathing was ragged.

Don't stop. She said it aloud, 'Don't stop.'

His laugh was unsteady. 'Isabella—'

'Not yet,' she begged. 'Please don't stop.' *Don't ever stop.*

Nicholas exhaled a shaky breath. *I should take her home.* But instead of drawing back, he bent his head and kissed Isabella again.

Long minutes passed, minutes when he was oblivious to the world, blind and deaf to everything except pleasure: the pleasure of her mouth, the pleasure of his hands tangling in her golden hair, the softness of her lips, the smoothness of her skin, the tiny sigh she uttered as he kissed her throat, her fingers clutching his coat, the spiralling pleasure of his arousal—

Stop this. Now.

Nicholas drew back, releasing her. He stood abruptly and walked to the fireplace. He stirred the fire with the poker, added another log of wood, and tried to gather his control, tried to drag enough air into his lungs that he could breathe properly again.

When he had regained some semblance of control he turned back to Isabella. She was sitting on the sofa, watching him, her eyes dark in the firelight. Her throat was pale and smooth where he'd kissed it, tasting her skin.

As he watched, she shivered.

'Cold?'

'A little.'

Nicholas held out his hand to her and she came, rising to her feet, walking towards him. He took her hand firmly. *Mine.* 'Here,' he said. 'Take this armchair.'

But Isabella preferred to sit on the rug before the fireplace, gypsy-like, with her legs crossed under her. Nicholas sat at an angle to her, his legs stretched out, leaning against the leather arm of the chair, holding her hand, watching the firelight cast shadows over her face, the smooth, pale skin of the throat, the hollow of her collar bone.

The earrings swayed gently from her earlobes, ruby and pearl, barbaric in the firelight. He reached out with a finger and touched one.

She glanced at him and smiled. 'You like them?'

Nicholas nodded. He liked the rosettes of pearls fastening the robe across her bosom even more. They gleamed against the darkness of the red. *Unfasten me*, they begged.

He curled his fingers into his palm and tried to ignore the rosettes. *I should take her home now.* But there was deep contentment in sitting with Isabella like this, in quiet closeness, in firelight and shadows. He searched for a topic of conversation, something that would take his mind away from those glinting pearls on her gown. 'Have you found a home for the last kitten?'

'I'm keeping her,' Isabella said. 'She purrs whenever I pick her up. I can't give her away.'

'What will you name her?' What had she named the black one? Ah, that was it: Boots. 'How about Puss?'

Isabella grinned at him. 'I thought of that. But no.'

The most beautiful thing about her face, Nicholas decided, was the crookedness of her lower teeth. Without that she would have been too perfect, untouchable; with it she was—

The shaft of desire was intense. The sense of possession was equally fierce. He tightened his grip on her hand. *Mine.* 'What then?' he asked.

'Something beginning with M.' Isabella touched her fingers to her forehead. 'She has an M, right here.'

Nicholas thought. 'Martha.'

'No,' Isabella said, showing her teeth again in another grin.

'Mary. Mabel.' If she grinned at him again he was going to have to kiss her. He focused his gaze on the fireplace. 'Er…Minerva.'

'Minerva!'

'I have an aunt called that,' Nicholas said, risking a glance at Isabella. She was still grinning. He swallowed and looked away again. 'How about…Medusa?'

Isabella laughed.

The sound drew his head around. He couldn't *not* look at her. And having looked at her, he couldn't not lean towards her and kiss her.

They kissed for long minutes—*heat, pleasure*—until the pain of arousal made Nicholas draw back. 'Isabella…' He was trembling. *I have to take you home now.* He turned his face away from her and dragged air into his lungs.

'Don't stop,' she said. Her fingers touched the back of his hand, a tentative gesture.

His laugh was unsteady. 'I have to.'

'No,' she said. 'Nicholas, please don't stop.'

The tone of her voice registered: low, as breathless as he was, and oddly serious. He turned his head and looked at her. 'What?' he said.

'Please, Nicholas,' she said in that same quiet, serious tone. 'Don't stop.'

'Isabella—' He halted. She knew what she was asking. He saw the knowledge on her face.

Nicholas cleared his throat. 'Why?'

Was she giving herself to him as an act of penance? He tensed, ready to refuse.

Isabella removed her fingers from the back of his hand.

'Because I...I want you.' He saw embarrassment on her face, and honesty. 'I want all of you.'

I want all of you too.

Nicholas released the breath he'd been holding. 'Do you know what you're asking?'

She looked at him seriously. 'Yes, I do.'

He studied her face, and believed her. *I should refuse. She deserves better than this.* He thought of wide beds, of clean white linen.

'Please, Nicholas.'

And so he reached for her, knowing that this time he wouldn't stop. He kissed her mouth, her throat, the hollow of her collar bone, and then he undid the rosettes of pearl and the robe fell from her shoulders.

The minutes passed slowly, with low murmurs and soft whispers, as they unfastened each other's clothing and laid it aside—his neckcloth, his waistcoat, the linen shirt, her slip, the half-stays, the thin chemise. Finally she lay naked in the firelight. Nicholas looked at her in wonder. She was Venus, pale and golden. His hand trembled as he touched her, skimming over that smooth skin. *Like warm silk.* And then he bent his head and kissed her, tasting her mouth again, and then that firelit skin.

He touched her with his fingers, with his mouth, learning her, worshipping her: the weight of her breasts as he held them cupped in his hands, the soft gasp she uttered when he took those rosy nipples in his mouth, the way the muscles tensed beneath his hand as he stroked down her belly, the dip of her waist, the rich curve of her hip.

Arousal flushed her skin. She was quivering, trembling. 'Nicholas, take off your breeches.' Her hand was at his waist, her fingers trying to find the buttons.

'Not yet,' he said, capturing her hand, kissing the palm, placing it above her head. He bent to kiss her breasts again, her belly. The scent of her arousal made him pause, struggling for control. He squeezed his eyes shut—*not yet*—and then opened them, seeing pale skin gleaming in the firelight, the curve of her hip, the golden curls at the junction of her thighs. 'Not yet,' he said again, and then he slid his hand down her inner thigh.

Isabella caught her breath. She trembled.

'Not yet,' he said again, whispering the words, sliding his hand back up the smooth, silken skin of her thigh.

He explored with his fingers, stroking, watching as arousal heated her skin, feeling the urgency build in her, in her heartbeat, listening to her breathing become fast, become ragged. She arched against his hand. 'Nicholas.'

He lowered his head, smelling her scent. The muscles clenched in his groin, in his chest, and when she broke, pleasure shuddering through her, he almost broke too.

He turned, rising on his elbow, reaching for her, holding her tightly. Isabella clung to him, her face buried in his shoulder. Her lips were parted. He felt her breath against his bare skin, felt the tremors rack her body.

Her breathing steadied. 'Nicholas…' She sounded dazed. 'Nicholas, I…' She swallowed. Her voice was steadier, firmer, 'Nicholas, I think you should take off your breeches *right now.*'

He laughed, a shaky sound, and released her and stood, aware that she was watching as he stripped off his remaining clothing. When he was finished he looked at her, knowing she'd never seen a naked man before. Her eyes were wide.

'Don't be afraid.'

Isabella swallowed. 'May I…?' She reached hesitantly to touch him.

He captured her hand. 'Later.' When his control wasn't so precarious.

He lay down beside her, stretching his body alongside hers, holding her gaze. Her hair lay tumbled, a golden spill across the rug. The ruby-and-pearl earrings gleamed at her ears, barbaric, sybaritic.

'I'll try not to make it hurt,' he said. 'But the first time—'

'I know,' Isabella whispered, touching his cheek with a fingertip. 'Don't worry about it.'

The words made him pause. 'You know?'

'Parlour gossip.' Her cheeks coloured slightly.

Nicholas uttered a laugh. He bent his head to kiss her, brushing his lips lightly over her temple. 'Parlour gossip? You discuss lovemaking with your friends?'

'Not now.' Her breath hitched as he bit her earlobe gently. 'My first Season. There was some curiosity among some of the girls.'

He laughed softly, and kissed his way down her jaw until he found her lips again. He deepened the kiss, losing himself in the taste of her mouth, stroking a hand down her body, pulling her close, fire-warmed skin to fire-warmed skin, and then he raised himself above her, in the darkness, in the firelight. *Take it slowly.*

His control held, barely, as he slid inside her. There was a moment when Isabella tensed, when he held himself motionless, panting, unable to speak, unable to ask if he was hurting her, and then she relaxed and her body opened to him.

Nicholas sank inside her, into heat, into pleasure. A groan rose in his throat. He bowed his head and squeezed his eyes shut. *Control.* He tried to find the words to speak. 'Isabella…is it all right?'

'Yes.' A single, breathless word.

Nicholas raised his head. He stared at her, at the dark eyes reflecting the firelight, at the flushed cheeks and the soft, parted lips.

Mine.

And then his control broke. His world narrowed to this moment, to this woman, to this fire-lit rug, to the movement of their bodies together, to her hips lifting, matching his rhythm. Pleasure spiralled inside him, tighter and tighter, so tight it almost hurt—

His climax, when it came, rode a knife-edge between pleasure and pain. It left him dazed and breathless, trembling. *So this is what it's like when you love someone.*

He held Isabella close as their breathing steadied. He was aware of his heartbeat slowing, of sweat cooling on his skin, of the scent of their lovemaking. He pressed his face into her hair and inhaled deeply. *Mine.*

'I hadn't realised it was…that good,' Isabella said against his shoulder.

Neither had I.

She pulled back from him slightly and looked at him. Her mouth was soft and smiling. She lifted her hand and touched his scarred cheek with light fingertips. 'I love you, Nicholas.'

'I love you too.'

'I never thought it would happen.'

'Neither did I.'

Her fingers traced the ridges of scar tissue across his cheek. 'Lucky,' she said quietly.

He smiled at her. 'The luckiest man in England.'

He saw the shine of tears in her eyes before her arms came around his neck. She clung to him, her face pressed against his shoulder. Nicholas held her tightly. *Mine.*

He listened to their breathing, to their heartbeats, to the sound of the logs shifting in the fire. *I don't want to let her go. Ever.*

'When can we do that again?' Isabella asked, her voice slightly muffled against his shoulder.

Nicholas laughed, a joyful sound, and tightened his grip on her. 'Every day, when we're married.'

For a moment he imagined the future, imagined taking Isabella home to Elmwood, imagined living there with her, imagined the Jacobean manse echoing with the sound of children's voices. The rush of emotion was sudden and intense. His throat tightened.

Nicholas closed his eyes. He listened to the ticking of the

bracket clock on the mantelpiece for several minutes, delighting in Isabella's closeness, her warmth, her softness, before sighing and releasing his hold on her. 'I have to get you home. Your servants will be wondering where you are.' *And mine may return soon.*

He sat up.

Isabella sat up too. He let his eyes feast on her for a moment. She was beautiful, dressed in nothing but shadows and firelight, with the ruby-and-pearl earrings glinting like barbaric pendants at her earlobes and her wheat-gold hair tumbling in long coils over her shoulders. A goddess. *My goddess.*

'Botticelli's *Venus*,' he said aloud.

'What?'

'You look like Botticelli's *Venus*.' *Rising naked from the sea.*

Isabella pulled a face. 'I look like a Dresden china milkmaid.'

The comment, the unexpected accuracy of it, surprised a laugh from him. The golden hair, the milk-white skin, the rosy cheeks…she was absolutely correct. 'You don't like your colouring?'

'I would much rather be brunette,' Isabella said frankly.

'But if you were brunette,' Nicholas said, smiling, 'then you could not be Botticelli's *Venus*.' *My Venus.*

She made a sound of amusement. 'True.'

Nicholas pushed to his feet. He held out his hand. 'Let me get you home.'

Chapter Twenty-One

On his way to Clarges Street the next afternoon, Nicholas passed Reynolds House. To his surprise, the knocker was on the door. Had Gerald returned to London?

On impulse he ran up the steps. His hand was still on the knocker when the door opened. Hampton, his brother's butler, and his father's butler before that, favoured him with the slightest of smiles and gravely bade him enter.

'Is my brother in?'

'In the library, Mister Nicholas,' the butler said, relieving him of his hat and gloves.

'No need to announce me.' Nicholas strode down the hallway. His mood was buoyant. Isabella was right: the impossible was possible. If Gerald didn't have a vacant living at his disposal, someone else would. The problem of Harriet would be solved. It was only a matter of time.

He tapped once on the door to the library and pushed it open.

Gerald looked up from the newspaper he was reading. His heavily jowled face seemed to tighten. 'Nicholas. I thought you were out of town.'

And you wish I still was, Nicholas thought wryly. 'I returned yesterday,' he said, closing the door. 'And you?'

'Two days ago.' Gerald folded the newspaper, a brisk, irritated rustle of sound. 'What do you want?'

'I came to ask a favour of you.'

Gerald uttered a bark of laughter, a humourless sound. *'You?'* he said, giving the word an almost bitter inflection. 'Ask a favour of *me*?'

Nicholas stood silently for a moment, looking at Gerald, seeing the signs of anger: the pinched mouth, the flush of colour rising in his brother's cheeks. 'I'll come back later,' he said, and turned to leave.

'No,' his brother said, in a flat voice. 'Ask me now. I want to hear this.'

Nicholas turned back to face him. 'Very well,' he said mildly.

Gerald had been prepared for argument, his mouth already open. He sat for a moment in surprise, bristling, and then closed his mouth.

Nicholas walked over to an armchair and sat. For a moment there was silence, broken only by the ticking of the clock on the mantelpiece. Was Gerald going to offer him something to drink?

Gerald folded his arms across his chest. 'Well?' he asked. The word was short and pugnacious.

No drink, Nicholas thought wryly.

'What is this favour?'

Nicholas's thoughts strayed briefly to Isabella. Some of his optimism returned. 'I have a request,' he said. 'I don't know whether you'll be able to grant it or not.'

His brother grunted.

Nicholas gave a brief account of Harriet Durham's predicament, carefully avoiding identifying Isabella as the girl's benefactress. His pity for Harriet returned as he spoke. It was a dreadful fate she had found for herself: to be without family, with no means of supporting herself and with her reputation gone. He introduced Mr Fernyhough's existence, and explained the man's dilemma. 'If Mr Fernyhough were to receive another preferment, then he would be in a position to marry Harriet Durham.'

'A jilt!' Gerald said. 'What man would want to marry her?'

'Mr Fernyhough, apparently. If he were not indebted to Colonel Durham.'

Gerald sniffed.

Nicholas leaned back in the armchair. 'So that's the favour I am asking. If you have a vacant living, would you consider conferring it on Mr Fernyhough?'

Gerald's mouth was a thin line. One of his fingers flicked the arm of his chair, a sharp, angry sound: *tap tap tap*. 'Why do you care about this girl? She made a fool of you!'

'I feel some responsibility for her,' Nicholas said, mildly. 'She was to be my wife.'

Gerald sniffed again.

'I would like to have her future assured as soon as possible.' Nicholas eyed his brother—*should I tell him now?*—and came to a decision. 'I'm getting married.'

'You are?' The tapping finger stilled.

'Yes,' Nicholas said. 'Isabella Knox has agreed to marry me.' The emotions of last night—the joy, the exhilaration, the wonder—returned. He discovered he was grinning like a fool.

'Isabella Knox? You?'

'Yes,' Nicholas said, his grin widening.

Gerald didn't congratulate him; instead, he sat silently. His face seemed to swell, the flush on his cheeks to darken. Rage.

Nicholas's grin faded. 'Gerald?'

'I have a vacant living,' his brother said, in a voice that was thick and almost unrecognisable. 'But if you think I'll give it to your Mr Fernyhough, you are vastly mistaken.'

Nicholas stared at him blankly. 'Gerald? Why—'

'Why?' Gerald heaved himself out of his chair. 'Because it's what you deserve, you son of a bitch.' His hands clenched into fists. 'Don't ever ask a favour of me again!'

Nicholas stood slowly. 'Gerald—'

'Get out of my house!'

Nicholas looked at his brother's face, congested with anger, and silently obeyed. He shut the door behind him and stood for a moment in the hallway. What had just happened?

He walked slowly back to the vestibule. The butler met him with his hat and gloves.

'Lord Reynolds is not in the best of moods today,' Hampton remarked in a voice that was utterly expressionless.

'No,' said Nicholas. He accepted his hat and stood holding it, staring back down the hallway. What the hell had just happened?

'Master Charles has decided to join the army,' Hampton said, in that same, toneless voice. 'The Rifle Brigade.'

'Ah,' Nicholas said. Understanding dawned. He felt a brief flare of rage. *He thinks I talked Charlie into it. He thinks I broke my word.*

Nicholas took a step towards the library, halted, and turned back to the butler. 'I'll come back later,' he said.

'Very good, sir,' Hampton said, bowing. He opened the door. A blustery wind gusted in.

Nicholas walked slowly down the steps. He stood for a moment on the street, turning the hat over in his hands, frowning. *Gerald thinks I broke my word.* He glanced up at Reynolds House, at the flat, grey stone, the blank windows, feeling oddly disturbed.

Later. He gave himself a shake. He'd deal with Gerald later. Now…now he was late to see Isabella.

His grimness stayed with him until he turned into Clarges Street, but with her house in sight it was impossible not to feel the lightness again, the sense of joy. *She is mine. She will be my wife.* And that word—wife—encompassed so many things: the person he would live his life with, would talk and laugh with, would make love to and sleep beside. The person he would raise a family with. The person he belonged to. *I belong to her, as she belongs to me.*

Wonder filled him. How had this come to be? That he belonged to Isabella Knox, and she to him?

Nicholas paused in front of Isabella's house. He recalled her words the evening they had met: *I am an eccentric.* He shook his head in disagreement as he climbed the shallow stone steps to the door. Isabella was different from other ladies of the *ton*, but she was not eccentric; she was herself.

Now, if she took to dressing Rufus in clothing and letting him dine at the table—

He swallowed a laugh and plied the knocker to the door.

The butler bowed him in, took his hat and gloves, and told him he was expected. Nicholas trod up the stairs behind a footman with a light heart.

The footman opened the door to the morning room. Isabella stood at the window, bathed in sunlight. She turned to face him. The smile in her eyes—*for me alone*—made him breathless. She came towards him with her hand outstretched. He took it as the footman closed the door, drew her to him, embraced her. *Mine.*

When one of the kittens began to sharpen its claws on Nicholas's boots, they broke apart laughing. Isabella picked up the kitten. It started to purr immediately, a warm rumble in the palm of her hand. 'See?' She stroked a light finger over the kitten's brow, tracing the letter. 'She needs a name that begins with M.'

'Margaret,' Nicholas said, bending to pat Rufus.

Isabella sat on the yellow damask sofa, holding the purring grey-striped kitten. 'She's not a Margaret.'

Nicholas sat beside her, a smile in his eyes. *How did I ever think of him as hard-faced?* 'Molly,' he suggested.

Isabella considered the name for a moment, and then shook her head. 'One of the maids is called Molly.'

Nicholas leaned closer. 'Marry Me,' he said.

Isabella pursed her lips. 'Marry Me? That doesn't really sound like a name for a kitten.'

Nicholas leaned closer. 'How about, Kiss Me?' he asked softly, in her ear.

'That doesn't begin with M,' Isabella said primly. She glanced sideways at him, trying not to let a smile escape, and failing.

'Doesn't it?' One of his fingertips trailed along her collar bone. It traced a light, tickling path up the side of her neck, and then along her jaw, stopping beneath her mouth. 'Are you certain?'

'Yes,' she whispered, leaning towards him, lifting her mouth, kissing him.

Long, lazy, sunlit minutes passed, minutes when her hand lay curled on his chest above the beating of his heart, minutes when he kissed her, gently, thoroughly, minutes when she kissed him back, trying to tell him without words how much she loved him.

'I think Kiss Me is a good name,' Nicholas said, when at last he raised his head. He put an arm around her, settling her against the warmth of his body, and pressed another kiss lightly on her hair.

'Marry Me is even better,' Isabella said, turning her face into his shoulder. She drank in the sensations—the heat of him through the brown superfine of his coat, the firmness of his shoulder and the strength of the arm that held her, the beating of his heart in the hollow of her palm, the clean male scent of him. Contentment filled her, so pure it almost hurt.

She closed her eyes. *What did I do to deserve this man?*

'When would you like to marry?' Nicholas asked, his fingers idly stroking her hair.

'As soon as the banns have been read.'

A light, timid knock sounded on the door.

Her eyelids jerked open. She pushed herself away from Nicholas.

The knock sounded again.

'Come in,' Isabella said, as Nicholas stood and walked to the window. The grey-striped kitten was mewing in her lap. She placed a hand on it, soothing, shushing, as the door opened.

Harriet stood in the doorway. Her face was pale and her eyes, as she looked from Isabella to Nicholas and back again, were dark and frightened.

'Harriet?' Isabella glanced at Nicholas, standing at the window. His face was utterly expressionless.

'I…I wanted to speak to you.'

'To me?'

'To both of you, ma'am.'

'Then please come in.'

Harriet stepped inside and closed the door. Rufus trotted over to greet her. The girl shrank back.

'Rufus.' Isabella clicked her fingers. *Poor Rufus,* she thought, rubbing the dog's warm, silky head when he came to her. *Nearly a month and she is still afraid of you.* 'What is it, my dear?'

Harriet came no further into the room. She stood with her back pressed to the wood. 'I wish to…' She swallowed. Her gaze flicked to Nicholas and away. An emotion crossed her face, too swiftly for Isabella to identify it. Fear? Revulsion?

'I wish to apologise for…for jilting you, Major Reynolds.' She spoke the words to his shoulder, not his face.

'Thank you, Miss Durham.' Nicholas bowed slightly. His voice was light and pleasant, polite.

'And…' Harriet clasped her hands tightly together and visibly gathered her courage. 'And I wish to marry you.'

Isabella had the impression that everything stood still for a moment: that she stopped breathing, that the clock on the mantelpiece stopped ticking, that the kitten stopped purring, that everything was frozen.

Nicholas stirred slightly, breaking the silence. 'I beg your pardon?'

Harriet lifted her chin. Her hands, gripping each other, were white-knuckled. 'I wish to marry you.'

Nicholas cleared his throat. 'I…ah, I was under the impression that you did *not* wish to marry me, Miss Durham.'

'I have changed my mind.'

Isabella swallowed. She forced herself to inhale, to speak through stiff lips. 'Why, Harriet?'

'I will not be a jilt!' the girl burst out. Her face was flushed now, and tears stood in her eyes. 'I want to do my duty! I want…I want to marry Major Reynolds!'

'Harriet…' Isabella tried to speak calmly '…there is a possibility that Mr Fernyhough will find a new preferment. He will be able to marry you—'

'I won't be a jilt,' Harriet said in a low, trembling voice. 'I won't! I will do my duty to my grandfather. I will do my duty to Major Reynolds.'

'But, Harriet—'

'I will marry Major Reynolds!' The girl's voice was almost fierce. 'He asked me, and I *will* marry him!'

There was another endless, echoing moment of frozen silence, while dust motes spun lazily in the sunlight and the kitten purred in her lap, then Nicholas bowed. His voice was utterly expressionless. 'Very well, madam.'

Isabella opened her mouth—*no!*—but no sound came from her throat.

Harriet made a stiff curtsy. She turned, fumbled for the doorknob and almost ran from the room. The *snick* of the door closing was loud in the silence.

'Isabella—'

She looked at Nicholas blindly. Her throat was tight, too tight for breath, too tight for speech.

'I have to,' she heard him say. 'I have to honour my commitment to her.'

Her eyes focused. Nicholas was pale beneath his tan, his skin almost grey. The scar stood out starkly. 'Isabella…' he said again. He walked slowly towards her, placing his feet carefully, as if he too was blinded.

Isabella scooped the kitten from her lap and stood. 'I will talk to her!' she said, as the little creature shook itself on the sofa and squeaked indignantly. 'I will ask her to relinquish her claim on you. I will *beg* that she…that she—' The words stumbled to a halt on her tongue. *I can't do that, and neither can Nicholas.*

'I gave Harriet my word that I would marry her.' His voice was quiet, his expression bleak. 'Isabella, I must honour my word.'

I know.

Isabella bowed her head. She closed her eyes.

Nicholas touched her cheek hesitantly, as if he no longer had any right to. 'Isabella…'

'I love you,' she whispered.

'And I you.' He caught her in a fierce grip, so tight she could barely breathe. For a second she inhaled his male scent, felt the beating of his heart—and then Nicholas released her, thrusting her from him, stepping back. 'I must find Colonel Durham.' His voice was rough and his face, when she looked at it—

Pain.

He swallowed and hesitated, and for a moment she thought he would say something more, then his face tightened and he turned from her and opened the door.

Nicholas walked out without looking back. The door shut behind him quietly.

Chapter Twenty-Two

Isabella sat numbly, while the ormolu clock with its bower of bright flowers quietly ticked away the minutes and the patches of sunlight that came through the windows lengthened and moved across the floor. When the clock struck the hour for the second time, she went in search of Harriet. The girl was in her bedchamber, lying face down on the bed, weeping.

Isabella halted inside the door, listening to Harriet sob. It was impossible to hate the girl. *Barely more than a child, without home or family or money.* The future, viewed through Harriet's eyes, must be terrifying. Nicholas represented security. He was an ogre, but one who would give her a home, who would take care of her.

Isabella released her grip on the door handle. *If I could just beg her—*

But she knew she wouldn't. She couldn't.

'Harriet?'

The girl lifted her head, showing a tear-stained face. 'Ma'am?'

Isabella crossed the room. 'I came to see how you are.'

Harriet wiped her face with a sodden handkerchief and sat up. She sniffed loudly.

Isabella sat on the end of the bed. 'Are you certain this is what you want?'

The girl inhaled a shuddering breath and nodded.

Isabella looked down at the counterpane, tracing the embroidery with a fingertip. Blue flowers, with tiny white hearts.

'I know how it must seem to you, ma'am. I ran away from him and now…' Harriet's voice trembled. 'And now I want to marry him.'

Isabella looked up. 'Major Reynolds will look after you,' she said quietly.

Harriet nodded. Her mouth twisted, as if she was trying to hold back more sobs.

Isabella looked down at the counterpane again. She traced the blue petals of a flower. 'There is the possibility that Mr Fernyhough may receive a new preferment soon. Are you certain you do not wish to wait?' She glanced up at the girl. *How much do you love him?*

Harriet's face was stony and resolute. 'I am certain.'

Isabella bit her lip. Arguments clustered on her tongue. She looked down at the counterpane again, but her gaze was turned inward. The blue flowers were a blur. *If I was in Harriet's position, would I wait in hope, or would I take what I could be certain of now?*

Mr Fernyhough was in no position to offer Harriet anything. He might never be. And if he were, he might choose not to make that offer. Harriet's reputation was ruined. Even marriage to Nicholas would not fully restore it.

Looked at in that light, Harriet's choice was…sensible.

Isabella sighed. 'Very well,' she said. She stood and looked down at the girl. She wanted to feel anger; instead there was merely a numb pity.

'I'm sorry to have been such a nuisance, ma'am.' Harriet's face crumpled. She raised the sodden handkerchief to her eyes.

'You haven't been a nuisance,' Isabella said. She stood for a moment, looking down at the girl, but it was Nicholas's face, grey and bleak, that she saw, not Harriet's. *You have merely ruined his life. And mine.*

She turned and walked across the room, opened the door and shut it behind her. For a long moment she stood in the corridor, utterly motionless. Finally she gave a laugh, a soft sob-like sound. 'Overly dramatic,' she whispered, walking down the corridor with slow footsteps. Her life wasn't ruined. She had lost nothing; her freedom was still hers, her fortune. Many women would envy her that.

Isabella sighed. She started down the staircase. The banister was cool and smooth beneath her hand.

And Nicholas…his life wasn't ruined either. He would have the quiet, passionless marriage he had once wanted. An awkward marriage, probably, at first. But once the children came…

He will be happy.

On Thursday morning Isabella's nightgown was slightly stained with blood. She sat staring at it for a long time.

I should be feeling relief right now. Why then this sense of loss?

Because that bloodstain represented life, it represented children. *His and mine. Ours.*

I want life, Nicholas had said. She could hear his voice in her ears, hear the carriages in Hyde Park, the *clop* of horses' hooves. *I want children. I want to see them grow.*

Isabella clenched the bloodstained fabric in her hand. *I want it too.*

The numbness broke then, and in its place was pain and grief and a sense of loss that was so overwhelming that for a moment she couldn't breathe.

'Don't cry,' she whispered to herself. 'Don't cry.' Because if she shed one tear, then she might never be able to stop.

* * *

Isabella was inspecting linen with Mrs Early—a task that suited her numb weariness—when the butler came upstairs to inform her that Major Reynolds had called and was awaiting her in the library.

'Major Reynolds?' Isabella gripped the sheet tightly.

'Yes, madam.'

Isabella swallowed. 'Very well.' She thrust the sheet at the housekeeper. 'Please continue, Mrs Early.'

Nicholas stood at the window, a dark silhouette against the bright sunlight. His height, the quiet strength of his body, the soldier's carriage, the tilt of his head as he stared out at the street, were so familiar that her throat tightened painfully. 'Nicholas?'

Nicholas turned. 'Isabella.' He swayed slightly, as if he held himself from going to her. His hands flexed, forming fists, and then relaxed. 'Yesterday...' His face was as grey as it had been when she'd last seen him, and, if anything, bleaker. 'Yesterday I forgot... Isabella, if you are pregnant—'

'I'm not.'

He shook his head and took a step towards her. 'You can't know that,' he said fiercely, his hands clenching again. 'Sometimes, the first time is all it takes—'

'My monthly flow started this morning.'

'Oh.' His fists tightened until the knuckles were white, and then the tension seemed to drain out of him. His hands hung limply, but the bleakness seemed to be etched more deeply on his face. He looked terribly, unutterably weary.

Did he want me to be pregnant?

Nicholas turned back to the window. He rubbed a hand over his face. Relief or sorrow? The tightness of his jaw, when he turned again to her, told her. His eyes rested on her face for a long moment. 'I must go,' he said quietly.

'Where?'

'To find Colonel Durham.' His voice was as weary and

bleak as his face. 'I will press for an early date. I think it's…best if we do this as quickly as possible.'

Isabella nodded.

Nicholas walked slowly across the library to where she stood. For a moment he stood, looking at her. He said nothing. His eyes, dark with regret, spoke for him. Then he bowed and turned away.

'Nicholas—'

He halted, half-turning towards her.

Isabella reached for him, gripping his hair, pulling his head down, and placed a kiss on his ruined cheek. The scar tissue was smooth and ridged beneath her lips. 'I will always love you.'

'And I, you.' His arms came around her for a brief second, tight, so tight she couldn't breathe, and then he released her.

Isabella inhaled, breathing in the scent of him, and then allowed his hair to slip through her fingers. She stepped back, fixing the sight of him in her memory. Green eyes. A scarred face.

Nicholas bowed, and then he was gone.

Nicholas checked at Colonel Durham's club, where he was told the Colonel was no longer in London. He then visited his own club, an establishment frequented by military men, where he was greeted as Ogre by his acquaintances and learned nothing new about Colonel Durham's whereabouts. The Colonel was thought to have returned to his home in Sussex.

Nicholas walked back to Albemarle Street. 'Have the curricle brought round in an hour,' he said to his butler as he stepped into the coolness of the entrance hall. 'I'm going out of town.'

He instructed the valet to pack him sufficient clothes for three days, went through his post, and sat down to write a note to Isabella, informing her that Colonel Durham was no longer in town. He folded the sheet of paper and inscribed her name on the front. *Lady Isabella Knox.* His regret, as he wrote those letters, black ink on white paper, was so sharp that he felt it as a physical pain, as if a chasseur's sabre had buried itself in his chest.

Nicholas was reaching for a wafer when he heard voices in the hall. 'Don't bother to announce me,' someone said cheerfully.

A tap sounded on the door, and his nephew strode into the room, grinning. 'Sir! I have something to tell you!'

The eagerness in Charlie's voice, the excitement shining in his eyes, made Nicholas feel tired and elderly. *Was I ever that young? That excited about life?* He pushed the letter away, closed his eyes briefly, and rubbed his brow. 'You have joined the Rifle Brigade,' he said. 'Yes, I know.'

Charlie's grin faltered. 'Aren't you pleased, sir? I thought you would be.'

Nicholas rubbed his forehead again. *I don't care. I don't care about anything.* He sighed tiredly.

'Sir?'

Nicholas lowered his hand. With an effort he mustered a smile and some words of congratulations. Both the words and the smile were stiff and unnatural, but Charlie didn't notice. His grin came back. He pulled up a chair in front of Nicholas's desk and sat, leaning forwards, words tumbling from his mouth as he explained with eager detail his decision to become a soldier. Nicholas watched his face, youthful, alight with enthusiasm, and felt a faint stirring of apprehension. *This could make a man of him, or kill him.*

'Did Mayhew put you up to this?' he asked, into the first pause that was offered.

Charlie looked affronted. 'No one put me up to it! I decided myself.'

Nicholas stroked his cheek with a light finger. 'It's not a game. You know that?'

'Yes, sir,' Charlie said, looking even more affronted. 'I'm not a child, sir.'

A month ago you were a sullen boy. But the young man seated in front of him, meeting his gaze levelly, was an adult. There was no bluster or bravado in his manner, just a quiet resoluteness.

Nicholas nodded, an acknowledgement. He stood and offered Charlie his hand. 'I wish you all the best.'

Charlie grinned. The excitement lit his eyes again. 'Thank you, sir.' His grip was firm.

Nicholas sat again. This time he listened to Charlie's words, asked questions, and gave answers to the questions the boy asked. *No, he's not a boy any more. He's a man.*

'How did you purchase your commission? I understood your pockets were to let.'

Charlie flushed and laughed. 'Oh, that. It was a horse, sir, at the races.' His flush deepened and his expression became half-embarrassed, half-defiant. 'Its name was Ogre's Luck.'

Nicholas grunted a laugh.

Charlie looked relieved. 'You don't mind, sir?'

'Ogre?' Nicholas shook his head. It was a connection he had with Isabella, one that no one knew about. *She named me.* He touched two fingers to his cheek. 'Half of London calls me that now.' But with no malice, no hint of ridicule. It was a nickname, nothing more. 'It's…' He shrugged. 'It doesn't bother me.'

Another ten minutes passed before Charlie stood to leave. 'You must be busy, sir.'

Nicholas looked down at the letter on his desk. He touched it with a fingertip. Busy. 'Yes,' he said.

Charlie took his leave. His steps, as he crossed the study, were brisk and eager. Nicholas watched him, feeling old and very tired.

A thought occurred. 'Charlie?'

His nephew halted, one hand on the door handle. 'Sir?'

'Do me a favour. Tell your father that your decision to join the Rifles was not due to my persuasion.'

Charlie grimaced. 'He's in a foul mood.'

'I know.' *He's afraid for you.*

Charlie nodded, raised his hand in a gesture that was vaguely like a salute, and closed the door behind him. His voice came faintly as he favoured Frye with a cheery salutation.

Nicholas sat for a moment, feeling elderly and drained of energy. Then he reached for the wafer and sealed the note. *Lady Isabella Knox,* his handwriting said. He touched it with a fingertip. The ink was dry. It didn't smear.

He sighed and pushed himself up from the chair. It was time to find Colonel Durham.

Friday passed as Thursday had, with slow monotony. Isabella stayed at home. Hyde Park, with its bustling parade of people and horses and carriages, was not something she felt able to cope with. Nor were the events that the gilded invitation cards on her mantelpiece advertised: the balls, the assemblies, the card parties, the visits to the opera. *I begin to understand what Nicholas means about London.* The noise, the intricate maze of manners, the bright-eyed gossip, the crush of people, were simply too much.

She wanted fresh air and wide open spaces and the time to be alone. Birdsong, not the clatter of carriage wheels and the shouts of street sweepers. *And maybe I will find my serenity again.*

Isabella spent many hours at the pianoforte. The sonata no longer sounded like noise. Her fingers knew the notes, she barely needed to look at the sheets of music. The soft lamentation of the first movement came from beneath her fingertips as mournfully as Beethoven could have wished.

The day dragged to its end, enlivened only by a brief visit from Gussie, ostensibly to bring her daughter to play with the two remaining kittens, but really, Isabella knew, to see how she was.

'A little under the weather. Nothing serious.'

Gussie accepted this with a nod. 'Will you come to the theatre with us tonight?'

All those people. All that noise. 'No,' Isabella said.

Gussie opened her mouth, and then shut it again. She turned her attention to her daughter. 'Gently, Grace.'

When they were gone, Isabella stayed in the morning room, Rufus asleep across her feet and the two kittens curled up in her lap. She stroked their soft fur lightly. 'I shall call you Puss,' she told the grey-striped kitten. She remembered Nicholas's grin as he'd suggested it, the laughter in his eyes. 'Puss and Boots.'

With a sigh she went upstairs to change her gown for dinner. It was a silent meal. Isabella ate slowly, without appetite, trying not to notice as Harriet wept silently into her soup.

The first course was removed and the second brought up from the kitchen. The new cook was equal in skill to Mrs Shepherd. Isabella looked at the basket of pastries and the Rhenish cream without interest.

Harriet sniffed into a handkerchief. Her face was woebegone above the sprigged muslin gown. *She sees herself as the only victim in this, when we are all victims.*

The girl's self-pity was abruptly too much.

'For heaven's sake,' Isabella said sharply. 'Major Reynolds is not the ogre you have painted him! He's a good, honourable man. A kind man. You could do no better than to marry him!'

She halted, aware that both her cousin and Harriet were staring at her. She inhaled a deep shuddering breath, appalled by how close her own tears were, and pushed back her chair and stood. 'Excuse me,' she said, and hurried from the dining room.

Tears and anger rose chokingly in her throat as she climbed the stairs. Isabella wrenched the door to her bedchamber open. 'He is the best of men! Why can't she see past the scar?' She closed the door forcefully. 'He deserves better than—'

She halted suddenly, aware that Partridge was standing in the room, staring at her, aware that there were tears in her eyes and in her voice.

They stood in silence for a moment, looking at each other, and then Partridge spoke. 'Are you all right, Miss Isabella?'

Isabella turned away from her, towards the bed. She scrubbed the back of her hand across her face. 'I…I have a headache, Partridge. I wish to be alone.'

Partridge left quietly.

Partridge returned some time later with Rufus, liberated from the kitchen where he had spent the dinner hours, at her heels. She helped Isabella undress silently—the gown with its row of tiny buttons, the lacings of the corset, the chemise, the silk stockings tied at each knee with a garter.

Isabella pulled on her nightgown. She washed her face and sat in front of the dressing table while Partridge unpinned her hair. She watched the woman's fingers in the mirror, extracting pins, laying them aside. Partridge's face was as bland, as expressionless, as it always was.

How much had the woman guessed? *Most of it, probably.*

Isabella brushed her hair slowly as Partridge tidied away the clothes. What had the woman thought on Tuesday night? *When I came home with my hair tumbled down my back and joy in my heart.* Partridge must know, must have guessed.

Isabella lowered the brush. She fingered the tooled silver back, tracing the crest. 'We will go into the country, Partridge, once…once Miss Durham is no longer with us. I have had enough of London.'

In the mirror she saw Partridge pause and glance at her, and then resume her task.

Isabella sighed. Perhaps Julian would let her have the Dower House, so that she could truly be alone. *Just me and Rufus and the kittens.* And her serenity, if she could find it again.

Someone tapped timidly on the door. Rufus sat up, his ears pricked.

Isabella met Partridge's eyes in the mirror. 'If that is Miss Durham, tell her…tell her that I have the headache and do not wish to be disturbed.'

Partridge nodded and went to open the door.

It was Harriet; she heard the girl's hesitant voice, Partridge's reply. It was a long reply, its tone almost scolding, the words too low to hear.

Isabella put down the hairbrush. *I will have to apologise to Harriet tomorrow.* She rubbed her face and sighed. She looked at Rufus, at the mismatched eyes and the wagging tail, and envied him the simple happiness of his life. And then she remembered the puppy he had been, beaten and bloodied, cringing from her touch, his ribs almost breaking through his skin.

Her throat tightened in memory. 'Come here, boy.' She knelt on the floor and hugged him, warm, so full of life and joy and vigour. 'We'll go into the country. You'll be happier there.' *We will both be happier.*

Chapter Twenty-Three

On Saturday morning, Isabella apologised to Harriet for her sharp words the previous evening. This caused the girl to weep again. 'You've been so kind to me, ma'am,' she sobbed into her handkerchief. 'I don't mean to be a burden.'

'You're not a burden, my dear.'

But Harriet cried bitterly and refused to be comforted.

It took the best part of an hour to convince the girl she was not—as she phrased it—an affliction to Isabella's household.

Finally Isabella felt able to leave. She glanced back at Harriet before closing the door. The girl had a wet handkerchief clutched in her hand and a look of worship in her damp, brown eyes.

Isabella walked down the stairs slowly, with guilt in her heart. *I don't deserve her worship.* Her kindness to Harriet had nothing to do with love; it was the product of pity. *And she is right: I wish her gone.*

The episode did have one positive outcome: Harriet made a valiant effort to control her tears. There was no more weeping at the dinner table. Her misery was silent. She sat, pale faced, and pushed her food around her plate. Isabella watched the girl, and then looked down at her own plate, at the food she had no desire to eat. *Hurry up, Nicholas. End this quickly, please.*

But Sunday brought no messages from him, and nor did Monday. On Tuesday evening, as they were about to retire to bed, a note was delivered by hand. Isabella recognised the writing. She opened it briskly, with fingers that weren't quite steady. Her heart sank as she read the half-dozen lines.

'Your grandfather is away from home,' she said, glancing across at Harriet. 'The servants don't expect him back for another fortnight.'

'Oh,' Harriet said faintly.

Isabella looked down at the letter, at the bold strokes of black ink. The girl's dismay matched her own. *Another fortnight of this?* She cleared her throat. 'Nicholas—Major Reynolds says that he went to Bath, as there was a possibility of your grandfather being there, but he was unable to find him.' She read the final line. *It seems we can do nothing but wait*, Nicholas had written. *I am sorry.*

The following morning Harriet didn't join them for breakfast. To her shame, Isabella was relieved. The meal was more pleasant without the girl's pale, resolute face, her silent misery, the unshed tears in her eyes.

Isabella laid aside her napkin with a sigh.

'Is that all you're eating?'

She looked down at her plate. 'Yes.'

Mrs Westin put down her knife and fork. 'Isabella, I don't mean to pry, but—'

Mrs Early entered the breakfast parlour. Her plump face was flushed, her manner flustered. 'Ma'am,' she said to Isabella, 'Miss Durham isn't in her bedchamber.'

'Not? Have you checked the morning room? The kittens—'

'She left these,' Mrs Early said, laying two letters on the breakfast table. 'One for you, ma'am, and one for Mrs Westin.'

Isabella met her cousin's eyes. She snatched up the letter addressed to her, tore it open, and read swiftly and with a growing sense of shock. *I did not realise how things stood between you and Major Reynolds*, Harriet wrote in a looping, childish hand. Tearstains blotched the ink. *I cannot repay your generosity and your many kindnesses by marrying him.*

Isabella squeezed her eyes shut. *Don't hope*, she told herself. *Not yet*. But already hope was running like quicksilver through her veins, making her heart beat faster and her fingers tremble. If Harriet didn't marry Nicholas, then—

Don't hope, she told herself again fiercely. *Not yet*.

She inhaled a shaky breath and opened her eyes and read further. *I am certain that you and Major Reynolds will be very happy*, Harriet wrote.

How had the girl known? Isabella glanced at her cousin. 'Elinor—?'

'Harriet says that she has borrowed some money from my reticule,' Mrs Westin said in an astonished voice. 'She promises to repay me.' She looked up at Isabella. 'Wherever can she have gone? And why?'

Yes, Isabella seconded. *Why?* There was no need for flight. If Harriet had just *said* something—

But this, apparently, was how Harriet solved her problems: by running away from them.

Isabella pushed up from her chair. 'Mrs Early, who has been waiting on Miss Durham? I wish to speak to her.'

The new housemaid, Molly, had been attending to Harriet's needs. Miss Durham, she said with wide and anxious eyes, had asked her to run some errands for her.

'I posted some letters for her, ma'am,' the housemaid said, pleating her apron nervously between her fingers. 'Several days ago. I didn't know it was wrong.'

'It wasn't wrong,' Isabella said, with a reassuring smile. 'Do you remember the addresses?'

The housemaid shook her head, still looking frightened. 'I don't read that well, ma'am.'

'And the other errand?'

'I bought a ticket for her, on the stage. Had her name put on the waybill. Miss H. Durham. She wrote it down for me.'

'Do you remember where she was going?'

'Chippenham,' the housemaid said. 'I'd never heard of it before.' And then she added helpfully, 'The stage left this morning, quite early. Miss Durham asked me to arrange for a hackney to come. But the jarvey wasn't to knock on the door. She was most particular about that.'

And you didn't wonder why? You didn't think that it was strange?

'Thank you, Molly,' Isabella said, trying to keep her tone even. 'You may go now.'

When the maid had gone, Isabella looked at her cousin. 'Chippenham? Why there?'

'I think I know,' Mrs Westin said, in a quiet, worried voice. She rose and left the room, returning in a few minutes with a newspaper. 'There was a position outside Chippenham, for a lady's companion. I noticed that Harriet had marked it.' But the page with the advertisement was gone.

'We have to find her!' Isabella said, pushing to her feet. 'Dear God, she's far too young—' She pulled the bell rope. 'Have my carriage brought around,' she said to the footman. 'Immediately.'

This is my fault. If anything happens to her—

She halted in the doorway, looking back at her cousin. 'Elinor, did you tell Harriet about...about Major Reynolds and myself?'

'No, my dear,' Mrs Westin said. 'For you have told me nothing yourself.'

Isabella bit her lip, abashed. 'Do you wish to come with me, cousin?'

Mrs Westin shook her head. 'You'll travel faster without me.'

Isabella acknowledged this truth with a nod; Mrs Westin was a poor traveller. She shut the door, picked up her skirts, and ran upstairs. 'Partridge! My carriage dress, quickly!'

Partridge was brisk and silent, but it still took far too long. *My fault. If anything has happened to Harriet—*

Isabella tried to stand still, to not fidget, to not snap at Partridge to fasten the buttons more quickly. How had Harriet found out? *Was I that transparent?*

A thought occurred to her as she fastened her gloves at the wrist. 'Partridge? Did you say anything to Miss Durham about…about Major Reynolds and myself?'

She watched in the mirror as a faint flush rose in Partridge's thin cheeks. 'I may have said something, ma'am,' Partridge said in an extremely neutral tone.

'When?' But she knew—the evening she'd spoken so sharply to Harriet at the dinner table, when the girl had come to her bedchamber and Partridge had turned her away from the door with a low-voiced rebuke.

Isabella bit her lip. *I should reprimand her.* 'Miss Durham has run away,' she said.

Partridge glanced up. Their eyes met in the mirror. Isabella saw how appalled the woman was. 'Ma'am, I didn't mean for—'

'I know.' *You were trying to help me.* Isabella sighed. 'Fetch your cloak, Partridge. We're going after her.'

Nicholas walked slowly up the three steps to his front door. *That was a waste of time.* No one at the Colonel's club knew where the man was. He could be anywhere in the country. Anywhere but Bath.

'These were delivered while you were out, sir.' The butler held out two letters. 'By hand.'

Nicholas looked at them without interest. Gerald, and someone whose handwriting he didn't recognise.

He slit open Gerald's letter with a finger as he walked down the corridor to his study, tearing the paper slightly and unfolding it one-handed as he reached for the brandy decanter. *I'm drinking too much these days.*

He poured himself a glass and read the note, grunting sourly when he reached the end. The living at Nidderdale was his to dispose of, if he wished. *An apology, Gerald?* If it was, it was too late.

Nicholas put Gerald's letter aside and opened the second one, taking slightly more care, managing not to tear it. He raised the brandy glass to his mouth and read the first lines.

> *Nicholas,*
> *I write to you with dreadful news. Harriet has run away again. She has taken the stage to Chippenham—*

Nicholas put the brandy glass down. He read swiftly. 'Frye!' he shouted, striding from the study. 'When was this letter delivered?' He thrust it at the man.

'About two hours ago, sir.'

Two hours. Nicholas reread the final line. *I am departing London immediately and have hopes of catching her by Marlborough*, Isabella had written.

'Have my curricle brought around,' Nicholas said, refolding the letter. 'At once!'

By Hungerford, the stage was a mere hour ahead of the chaise. One of the serving maids at the inn confirmed that Harriet had been aboard. 'Little thing with brown hair?' she said, wiping her hands on her apron. 'Looked as if she'd been crying.' Harriet had purchased a glass of lemonade, but declined the ham sandwiches offered by the establishment.

Isabella glanced up at the sky. Grey clouds were gathering on the horizon. She wrapped her travelling cloak more tightly around herself and climbed back into the carriage.

The rhythm of the carriage wheels wasn't soporific today. Isabella sat tensely, staring out at the countryside. *Too soon to hope*, she repeated in time to the wheels, crushing that emotion in her chest, digging her fingers into her palms. *Too soon.*

So much could still go wrong. Disasters loomed in her mind: Harriet changing her mind again; Nicholas insisting that his obligation to Harriet outweighed his obligation to her.

At Froxfield, they had closed on the stage, and the sky was low and grey. The sun was no longer visible. 'Fifteen minutes?' Isabella asked.

'Yes'm,' the ostler said.

A long blast on a horn sounded, signalling a traveller wanting a change of horses. The ostler touched a grimy hand to his hat. ''Scuse me, ma'am,' he said, and hurried off.

A curricle clattered into the inn yard, its horses streaked with sweat. Isabella's heart leapt. 'Nicholas!'

Nicholas thrust the reins at his groom and jumped down. Isabella scanned his face as he strode across the cobblestones towards her. She had expected anger, or at the very least, grimness; instead, there was something close to a grin on his face. 'I thought I'd have caught up to you before this,' he said, reaching for her hands. His green eyes smiled at her. 'You must have been springing your horses!'

'I have been,' Isabella said, returning the pressure of his fingers. 'We're only fifteen minutes behind them.'

'Do you wish to ride with me?'

Isabella glanced up at the sky, at the lowering clouds, at the rain already misting the horizon. 'Yes.'

She gave orders to her coachman while fresh horses were

harnessed to the curricle, and climbed up into the seat vacated by Nicholas's groom.

The ostler stood away from the horses' heads and deftly caught the coin Nicholas tossed him, the curricle lurched forward, and they were off.

Nicholas kept a sedate pace until they were out of Frox-field, then he let the horses have their heads. Hedgerows and ditches flashed past them. Air scented with the smells of the countryside—grass and cow manure and woodsmoke—tugged at her bonnet. Isabella put a firm hand on it and glanced at Nicholas's profile. His attention was on the horses, one of which showed a tendency to pull to the left. 'Nicholas, I must apologise for allowing Harriet to—'

'Apologise?' he said, a note of surprise in his voice. He glanced at her, a swift flick of his gaze before his attention returned to the horses.

'Yes,' Isabella said. 'It was my fault that she—'

'You have nothing to apologise for,' Nicholas said firmly, feathering the reins as the curricle swept around a bend.

Isabella studied his face. The scar told her nothing. The puckered flesh, the ridges of melted skin, hid his expression. 'You're not angry?'

'Should I be?'

They rounded another bend. A long stretch of road opened before them. A few miles ahead was another coach, a speck in the distance. 'Ah,' Nicholas said. 'Do you think…?'

Isabella held on to her bonnet as Nicholas urged the horses to a stretching, ground-eating gallop. The distant vehicle slowly resolved itself into a large, top-heavy coach, moving with sluggish speed, and then, as they drew closer, into the Bristol stagecoach, piled with luggage and with three mis-erable passengers hunched on the outside seats.

Nicholas drew alongside and shouted at the coachman to stop. The man stared steadfastly ahead, ignoring him.

Nicholas muttered under his breath. The curricle surged

past the swaying coach and swung in front of it. Nicholas slowed his horses to a trot, keeping the curricle firmly in the middle of the road, with no room to pass.

Isabella clutched her bonnet even more tightly as the stagecoach loomed behind them. Noise enveloped her—the thunder of hooves and wheels, the shouted voices of men— and then the stagecoach slowed too.

Nicholas brought his horses to a walk, and then a halt. 'Here,' he said, thrusting the reins at her. 'Hold them.'

Isabella did, twisting in the seat to watch as Nicholas strode back to the coach. He overrode the coachman's indignant voice. 'Looking for a runaway,' he said curtly, and wrenched open the heavy door.

The reins tugged in her hand as one of the post horses pulled at its bit. Isabella glanced at it, and then back at the stagecoach. Nicholas was closing the door. His expression was frowning. He spoke to the driver. Isabella couldn't hear the words, but from his gestures he was describing Harriet.

The coachman shook his head. His answer was brief.

'Where is she?' Isabella asked as Nicholas climbed up into the curricle and reclaimed the reins.

'She got off at Froxfield,' Nicholas said, guiding the curricle to the side of the road.

'Froxfield? But she was booked to Chippenham.'

'So the coachman said,' Nicholas said, as the stagecoach rolled past, the outside passengers craning their necks to look at them.

'But why—?'

'She was in conversation with a man. Not a passenger, a man who was at the inn. And she got off the stagecoach and asked for her luggage.'

'A man!' Cold fear clenched in Isabella's chest. Not one of the disasters she had envisaged. *Worse. Far worse.*

'Yes,' Nicholas said grimly, turning the horses. 'We'd better get back to Froxfield. Fast.'

Isabella glanced at his face, and past him to the undulating hills. They weren't far from where Harriet had grown up. 'Perhaps Colonel Durham? Did the coachman say how old—?'

'A young man.'

'Did…did he say whether Harriet knew him?'

'He said that she was upset. Crying.'

'Oh.'

They drove in silence, fast, pausing only once to redirect her chaise. 'Back to Froxfield,' Nicholas said curtly, not waiting to give an explanation.

Isabella sat in tense silence as Froxfield came into view. She kept her eyes anxiously on the church spires, watching them grow nearer. At the inn, she scrambled down from the curricle before it had come to a complete halt. She ran across the courtyard and pushed open the door, almost knocking over the innkeeper. 'A girl,' she said breathlessly. 'A girl got off the stage. About half an hour ago. She met a man.' She was conscious of Nicholas behind her, blocking the doorway. 'Do you know where they are?'

'They're in the parlour, ma'am.' The innkeeper gestured down the hallway. 'But—'

Nicholas pushed past them both. His footsteps rang on the flagstones. He wrenched open the door to the parlour and stepped inside.

'Excuse me,' Isabella said, and hurried down the hallway. 'Harriet—'

She halted in the doorway, taking in the scene: the small parlour with a sofa and two armchairs covered in green brocade and the little oak side table, the man standing silhouetted against the window, his face freckled and earnest, his mouth half-open in shock, Harriet shrinking back on the sofa, a wet handkerchief clutched in her hand and her eyes red from crying, and Nicholas standing in the centre of the parlour. He was a tall man, and in this low-ceilinged room seemed even taller. A giant. An ogre. He stood silently, not moving, and yet he filled the room with his rage. The sense of threat was so palpable that she could understand Harriet's cringing terror.

'Mr Fernyhough,' Isabella said, stepping into the room. She closed the door on the innkeeper. 'How very glad I am to see you.'

Nicholas's head swung around. His expression relaxed slightly. 'Mr Fernyhough?'

'Yes.' Isabella smiled at the young man. She held out her hand. 'How do you do?'

Mr Fernyhough glanced at Nicholas, swallowed, straightened his spine, and pushed away from the window. He skirted Nicholas with another wary glance.

I don't blame you, Isabella thought, as Mr Fernyhough bowed over her hand. *I would be frightened of him too*. How did Nicholas do it? There had been no shouting, no bluster, and yet he was clearly and quite unmistakably dangerous. 'What are you doing here?'

Mr Fernyhough glanced nervously at Nicholas again. 'Harriet—that is to say, Miss Durham wrote to tell me that she was…was leaving London for employment in Chippenham.' His chin rose. The look he sent Nicholas was slightly defiant. 'So I came to stop her.'

'How very good of you,' Isabella said warmly. She looked at Harriet, huddled on the sofa. The girl looked white-faced enough to faint. 'Shall we partake of refreshments while we talk? Nicholas, if you wouldn't mind asking the innkeeper?'

Nicholas gave a short nod. With him gone, the level of tension in the room dropped markedly.

Isabella untied the ribbons securing her bonnet and removed it. She placed in on the little oak table and laid her gloves alongside. 'Harriet, my dear,' she said, going to sit beside the girl, 'there was no need in the least for you to run away!'

Harriet began to cry again.

Mr Fernyhough knelt before her and captured one of her hands. 'Don't cry,' he said. 'Everything will be all right.'

His voice held an uncertain note, but Harriet appeared not to hear it. She lowered the handkerchief and looked at him, her eyes glistening with tears.

'Everything will be all right,' Mr Fernyhough said again, this time more forcefully.

Harriet spoke tremulously, 'But Major Reynolds—'

'I shan't let him harm you,' Mr Fernyhough said stoutly, before casting a nervous glance at the door.

'Of course Nicholas won't harm you!' Isabella said.

Harriet looked at her doubtfully.

'No one will harm you,' declared Mr Fernyhough, gripping Harriet's hand. 'Not while I'm here.'

Nicholas re-entered the parlour. His expression was mild, but both Harriet and Mr Fernyhough flinched slightly. Isabella lost her smile. *Can't they see past the scar?* And then she absolved Mr Fernyhough of stupidity. Given the circumstances, it would be foolish of the man *not* to be afraid of Nicholas.

Harriet's gaze darted to Nicholas's ruined cheek and fell. She stared at the handkerchief.

'Mr Fernyhough,' Nicholas said, with a gesture at the door. 'A word in private, if you don't mind.'

Mr Fernyhough swallowed audibly. He released Harriet's hand and rose to his feet. 'Of course, sir.'

Harriet began to sob again as the door shut behind the men. 'He'll kill him—'

'Of course he won't!' Isabella said, exasperated. She inhaled slowly and made herself smile at the girl. 'My dear, while I appreciate that you ran away with…with the best of intentions, I must tell you that it was completely unnecessary! Why didn't you talk to me?'

Harriet shrank back and shook her head, not meeting Isabella's eyes, and whispered that she hadn't dared.

'Am I so terrifying?' Isabella asked, trying to be amused instead of annoyed.

'Terrifying? Oh, no, ma'am!' Harriet looked up. 'You are an angel! You've been so kind to me, and I—' Her voice caught on a sob.

'I'm no angel,' Isabella said. *Any more than Nicholas is an ogre.* She sighed. 'My dear, you cannot solve your problems by running away from them.'

Harriet sniffed into her handkerchief. 'Malcolm said that too.'

'Malcolm?'

'Mr Fernyhough.' Harriet began to weep again, forlornly.

How do I stop her crying? Isabella thought helplessly. To her relief the door opened. Mr Fernyhough stood on the threshold. His expression made her look at him more closely. Joy? She glanced enquiringly at Nicholas, standing behind him in the doorway.

'Harriet,' Mr Fernyhough said, stepping into the parlour, 'there's no need to cry.'

Harriet gulped and stopped crying.

Now why won't she do that for me?

'I think we can safely leave Miss Durham in Mr Fernyhough's company,' Nicholas said, with a faint smile. He held out his hand to Isabella.

Isabella rose gratefully. She let Nicholas take her hand and draw her out into the corridor. 'What—?' she asked, glancing back at the parlour as Nicholas closed the door.

'Mr Fernyhough has something of a private nature to say to Miss Durham,' Nicholas explained, leading her down the corridor into the taproom. It was empty.

'But what—?'

'I believe he is asking her to marry him,' Nicholas said, escorting her to a cushioned bench beneath the window. Rain streaked the tiny panes.

'Marry?' Isabella said, sitting. 'But he's beholden to Colonel Durham!'

'Not any more.' Nicholas grinned at her, felt in a pocket, and pulled out a letter.

Isabella unfolded it and read swiftly. 'A living in Yorkshire?' The hope she had been holding back flooded through her. There was tightness in her chest, in her throat. It hurt to breathe. It hurt to hope. She lifted her gaze to his face. 'Nicholas…'

He was watching her, smiling faintly. 'Will you marry me, Isabella?' he said softly.

She couldn't speak, could only nod.

Nicholas pulled her towards him, settling her against his shoulder. His arms came around her, quite tightly.

Isabella pressed her face into his caped driving coat. 'I have a horrible feeling that I'm going to cry again,' she said in a shaky voice.

'I believe I'll cope,' Nicholas said.

Isabella closed her eyes. She breathed in the scent of him—of dusty roads, of horses. His shoulder was so broad, his hand so gentle at the nape of her neck, his arm so warm and strong around her.

She heard the sound of his breathing, his heartbeat, and beyond that the patter of raindrops striking the windowpanes and a sudden clatter of noise in the inn yard.

'I think your chaise has arrived,' Nicholas said.

Isabella drank in the sensations of him a moment longer—heat, strength, gentleness, the smell of horses—and then slowly sat upright. She looked at Nicholas. His green eyes were smiling at her. Dim daylight fell across his left cheek, illuminating the scar. 'Nicholas—' The love she felt for him was so intense that it choked the words in her throat.

She raised a hand and touched the damaged skin lightly, tracing the ridges, the smoothness and the roughness, with a sense of wonder and joy. 'My ogre,' she whispered.

Nicholas captured her hand. His grip was tight, matching the intensity of his eyes. 'The luckiest ogre in England,' he said.

Isabella laughed, shakily. She leaned towards him and kissed him.

'Your servants—' Nicholas said.

Isabella glanced out at the courtyard, at the carriage and the rain. 'We have another minute.' She pulled his head down, burying her fingers in his hair, kissing his mouth, his jaw, his cheek. *My ogre. No one else's but mine.*

* * * * *

*Rancher Ramsey Westmoreland's temporary cook
is way too attractive for his liking.
Little does he know Chloe Burton came to his ranch
with another agenda entirely....*

That man across the street had to be, without a doubt, the most handsome man she'd ever seen.

Chloe Burton's pulse beat rhythmically as he stopped to talk to another man in front of a feed store. He was tall, dark and every inch of sexy—from his Stetson to the well-worn leather boots on his feet. And from the way his jeans and Western shirt fit his broad muscular shoulders, it was quite obvious he had everything it took to separate the men from the boys. The combination was enough to corrupt any woman's mind and had her weakening even from a distance. Her body felt flushed. It was hot. Unsettled.

Over the past year the only male who had gotten her time and attention had been the e-mail. That was simply pathetic, especially since now she was practically drooling simply at the sight of a man. Even his stance—both hands in his jeans pockets, legs braced apart, was a pose she would carry to her dreams.

And he was smiling, evidently enjoying the conversation being exchanged. He had dimples, incredibly sexy dimples in not one but both cheeks.

"What are you staring at, Clo?"

Chloe nearly jumped. She'd forgotten she had a lunch date. She glanced over the table at her best friend from college, Lucia Conyers.

"Take a look at that man across the street in the blue shirt, Lucia. Will he not be perfect for Denver's first issue of *Simply Irresistible* or what?" Chloe asked with so much excitement she almost couldn't stand it.

She was the owner of *Simply Irresistible*, a magazine for

today's up-and-coming woman. Their once-a-year Irresistible Man cover, which highlighted a man the magazine felt deserved the honor, had increased sales enough for Chloe to open a Denver office.

When Lucia didn't say anything but kept staring, Chloe's smile widened. "Well?"

Lucia glanced across the booth at her. "Since you asked, I'll tell you what I see. One of the Westmorelands—Ramsey Westmoreland. And yes, he'd be perfect for the cover, but he won't do it."

Chloe raised a brow. "He'd get paid for his services, of course."

Lucia laughed and shook her head. "Getting paid won't be the issue, Clo—Ramsey is one of the wealthiest sheep ranchers in this part of Colorado. But everyone knows what a private person he is. Trust me—he won't do it."

Chloe couldn't help but smile. The man was the epitome of what she was looking for in a magazine cover and she was determined that whatever it took, he would be it.

"Umm, I don't like that look on your face, Chloe. I've seen it before and know exactly what it means."

She watched as Ramsey Westmoreland entered the store with a swagger that made her almost breathless. She *would* be seeing him again.

Look for Silhouette Desire's
HOT WESTMORELAND NIGHTS by Brenda Jackson,
available March 9 wherever books are sold.